Outside Wonderland

Outside Wonderland

LORNA JANE COOK

St. Martin's Griffin
New York

OUTSIDE WONDERLAND. Copyright © 2011 by Lorna Jane Cook. All rights reserved. Printed in the United States of America. For information, address St. Martin's Press, 175 Fifth Avenue, New York, N.Y. 10010.

www.stmartins.com

Library of Congress Cataloging-in-Publication Data

Cook, Lorna J.
    Outside wonderland / Lorna J. Cook. — 1st ed.
        p.   cm.
    ISBN 978-0-312-62569-6 (trade paperback)
    ISBN 978-0-312-60696-1 (hardcover)
    1. Brothers and sisters—Fiction.   2. Man-woman relationships—Fiction.   3. Parent and adult child—Fiction.   4. Domestic fiction.   I. Title.
    PS3603.o573o87 2011
    813'.6—dc22

                                        2010040446

                First Edition: March 2011

        10   9   8   7   6   5   4   3   2   1

In memory of my belle-mère,
Betty Elaine Humphries Cook

ACKNOWLEDGMENTS

I would like to thank Lisa Bankoff for being a loyal, trusted agent; Dori Weintraub for her enthusiasm as my editor; and everyone at St. Martin's Press for fostering this book. Also, for reading the novel at various stages and offering helpful insights, I am grateful to Christine Kole MacLean, Carla Vissers, Julia Haidemenos, Steven Tobey, Clark May, Wendy Willoughby, Michele Lonergan, Rick Ganzi, and Lois Ganzi. And thank you to my family for a multitude of support.

Distance lends enchantment to the view.

—fortune cookie message

PROLOGUE

I was not privy to the early years after my departure, but I caught my first glimpse on a breezy May morning in 1973. I watched them arrive in Athens as in a dream, an American father and three children, aged nine, twelve, and a ripened fifteen. James Stenen was (still) leggy and intense; the jet-lagged children were mimicking his gait, though the eldest, Alice, was uncannily a mirror image of me, her late mother. I was pleased by this, but more so by my family's new location. James had finally gotten his wish—the sabbatical in Greece he'd talked about since the day we wed.

They settled into a chalk-white building jutting from a hillside with postcard views of jumbled houses and cobbled streets, and the Parthenon glowing golden every night. Eagerly, I surveyed my family's treks around the city and along the worn, waxy paths of the Acropolis; James, a professor of classics, canvassed nearly every inch, while the children bided their time on the cool marble ledges in the shade, daydreaming or eavesdropping on tourists. And I eavesdropped on them.

Over the first weeks they began to adapt and explore. James studied ancient vases and vessels, while Alice watched handsome men with dark eyes and tight jeans (and they watched her). Dinah discovered a love of all things Orthodox—gilded churches, melting votives, tiny shrines festooned with roses. And Griffin fell into a robust camaraderie with local boys who didn't care that his Greek was sloppy as long as he kept up and passed the ball. They slung skinny arms around his neck and pulled him into their royal blue circle.

On weekends, the family drove away from Athens in a dented green Fiat. They combed tiny fishing villages for stones and treasures, Griffin trolling the shore and poking at suspicious objects, hoping for a shock, something to report. I listened as the girls sat on the beach and discussed things they missed about home in Maryland—cheeseburgers and ice cubes and television.

"And Joan," said Dinah, referring to the grandmother who had helped raised them. "I hope she's not too lonely."

"She probably likes a little peace and quiet for a change," Alice said.

"Yeah, without Griffin around," said Dinah. Her sister laughed.

At sunset they all gathered underneath café umbrellas, swinging their brown legs and telling jokes while they ate moussaka and sipped lukewarm colas. James smiled at his children, and I know he was wishing I could see them now. If he only knew.

They spent the summer on a scorching island with a

hotel pool that overlooked the sea, blue upon blue. The children swam and read novels while their father worked in the cavelike ruin of Akrotiri, where the earth coughed up history with each turn of a shovel. James seemed happy for the first time in years, his sorrows lost in the wonderful soil. Dinah asserted that they should stay "forever," and from afar, I smiled.

Their bliss lasted until November. Students at the university in a northern corner of Athens began to gather in groups and throngs, then with workers, thousands strong, to protest junta leaders. Rumors of the unrest floated up and down the boulevards like litter. And James, in casual conversation at a market, was spat upon by a bitter *gria*, simply for being an American, whose government backed the junta. On the third day, at early dawn, tanks lumbered toward the crowds to crush the rebellion. Chaos and more rumors spread: that hundreds were killed—or was it just four? No one seemed to know.

Afterward, while history shifted in favor of the Greek citizenry, it was altered tragically (again) for three American children, whose father crumpled in the middle of Avenue Vassilissis Sofias, struck down not by bullets but by his own faulty heart. James cried out for help, grasping for the right words—"*Voithia, parakalo*"—though they weren't enough to keep the world from spinning, or him from spinning from its surface.

Just like their mother, who once lurched from a step stool in the pantry in Takoma Park, still holding a can of tomato soup when she lost her balance. Nothing to hold on to.

There, and then gone.

When it happened, eight years earlier, for a split second

I thought I was mistaken; I'd only hit my head and I would get back up. I had to make the soup, and fix the sink, and feed the baby—there was too much to do! And then came a flickering moment of comprehension and astounding regret: *Oh no! The children, the baby, James, I didn't, I wish,* and, *why now?* I didn't think it would happen so soon (I was twenty-eight!) or that it would be so permanent. I knew, but I didn't really know.

Then I was pulled away from all of that. Freed, as from a tangled net. Regrets were erased; and calm filled the atmosphere like new weather as I crossed over. The temporal world with all of them in it—my husband and three small children—vanished from view, as clouds filling an airplane window obscure the earth below.

So it was for James, after he found himself hurtling through sparking lights and thousands of moments of his life, still clinging to There, before he let go and landed Here, where I was waiting.

❧

Here, time no longer exists. We stroll through spongy grass, leave scarce ripples on glassy lakes as we walk across, or nestle into the arms of a velvet tree. We understand the stars and the thoughts of snails now. The music is, of course, unearthly. We keep as busy and idle as we wish, surrounded or alone, much like life on Earth. Not-time passes, or stays still, however one chooses to look at it. Thus, twenty years have passed before we next glimpse our children. Each time, I am amazed—not only that time has passed in our absence or that our children have grown and changed, but also that they are still the same, earnestly making their way in a fractured life. The human spirit, padded in ignorance, is a wondrous thing. They move within their own orbits—each of them seemingly lost, or intentionally lost in his or her own endeavors—while shifting into and out of one another's lives.

Our glimpses of them are random and not of our doing, like a satellite turning toward a clear and sudden vision.

PART I

A Gift, a Flight, a Dog

One

It always began, and ended, with a gift—a filmy scarf, a box of square chocolates with hand-drizzled icing, and, of course, flowers. Wiser men dismissed the cliché of roses and opted for white freesia or peonies, fat pink blooms like layers and layers of lace—an inverted petticoat, something sweet and old-fashioned, yet hinting of sex. Perhaps it was her own perversion that turned something as innocent as a flower into a come-on. But in Alice's experience, that was exactly what it was. Admirers sent them backstage, or waited outside behind the ropes and stanchions, clutching bouquets to their tweed or corduroy chests, hoping to elicit a smile at the very least.

"Alice!" they called, as if they knew her personally after seeing her onstage, her name on the posters and marquees: Alice Stone, an Off-Broadway celebrity. A reviewer had said she was destined for greater things, and perhaps because of that endorsement, members of the audience always wanted to see what she looked like up close, "in real life." Onstage, she was beautiful; in real life, a little less so, though she was curvier than some costumes revealed (she always ate the chocolates); her face more arresting without the makeup.

Alice was amused that adults could have trouble separating real life and fantasy—wanting so desperately to believe in fairy tales, true love, and happily-ever-afters. Women in the plush mohair seats breathed softly when Alice collapsed into the arms of the magnetic lover, the wrong man, the right one, whatever. The men beside their dates or wives simply watched Alice move across the stage, imagining they were the ones grasping her arm, or ripping off her dress. Of course, the latter never happened onstage, but several lovers had acted it out in Alice's apartment.

Acting was so simple. Alice thought of it like swimming: Dive in and float or thrash about, and then climb back out. Often she was reaching for her regular self like a towel the moment the curtain fell. Other actors—starry-eyed, smitten with *theatre*—held on, claiming characters had them in their grip for days or even weeks after a play ended. Alice knew it was the other way around. They didn't want to let go of being Stella or Stanley or Laura or Desdemona or even Puck. It was intoxicating. It was also, Alice thought, childish, though she couldn't blame them. In a way, she envied them.

Once upon a time, Alice believed in fairy tales. Her mother had recited them from memory on the edge of her bed while Alice closed her eyes and imagined. The night became starrier, the covers silkier, and the wind through the window filtered with magic particles and the whispers of elves beyond the sill. Her mother's favorite stories were from *Alice's Adventures in Wonderland* and *Through the Looking-*

Glass. She had named her three children after characters in the books—Alice (obviously), Griffin (modified spelling), and Dinah (the cat).

Then she slipped, as through a looking glass, and disappeared. Off to Wonderland, or Heaven, or somewhere far away and out of reach.

Alice was seven, and sitting four backyards away with a friend, languidly stringing garlands of untrimmed blades of grass and lily of the valley stems—while at home, life as she knew it was ending.

Everything changed the instant Alice's mother lost her footing on the rubberized step stool in the pantry—while her husband lectured at work; while her baby napped in the crib; while her four-year-old watched cartoons, sucking his thumb; and while Alice, her eldest, crushed fragrant flowers to smell the sweetness in her palm. A neighbor returning a casserole dish happened by the house just after the fall and called for help, but it was too late.

After that, Alice accepted that bad things rose out of thin air, in the middle of normal life—when you weren't even looking, even if you were being careful, or good. Normal people tripped or had heart attacks in foreign countries. Thus, you could lose your mother—and then, stunningly, also your father. Alice realized that she had a choice: either collapse or brace herself for what might come next. She opted for the latter.

For years, she was careful to the point of obsession—locking and relocking doors, boring her gaze into traffic lights and oncoming cars, consuming only organically grown food, vitamins, filtered water. As a teenager, she'd kept watch over her siblings and Joan, and until she moved to New York after college, where she had to fend only for herself. It was a relief not to worry about the others, but she didn't feel less anxious. In her early twenties, she went to a kindly but faintly inept therapist, who advised her to "tamp down" her fears, as if they were mere campfires and it was her own fault for letting them flare up. And one day, he actually chided Alice for being "so negative," and encouraged her to "always look on the bright side of life." Later, when she heard the Monty Python song, she recognized the line and laughed. There was no end to advice, no matter how absurd the source. Alice left the therapist and never went back.

Besides, on her own she'd found that time had passed and nothing else terrible had happened. She relaxed, a little. Drank, at times, a lot (it seemed to help). And best of all, she discovered acting. Or rediscovered it. She'd always acted, even as a child, playing at being other people, improvising when life called for it. It was, in fact, her calling.

Onstage, in rehearsals or performances, Alice Stone was in perfect control; it was because at the same time she was letting go of Alice Stenen. She disappeared beneath a character's skin and clothes and had to move only within the orbit of a stage, everything laid out and planned beforehand. Thus she was free, and, as an admiring cast mate had observed, "buoyant." Buoyancy was not a normal state of being for Alice in real life. She was not good at letting herself go. But she was not good at holding on, either. It was why her relationships were mostly fleeting.

Standing alone in her dressing room, Alice surveyed her latest gift, already knowing what it meant.

The box was a slender rectangle, as if for a tie, but when she lifted the lid, Alice smiled wryly. Of course, it was a necklace—this one a silver strand, teardrop gem shimmering in the vanity lights—which meant "I can't live without you," and "I'm sorry," and also, inevitably, "It has to end." For some reason, a necklace was the farewell gift of choice for most; maybe it symbolized a noose.

Without reading the attached note, Alice knew it was from Alex, fifty-four and just through a costly divorce, lavishing his spare time and half of his selfish heart on her. The other half belonged to his college-age children, whom he didn't wish to hurt. Alice suspected that the ones he really was afraid of hurting most were himself, his bank account, his orderly life. A girl on the side (even a girl of thirty-five) was what kept him sane, and "alive." As if a tumble in her bed—or on the floor, or the backseat of a cab—were akin to an oxygen mask, or the slap of defibrillators to a chest. Perhaps it was, and Alice had been happy to oblige, to help save a drowning man from a boring life.

Finally, she read the note. Alex—kindly, greedy, charming, needy Alex—was calling it off: "I actually love my wife" (*What happened to the "ex" part?*), "and I can't risk losing everything." It occurred to Alice that she could use the note as blackmail if she wanted to. But she had no desire to turn someone's life upside down. Men like Alex could do that all by themselves.

Alice sighed and slipped on the necklace. Maybe she'd wear it for tonight's performance. The necklace would be perfect, the gem catching the overhead spotlight and glinting like a diamond. She inspected. It wasn't a diamond, but pale bluish green. Amethyst? Quartz? The setting and the silver looked expensive, but it could be something Alex had found on a quick run-through at a department store. Yet even if he had bought it with care at Tiffany's, the implication was the same: *Here. I'm going. Get lost.*

Alice stuffed the box and note in the trash and turned to get dressed, ignoring the chatter of the other actresses crowding the mirrors, singing and shrieking their lines to warm up and calm nerves. By the time she stepped onstage, diving effortlessly into character, Alice had left Alex far behind on the shore.

The audience that night was spotty, many rows empty, but Alice attributed it to the day and the weather—Wednesdays were always slow, and cold, torrential rain didn't help. Who would come out on such a night to see a play about a dysfunctional family, even if it was by Tennessee Williams? Which it wasn't. It was a small, experimental two-act play written by a talented but mostly unknown playwright whose following so far consisted of friends and admirers.

Afterward, the other actors invited Alice out for drinks. Creatures of habit, they liked to convene at nearby bistros or bars and rehash the night's performance. Five of them were gathered on the sidewalk now, lighting cigarettes underneath umbrellas while someone hailed a cab.

"I'll think I'll pass," Alice said, huddling inside her coat.

"Come on, Alice," implored Janine, a baby-faced newcomer who played the younger sister of Alice's character. "We're going to have champagne to celebrate ten weeks. You *have* to come!"

"No, thanks," said Alice. "I'm really tired. And if it really has been ten weeks, I think you're going to need something stronger than champagne."

Janine laughed. "But it beats *Cats*, right?" She kissed Alice on the lips, impetuous as usual, and skipped away through puddles to join the others.

Alice pulled her collar tighter against the rain and headed in the other direction. Her apartment was a thirty-five-block walk to the Upper West Side, but she'd lied—she wasn't tired at all. She needed to breathe. And she needed to vent.

She hated to admit how much she had allowed herself to care about Alex, how hurt she was, preferring to think about how predictably callous and selfish he'd turned out to be. As she walked up Amsterdam, she decided to work through the alphabet: *asshole, bastard, coward, dickhead, effing asshole, fucker.* She felt a little better by the time she reached *l* (*liar, limpdick*).

She thought of her brother and Theo, so perfect together. And her sister, Dinah, with her quaint, old-fashioned approach to romance. As far as Alice knew, Dinah was tirelessly monogamous, and believed in true love. Sometimes Alice envied her. Dinah didn't take careless risks and she was patient and loyal, even though, at the moment, also single. Alice had the impulse to phone her sister when she got home, to commiserate, but knew it was too late. Even if Dinah were awake, their grandmother, Joan—with whom she still lived in Takoma Park, Maryland—would be asleep, lunging for the phone with panic in her voice.

It was after midnight when Alice reached her building and trudged wetly up four flights of stairs to her apartment.

When she reached the door, touching her key to the lock, it opened without resistance, the heat rushing to engulf her. She gasped, jerking her keys away. The doorknob dangled, clearly jostled loose.

Slowly, Alice backed away, heart pounding. Carefully, she closed the door behind her and then raced back down one flight of stairs and knocked on the door of Mr. Sechenov, an elderly friend. He always liked to hear about Alice's latest roles, and she gave him free tickets to her matinees, mainly so he would get out now and then. He had a prosthetic leg he kept propped by the door just for outings, and when he opened the door now, he was in pajamas, leaning on his cane, one-sided.

"Oh, hello, sweetheart," he said, his face lighting up.

"I think I've been robbed," Alice blurted. It occurred to her as soon as she spoke that she was crazy to call on a defenseless old man. "I'm so sorry, Mr. Sechenov, I shouldn't have woken you," she said. "But do you mind if I use your phone?"

"Of course not, doll! Come inside." He hopped out of the way and waved her in, glancing anxiously toward the hallway before bolting the door.

The apartment was just like Alice's, only reversed— the kitchen to the left of the door instead of to the right, windows facing east instead of west—and it smelled faintly of old age. But he had the same square living room, with a false fireplace and parquet floors. Alice had noticed before that his phone was even on a table in the same place she had hers, and that he also piled take-out menus there and kept pens in a drinking glass.

Alice dialed the police, then sat down to wait. "I wonder if I should go back up there," she said.

"No, no! You should stay. We'll hear the police when they come and we'll go up together, okay?"

Alice nodded. She perched on the edge of the olive corduroy sofa, its back covered touchingly with lace doilies. Remnants of the late Mrs. Sechenov, probably. There were no other signs of a shared life—a single chair was pressed up to the table, a small pile of books braced the sofa, and only wing tips waited beside the door, one attached to the leg. Mr. Sechenov had lost his wife many years earlier, but Alice had learned that he didn't like to talk about her. When she'd started to ask once, his eyes had watered and he'd waved the question away like smoke.

Mr. Sechenov handed Alice a towel for her drenched hair, and offered tea and then water and then "a cordial," but Alice shook her head each time. She had had his tea before and it tasted oddly like dust. She thanked him, apologizing again for the late-night intrusion.

"No, don't worry. You can always count on me," Mr. Sechenov said, sitting down opposite Alice in a tweed La-Z-Boy. "It's not easy living alone," he added, his brow furrowed. "You never know what could happen to you."

Alice wasn't sure if Mr. Sechenov was referring to her or to himself. He seemed even more rattled than she about the break-in, but then, he was old, and disabled.

"I'm sure it's no big deal," Alice said, continuing to downplay her own fears to allay his. "Maybe I forgot to latch the door completely when I pulled it shut. Someone probably just found an open door and got lucky."

17

"I hope it wasn't one of those delivery guys. They make me nervous—all those tattoos, and that one from Thai Palace with the pierced lip? I don't understand that at all."

"Neither do I," Alice said. She didn't mention that she once had had a boyfriend with a lip ring and rather liked it.

"Aren't you scared, hon?" Mr. Sechenov asked.

"No," Alice said, "thanks to you." She smiled. "And it was probably nothing—you know, these things happen sometimes." She supposed it was just her time; everyone in the city was robbed or mugged or worse at some point. She should be glad it wasn't worse.

"Someone new just moved in next door," Mr. Sechenov said suddenly, brightening and tilting his head toward the wall at his left. "A young man, your age." Alice half smiled, half listening. The old man went on, mindlessly rearranging some newspapers on the floor with his bare toe. "Might be nice. Hard to tell from a brief meeting, but he was friendly. Had a lot of books, looked like, and CDs. And a child."

Alice heard the last part and laughed a little at the afterthought. She felt antsy, though, and had to resist the urge to get up and pace, trying to be polite.

"I don't think there's a mother in the picture," Mr. Sechenov mused. "Far as I can tell. They seemed close, chummy, you know. Like they have a bond. That's always nice to see in young fathers, I think."

"Mm," Alice said. In her mind she was going through her apartment and wondering what she might have lost. She wasn't really attached to material things, but she loathed the idea of someone rifling through them. The more she thought about it, the more she tensed, and then seethed. It was so utterly invasive. How *dare* they?

"I have to go," she blurted. She jumped up and went to the door, unable to sit still and do nothing. She would deal with it herself, she thought, if the police wouldn't come.

She nearly collided with them in the hallway, caught by the arm by an officer who merely said a soft *"Whoa,"* as if nothing ever surprised him, and held her like a wild pony.

"It was my apartment," Alice said impatiently, breaking loose and rushing ahead up the stairs. "I'm the one who called."

"Miss Stone?"

"Yes." She kept running.

"Wait," came the insistent response as they followed her.

There were two officers, the cowboy who'd roped her and the other, darkly handsome and close-shaven as a marine, both of them freckled with raindrops. Alice felt better with them at her heels, in their authoritative navy blue, knowing that whoever was in her apartment would have a fight on his hands, if he was still there.

At the door, the marine firmly held Alice back as his partner nudged it open with a nightstick and flipped on the light switch. They went inside and were out of sight for several moments while Alice paced in the hallway. She started when she heard thumping on the stairs, but it was only Mr. Sechenov coming up to check on her. He had thrown a coat over his pajamas and attached his prosthetic leg with its shoe, though his other foot was still bare.

"Did they catch him?" he whispered loudly.

"I don't know," Alice said.

The marine reappeared in the doorway. "You can look around and tell us if anything in particular is missing." He glanced at the old man with his mismatched feet. "You'll have to wait out here, sir."

"It's okay, Mr. Sechenov," Alice said. "You can go back to bed now." She gave him a little hug, and he turned to go back downstairs, looking slightly disappointed to miss the drama.

Inside her living room, Alice surveyed the damage. The television and stereo were gone. Probably some jewelry, too, from ex-lovers, though Alice didn't even bother to look. It was beside the point. She suddenly felt as if she were standing in someone else's apartment; her home had been invaded, and thus nothing looked familiar, or safe. There was nowhere to hide, nowhere to relax and kick off her shoes. Now she would have to be alert, always—just like before.

The cowboy prompted, "Anything missing? Valuables?"

Alice murmured, "An old TV that hardly worked and the stereo. It was cheap."

The marine said, "Well . . ." and then hesitated. He didn't need to say it probably was a waste of the thief's time, and a waste of the officers' time to investigate such worthless losses, though of course they were glad to do their job. The cowboy in particular looked in no hurry to leave; he stared openly at Alice now that he had nothing else to do.

His partner turned to Alice. "Do you have some other place you could stay tonight, Miss Stone?"

She nodded. The cowboy put an arm around her shoulders and gave her a squeeze. "It's always hard when there's a break-in," he said, keeping his arm around her. "Makes you feel vulnerable. You really should stay with friends tonight, if possible."

20

Alice gently shrugged him off, and he politely stepped back.

The marine put in, "I hate to tell you, miss, but there are hundreds of these cases, just someone slipping in and hoping to find stuff to pawn or whatnot, then rushing back out. There's not much we can do except run a check on prints, though the petty ones usually don't get caught. I'm sorry. You should change your locks, by the way—this was way too easy to crack."

The two officers waited while Alice made a phone call and then followed her downstairs and hailed her a taxi.

She had thought about asking an old boyfriend to come for her—there were at least two she could think of who wouldn't hesitate—but she didn't want to deal with the implied expectation. And she couldn't impose overnight on Mr. Sechenov. Instead, she had called Janine, who had just come in from dinner and sounded slightly drunk on the phone but told Alice to come right over.

On the cab ride to Chelsea, where Janine lived beside a busy fire station, Alice began to regret her decision. She rubbed her head, which was throbbing, knowing she wouldn't sleep, no matter where she spent the night.

I find James staring at the Parthenon, his favorite vision. It blooms up now and then in its chalky perfection, every column and frieze intact, flowering vines curling toward the peaks. James has met some of the builders, and an artist whose vase he once handled in shards at Akrotiri. The man smiled when James told him; he reminisced about the coolness of the red clay when it had dried, the bottomless black of the ink. He was delighted that it had lasted millennia. Not everything lasts, obviously.

After spying Alice, James is contemplative. It's like that for a lot of us, whisked off in the middle of life. He wishes he could help her, wishes that he could tell her he's sorry he had to leave her—all of them—like that. (Not that it was his fault.) It is why Alice arms herself for the worst, then faces it down, a regular Joan of Arc, telling herself she can take the heat.

"When she was twelve," James says to me—and I light up. He often tells stories about our children's lives in the years after my "unexpected absence" (he euphemizes still, to my amusement), and every time a little puzzle piece clicks into place.

"There was a thunderstorm one night," James goes on. "Joan was out of town with the church choir, and I had a faculty meeting running late, so Alice was left in charge at home for a few hours."

The children later told him that the power went out, the house went dark, and they all gathered in a corner of the living room. Though she normally disdained babysitting, Alice knew it was up to her to keep her younger siblings calm. She lit candles, and then told them the story of *A Midsummer Night's Dream*, improvised from memory. Alice acted out some of the parts and made up lines, flitting around like Titania or Puck, in her element.

I see her through James's memory as if on a flickering screen, her wild hair tied with a shoelace, her newly adolescent body silhouetted in the eerie glow of candlelight, a mesmerizing fairy.

Suddenly, there was a loud clap of thunder and a crash in the kitchen. The younger kids shrieked, but Alice maintained the presence of mind to investigate, flashlight in hand, and returned to report that it was "just a little wind" knocking into the window. "So where was I?" she said, as if nothing had happened.

"I had left my meeting at Georgetown as quickly as I could when I realized the children were probably frightened home alone in the storm," James says. "Rushing into the dark house, I was surprised to find Griffin and Dinah in a festive mood. Then Alice came up behind them, white as a sheet but smiling gamely. And when I went into the kitchen and saw the window gone, glass all over the place, and a branch halfway through the room, like a javelin thrown in, I realized how scared she must have been. But I also realized that she could act the part required of her, and it alarmed, as much as impressed, me how naturally she did it."

"Deep down, she's always still a little scared," I say. "She just never lets on."

We watch the grown-up Alice in the taxi disappear around a corner in lower Manhattan amid the faint wail of sirens, and then out of our sight.

Soon the Parthenon will disappear again, too; even Here things come and go, though wondrously. If you missed something on Earth—the Pyramids, say, or glaciers, or the Sahara, Belize, the Ohio River from a tree-lined bluff, a white Christmas, the Louvre—you can take a tour and catch up, though the experience is fleeting, a kind of fantastic mirage.

When the entire Acropolis is gone, slipped away as into

fog, James strolls along a path toward some new-fallen snow petals, and I walk with him.

"You know, he's lucky," James says.

"Who?"

"The old man. Mr. Sechenov. He gets to see Alice anytime, and have tea with her, comfort her."

I smile. "I think she comforts him more."

Then James says, "You know that day in Athens—"

"When you died."

He looks at me, rolls his beautiful eyes. "Yes, okay, *died*. It happened so fast."

"I know," I say. It happened twenty years ago, but also, really, just yesterday.

"I should—"

"We can't—she'll figure things out."

"I know," James says, and smiles. He knows the boundaries between Here and There. The ones left behind are on their own (but not entirely), because once one crosses over, there is no going back. And so we walk on, arm in arm, kicking up snow and then flowers in a fantastic pink froth.

Two

Dinah watched people filling the seats in the cabin around her and imagined that, like her, each silently nursed a fear of flying. There were countless reasons: falling out of the sky, loss of pressure, claustrophobia, hijackings. Some just loathed the tiny tray tables and the cramped seats and sitting with strangers. The aisles were narrow, the food to come awful. In spite of a compelling paperback or a skein of wool, most probably just wanted the trip over with. They wanted to be on solid ground, the sky safely far, far overhead. Didn't everyone?

Hunched beside the scratched oval window, Dinah tried not to think about how much she hated flying—for none of the usual reasons. No one was beside her yet, so she reached up and fidgeted with the tiny light switch, the airflow knob. She dug in her bag and found stale bubble gum. She chewed it anyway, to distract herself.

A flight attendant with a braid flung over one shoulder

like a glossy, ropy scarf walked along the aisle, closing each overhead compartment with a tidy click. Her name badge identified her as "Ximena," and she addressed seated travelers in elegantly accented English or fluid Spanish, seeming to assess on the spot which language fit with which face; she usually was correct. When she reached Dinah's seat, however, she hesitated. Dinah had dark, bobbed hair and brown eyes; at various times she had passed for Greek, Italian, and Latin American.

"Do you need something?" Ximena asked. *"¿Hay algo que necesita?"*

Dinah glanced up and realized that she had pressed the call button accidentally. "No, thank you," she said. *"Gracias,"* she added, her Spanish skills still newly minted.

Ximena smiled, turned off the lighted button, and moved on. Dinah became aware then of voices all around her, a consistent hum of English and Spanish, with an occasional high chorus of Japanese coming from three college-age women in the next row. The cabin was full of students embarking on language courses or holidays, many of them enviably bilingual. She overheard a group of young men from Boston, she guessed, correcting one another's pronunciations, mocking the others' accents while their own leaked through.

"No, moron," one said. "The double *l* in *Ah*gentina is a *zjah* sound, not a *y* like in Mexico. Chicken is *pozjho*, not *po-yo*."

"Yeah, well, *poyo* this," another said, making an obscene gesture while his seatmates laughed. Then they chattered on in Spanish, surprisingly eloquent.

Dinah closed her eyes and consulted her own memorized lines but could only come up with *"¿Tiene cambio para cien?"*—"Do you have change for a hundred?" How far would that get her? she wondered. Would it guide her from Buenos Aires to Iguazú Falls? Would it help her find a man whose last name she didn't even know? Jimenez? Hernandez? He'd said it once, but she hadn't heard, or had forgotten. How could she *forget*?

If she told anyone—the old man now settling in to her right, for example, or the kindly, attentive Ximena—why she was on a plane to South America, she wouldn't know where to begin.

I was on a cruise in Alaska last July. . . .

It all started in Greece in 1973, the year my father died. . . .

When my mother died . . .

Perhaps there was no logical thread to follow, to explain. And logic wasn't one of Dinah's strong points anyway.

She was driven by a combination of pluck and faith, though her worldly elder sister would call it something else. But Dinah didn't think it naïve to believe in, and try to follow, one's destiny. She had read Psalm 139 over and over: *Thy eyes beheld my unformed substance; in thy book were written, every one of them, the days that were formed for me, when as yet there was none of them.* Even if the decisions one made on a given day seemed crazy, it helped to think that all things happened for a mysterious reason.

Dinah's faith was a mishmash comprised of the most promising aspects of Protestant doctrine, Catholic and Greek Orthodox rituals, as well as childhood convictions and a bit of superstition. Until now, though, Dinah hadn't really tested her faith by acting impulsively. Until now, she had been waiting patiently, or passively, for a sign from God.

Suddenly, it seemed she wasn't supposed to sit around anymore. A new door had opened, revealing some surprising things. Apparently, Dinah was capable of anything. She was capable of lying and finagling, of putting her own desires before the needs of others, and of taking an extra and undeserved vacation. On Capitol Hill, where she worked, none of that behavior, except taking an extra vacation, would be considered abnormal (ends sometimes justifying means). But for Dinah, it was antithetical.

Comó se dice—"What am I doing?"—she thought, pressed against the cabin window, swooning with a sudden gust of doubt.

"Business or pleasure?" the old man in the seat beside her was asking.

Dinah started and turned to look at him. He wore a full suit and tie, with a stark white shirt, and his gray hair appeared freshly oiled and combed. He smiled when he spoke and had the air of a lifelong flirt.

He repeated the question. "Is your trip to Buenos Aires for business or pleasure?"

Neither, Dinah thought, though actually it could be both. It also could prove to be an unmitigated disaster.

"I'm just going to visit someone," she said casually.

"Ah," he said. "Family or friend?" Apparently, in this man's universe, everything was either/or.

"Boyfriend."

The old man stared at Dinah long and hard, his dark, lively eyes searching. Didn't he believe her? Was it obvious that she was lying, or at least wasn't convinced herself? His staring was so disconcerting that Dinah, for once in her life, didn't notice that the plane had already taxied and was lifting off. But when she heard the engine churning, roaring, she turned to look out the window and gripped the seat belt, pulling it taut. Her faith was wavering. She swallowed hard and almost choked on her gum.

"Don't be scared," the old man said, patting her arm, leaving his wrinkled hand there, mapped with veins. "Whatever you are afraid of won't happen; it never does."

No, not true, she thought. *It already did. It often does.*

"You don't like to fly," the old man persisted, his voice now soft.

Dinah shook her head. The tears flowed as they did every time, even on the shortest flights. How many times had she wiped her nose with tiny, coarse airline napkins? She reached for one now, but the old man handed her a soft white handkerchief instead. He told her if she wanted to talk, he was a willing audience.

"It's an eleven-hour flight," he pointed out with a small shrug. "And I forgot to bring a book."

Dinah wadded up the handkerchief and held it loosely in one hand, not sure if she should give it back. She smoothed her shirt over her stomach with her other hand and looked away for a moment. She took a deep breath and composed herself.

And then she told him everything.

When Dinah was one, just weaned, her mother died after a freak accident at home, falling from a pantry stool and hitting her head on a jutting shelf. Dinah didn't remember that, of course. She didn't remember anything about her mother, and had only the borrowed memories of her older sister and brother. They had been seven and four, respectively. Alice told Dinah that their mother had had long dark curls (like Alice's) and a dimpled smile (like Griffin's). She sang when she pushed them on swings—"Swing Low Sweet Chariot . . ." or "Rock-a-bye, Baby"—songs that, when considered in retrospect, Alice noted, had to do with death. Griffin recalled their mother's penchant for squeezing lemon juice on everything: salad, noodles, chicken, and pancakes. "Her fingers always smelled like lemon," he said. Also, she loved to drive. Griffin claimed they spent their whole childhood in the backseat of the old Ford Galaxy, but Alice pointed out, not unkindly, that his four years with their mother hardly constituted a whole childhood.

Dinah's childhood seemed a blur but for one year—or rather, half of a year—the short time spent in Greece.

Most vividly, she remembered Easter, the sensational Greek holiday. Like the natives, Dinah's family ate traditional *tsoureki*, braided bread, and dyed their eggs the red of Jesus' blood. And that night, from their apartment window, they watched a magical procession of torchbearers wending from the top of Mount Lykavittos, lit up like candles on a cake. It was magical, and holy. After that, Dinah was drawn to the mosaic-tiled churches dotting the city and the villages they visited, where she felt the profound presence of God. Then her father died in the midst of a riot. Both events—her budding faith and her father's death—forever shaped her.

Now, twenty years later, Dinah remembered the flight home from Athens. Her brother, eyes wide and blurry, had clutched her hand to comfort her, pressing bruises into her palm. Across the aisle, her sister bowed over the tray table, her long hair nearly touching the floor. Their father's colleague, an American linguist, and his wife, who were accompanying them home, sat in the row behind, making somber to-do lists.

Dinah remembered the whispers around them as passengers learned of their tragedy, and the flight attendants' pitying looks as they bent to offer drinks, first-class snacks, pillows, and crayons—all of which were numbly rejected. Alice accepted only an aspirin, taking it like a Communion wafer on her tongue. Then she buried her head once more on the tray, not caring that it was mere plastic and looked in danger of snapping off.

Dinah turned ten that day on the flight home to the United States. It happened somewhere over the North Sea or the Outer Hebrides; she knew the hour of her birth and figured in the time zones on the map of an airline magazine to divert her mind. Then she scanned the duty-free items for sale, choosing pretend birthday gifts for herself: a stuffed panda, an embossed pen, and a large bottle of Chanel perfume, gold as honey. Anything to keep from thinking about her father in a coffin below with the luggage and the caged, drugged pets.

The linguist and his wife delivered the three children into the arms of their devastated grandmother at Dulles International Airport. While the family had been in Greece, Joan had been taking her own sabbatical—from a second round of motherhood thrust on her when her daughter-in-law died so suddenly.

Though stunned by the death of her son overseas, the children remained her priority. Joan shoved her grief away, dealing with it late at night when the children slept and she could give herself over to weeping uncontrollably, usually into a pile of laundry. Dinah, who had become nocturnal, often heard her. Also, sometimes she found a clean shirt on her bed the next day, neatly folded and with a little dried streak of snot. Stoically, she'd wipe it off.

Dinah grieved for months, too, but, surprisingly, her faith was not shaken. Rather, it grew, watered, it seemed, by her tears. In the room she shared with her sister, she lay awake in her twin bed, fingering the rib-cord spread, and silently discussed her father's death with God.

It was his time, she heard Him reply, though it could have been something she'd read scrawled on a sympathy card. Dozens of them filled a basket in the dining room. No one bothered to read them all, though Joan dutifully opened them with her son's teak letter opener, the one carved into the shape of the Minotaur. Dinah asked God why her father's time had to come so soon, and why she and Alice and Griffin had to be orphans. There was a long silence. Then God said, *Fear not,* and Dinah turned over onto the cool side of her pillow and tried to heed the advice.

The first time she believed she heard God speak was in Athens, right after Easter. Dinah had wandered alone into a small but high-ceilinged basilica and stood before an altar of candles. The flames flickered in unison like tiny dancers and then stood back up, erect. The air was pungent with incense, as if Dinah indeed were inhaling something holy. Suddenly, a voice seemed to whisper, *I know you,* and Dinah was overcome by a sense of deep calm. A sense of belonging. And though she couldn't have explained it at the time, she felt wholly intact and secure, surrounded by an impervious, invisible shield.

As an adult, she no longer heard God speaking directly—or at least not in literal words—and wondered if she had imagined it when she was young and desperate. Still, she was faithful, attended church, and her friends considered her amusingly saintly. It was an image she sought to dispel now and then by drinking extra cocktails or flirting at parties. But life was short, she'd learned, and it made sense to do something worthwhile, rather than hedonistic. She believed there had to be a purpose to life, after so much death. Otherwise, what was the point?

In Washington, D.C., she earned her living as a legislative assistant for a liberal, socially active New Hampshire congressman, but Dinah spent her spare time serving tomato soup and roasted chicken to denizens of a homeless shelter. And she never went anywhere without a sandwich in her purse (peanut butter, which didn't spoil), handing it to anyone she found clutching a cardboard sign on a square of clean-swept pavement. The city prided itself on order and cleanliness; visiting diplomats and tourists were met with a sparkling first impression of the nation's capital. But Dinah saw what lay beneath—or rather, shoved off to the sidelines: the lost, the forsaken, the lonely. It was easy for Dinah to help strangers; she almost preferred the anonymity of these encounters.

Her best friend, Touki, whom she'd known since she was seven, gently accused her of keeping others at arm's length. Touki had had the advantage of being part of the sprawling, noisy multigenerational family next door. Dinah had half lived there, too, though she realized at a young age how she stood out, partly for being white, partly for being orphaned. Often she quietly watched the goings-on like an anthropologist. It had nothing to do with race; she was trying to understand family life.

"I don't blame you, given your childhood," Touki said after Dinah's most recent breakup. "You don't get too close because you're afraid that everyone you love will die."

"No, I don't," Dinah argued. "Everyone will die eventually. But I'm not afraid of that."

"What are you afraid of?" Touki asked, her dark eyes gleaming.

Dinah shrugged. "Nothing," she said, but of course, it was a lie. The truth was complicated, and yet embarrassingly corny: *That I will die without someone to love.*

Her last boyfriend, Dan, a low-ranking Senate aide, had left for a better job with the embassy in Rome, and was gone by Christmas. The same November day that he announced his departure—over dinner on Dinah's last birthday (*surprise!*)—he also admitted that he was in love with a new colleague named Gina. Dinah knew she couldn't compete. But even if she'd been as sexy and high-heeled as she imagined the Italian to be, she suspected that Dan wouldn't have stayed. And it wasn't really his fault.

She could blame it on Joan, an easy mark. But the fact was that Dinah, the youngest, still lived with her grandmother by choice, long after her siblings had fled for their own lives in different cities. She felt guilty bringing boyfriends home to her childhood bedroom—and making them sneak out before dawn—and she didn't like to sleep at their apartments, leaving Joan to wonder where she was. But it was the price, Dinah thought, of free room and board—though she bought groceries, and the house was long since paid for. It was the price of putting family first.

Of course, Joan had never asked Dinah to move home, though she'd welcomed her back after college when she was trying to find an apartment. After a while it seemed to make sense that Dinah stay, since rent in D.C. was notoriously high.

"You'll save money," Joan told her. "And the company *would* be nice."

They settled into a phase of their life as roommates. Dinah commuted to Capitol Hill every day, and volunteered on Saturdays and sometimes after work. She saw friends, dated sporadically, and puttered in the garden. Joan tutored at inner-city elementary schools, played bridge, and raised herbs in the sunroom. She and Dinah actually had a lot in common. But sometimes Dinah felt the slight stranglehold of maternal love never far off. Or spinsterhood, an old-fashioned notion that seemed disturbingly prescient.

Even Alice had told Dinah repeatedly that it was high time she moved out of the Takoma Park house and into an apartment or condo in the city, closer to work. "You know you can afford it," Alice had said on the phone again not long ago. "And Joan can be by herself. It wouldn't kill her. She has friends; she has her church."

Dinah didn't mention that it was her church also. That she continued to attend every Sunday with Joan, that she actually enjoyed the ritual, the continuity; she even liked the coffee. And she didn't want to lecture Alice about the fact that Joan had recently had cancer; of course, Dinah couldn't have left her *then*. Someone had to be with her, and Dinah was already there. So she'd stayed.

And last July, she had taken a week's vacation to accompany Joan on a cruise from Vancouver to Alaska to celebrate a year's remission. Joan had survived a mastectomy and a bout of chemotherapy and was ready for a holiday. Dinah cheerfully complied, even though secretly she dreaded a week aboard a ship, sure she would be bored and claustrophobic.

On the first day, Dinah strolled along the wet deck of the *Silver Mariner,* squinting through rain at the gray horizon over grayer water. She circled the promenade decks, passing the same passengers huddled in their jackets, with their binoculars and cameras. Meanwhile, Joan dozed happily beside the indoor pool with a mystery novel spine-up on her lap. She had a tiny cap of curly gray hair, finally growing in, and wore a navy swimsuit with a prosthetic cup ("my rubber boobie") on the left side.

Sometimes while Joan napped, Dinah floated on her back and gazed up at the dark clouds beyond the skylights and wondered what had happened to her life.

By midweek, when the sun came blazing across the mountains, Dinah had to admit that the trip was worth it for the sight of a suddenly gilded sky, glossy orcas flanking the ship, and glaciers shattering into the sea, dislodging hunks of turquoise ice like giant sno-cones. She even pulled out a camera, like the rest of the gawkers.

That night, however, while she walked with Joan after dinner, the clouds skittered together again. "I guess the show's over," Dinah said morosely as they retired to their cabin.

"You sound peevish," Joan remarked, fumbling for the key.

"No, I'm not."

"I didn't say you are. I said you sound like you are."

Dinah rolled her eyes. "Here, let me," she said, taking the key away. Joan stepped back and gave Dinah an "I told you so" glance.

Once inside, Joan began her nightly routine in the tiny bathroom. She swathed her face in Pond's cream like an aging clown. "Why don't you go out for a while?" she suggested. "Maybe it will cheer you up."

Dinah sat at the child-size desk and glanced at the balcony, where long streaks of rain splattered the glass doors. "Sure, I'll go 'out,'" she said. "I think I'll just hail a cab and go see a movie."

"Very funny," Joan said. "But I do think they're showing that thriller you wanted to see. The one with what's-his-name, the smirky one." She paused. "I've never liked him, but I suppose the action is more the point. I saw a poster for it on the third level."

"Maybe," Dinah said. "Or maybe I'll just walk around till I find some strange man to pick up."

"You joke," Joan said, smoothing the face cream in slow circles around her cheeks, under her eyes, "but it's not unusual for some people." Dinah wondered if her grandmother was referring to Alice, with her succession of lovers. She knew, however, that her sister wasn't promiscuous, not really; and if she was, Dinah suspected it was only to fill the void of loneliness, while not letting anyone stay long enough to leave. Or die.

"Young people are much too flippant about sex these

days," Joan went on. "I mean the way you sacrifice the mystery and romance and *dignity* of sex by being so casual about it. 'Casual' should be for clothing that doesn't bind. Not for relationships." She frowned at her reflection.

"I know. You can get off the soapbox now," Dinah said. She was used to Joan's little lectures, as if she were still rearing her granddaughter.

"I know *you* have higher standards than that," Joan said more gently. "I didn't mean to sound critical of you personally."

"It's okay, really," Dinah said. She came up behind Joan and couldn't help smiling as she peered at her grandmother's white moon face in the mirror. "That's a nice look for you, by the way," she added.

"Hah," said Joan. "You may mock me now, while you're young, but someday this will all be yours," she said, nodding impishly toward her own reflection.

Dinah kissed her grandmother good night and went out to stroll the promenade deck. Again.

For a brief reprieve, the rain ceased and clouds tufted apart, revealing a small bit of sky, a black pincushion dotted with silver. The air was cold and breathtakingly clean. Couples brushed past Dinah—elderly ones with peaks of white hair and matching windbreakers, and younger ones on their honeymoon, or who had left children in the care of nannies or in front of TVs in their suites. Occasionally, she would spot teenagers sneaking off by themselves, little clusters of them laughing and tossing around packs of cigarettes. The ship was full of lively strangers, and Dinah felt lonely and unsettled. She didn't know if it was the dark sky falling into the darker sea or the sensation of lurching slightly all the time.

When the rain began to fall again, Dinah went back inside and found herself lured by the Midnight Bar. Like everything else aboard the ship, it perpetuated the illusion of another world. The setting was cinematic in its perfection, and also in the distinctly plastic sheen that seemed to cast everything in an unreal light. The waiters were a shade too friendly, the drinks a little too colorful, the piano music a touch contrived. But the zinc-topped bar sparkled from the tiny lights overhead, and if Dinah used her imagination, she could believe she was in a city and had just happened to come in out of the rain to relax.

"Big storm out there," an elderly man pronounced as she took a seat.

"Yes," Dinah agreed.

"But at least it's summer, or we might hit ice and end up like the *Titanic*."

"It is bad luck to speak that name on a ship," another man put in, his Spanish accent warm and thick. He leaned past the old man to wink at Dinah.

The old man scowled and grunted, not amused. He finished his drink and sidled away from the bar, and as soon as he was gone, the younger man slipped off his stool and came to sit beside Dinah.

"I did not mean to be offending," he said, glancing toward the door. Then he held out his hand in greeting. "I'm Eduardo."

Dinah shook his hand, smiled, and introduced herself.

"*Dinah*," he repeated. "It is a pretty name."

Eduardo, dark-eyed and breathtakingly beautiful, like an advertisement for musky cologne, was from Argentina. He told Dinah he spent his summers—Argentine winters—working for the American cruise line, and the rest of the year at a resort near Iguazú Falls, taking tourists on Zodiac rides near the base of the waterfalls. *Cataratas,* he called them. Dinah liked how words tripped off his tongue, and how familiar English words sounded more beautiful when he used them. Even her name, spoken with his accent, moved her. She wanted to hear him say it again and again.

As they talked over watery drinks, they leaned increasingly closer to each other, like plants tilting toward sunlight. Dinah had heard about people feeling a visceral, almost animal attraction to someone else—having to do with the other's scent or pheromones—but she'd never experienced it, until now. She could not have explained why, but she couldn't stop looking at Eduardo's eyebrows, for instance, enamored of every dark, perfect hair, or the curve of his earlobes—and how she actually wanted to bite them. She couldn't know, of course, if she was having the same effect on Eduardo, but he stared deeply into her eyes without once looking away. He lightly touched her arm or thigh every now and then as if to hold her interest, or maybe just because he couldn't resist.

"I cannot be here," Eduardo said suddenly.

"Why not?" Dinah asked, her heart sinking.

"I am not to associate with the guests," he said, as if reciting from an employee manual. He glanced at the bartender, who seemed not to care one way or the other. *"Ven conmigo,"* Eduardo whispered then, sliding off his stool. Dinah understood, and without hesitating, she followed.

Once outside the bar, Eduardo motioned Dinah into a shadowy alcove. As she started to speak, he kissed her mouth mid-sentence. When his lips tenderly clutched her bottom lip, as if it were stuck in a closed padded door, something opened inside her—something dormant, perhaps, or never before discovered.

Her recent melancholy evaporated, along with her so-called higher standards. With Eduardo's firm, muscled body pressed against her breasts, his heart beating in synch with hers, Dinah began to reconsider what it meant to be the "good girl." For one thing, she hadn't actually been a girl for quite some time. For another, why shouldn't she follow her impulses now and then—like Alice did? Why not open up to opportunity that arrived like a gift? After all, hadn't God created his people to fall in love, to kiss, to mate? Maybe, Dinah reasoned—digging deeply into her faith for a sign—Eduardo was, in fact, God's message to her to lighten up and enjoy life, to be grateful for surprises like this. Maybe this was what God had had in mind all along.

Thus, when Eduardo's hands traveled down Dinah's waist and her thighs and back up again, as if he were follow-ing a map, Dinah let new roads open up. Where he would lead, she felt instinctively she would follow.

For starters, Eduardo's room was two levels below Di-nah's and Joan's. It had the same blue-striped wallpaper and view, but twin bunks; he shared the room with another crew member. He promised, though, that the other man would not be back for hours. Dinah began to undress slowly, trem-bling a little. The hesitation gave her time to regret every-thing in advance, yet she still let it become a small avalanche.

Eduardo stepped forward to help Dinah unzip and

unbutton her clothes, pausing to kiss newly exposed skin. "Ah, *barriga*," he said. "Mmm, *nalgas*," he purred, turning her over on the bed. He kissed her as if drinking her in, and he kissed parts of her body she'd kept to herself for too long. He gently pried her legs apart and pressed into her, whispering things in Spanish that Dinah wished she understood, and then was almost glad she didn't.

For the next three days and nights, they met whenever they could; the clandestine sneaking about the ship seemed like an affair from an old romance novel or movie, and Dinah felt she was constantly half holding her breath. Joan asked her if she was ill; she looked "flushed." Dinah laughed and assured her grandmother that she was fine.

"*Really*," she added, smiling. As soon as Joan fell asleep, Dinah slipped out like a naughty teenager.

After the first time, Dinah gently insisted on condoms, which Eduardo willingly supplied; neither discussed the risks of their impetuous initial encounter, but Dinah knew her menstrual cycle. Odds were, she was safe.

The only other risk they took was getting caught, but Eduardo knew the ship, and he handily carried keys to countless doors. Once, he pulled Dinah into a towering linen closet and then locked it. They made love against piles of snow-white sheets and tablecloths, crisply starched. Afterward, they sat giggling as they carefully, dutifully refolded everything.

Then they borrowed a vacant cabin, and then one that wasn't, though the occupants were ensconced at the casino, something Eduardo had been careful to check. As soon as the door was latched, he ran his hands, encased in his uniform white gloves, up and down Dinah's body. She tried not to feel guilty as she spied the personal items scattered on the dresser, or lay naked atop the bedspread of some unsuspecting guests. Mostly, she felt thrilled.

On their last night, they simply curled together on deck beneath blankets and a black, moonless sky. Dinah had never taken such chances, had never been wooed so relentlessly and seductively. And in spite of all that was wrong with the scenario—they'd only just met, they lived continents apart, he wasn't really her type, and this wasn't like her at all—Dinah knew three nights would change everything, and they had.

"So, you really fell in love, just like that?" the old man asked. The leery glint had returned to his eye. Dinah knew how she must seem—romantic, naïve, easy. Insane. The old man had listened to her, enthralled, leaving the meal on his tray untouched, the plastic utensils still wrapped. Now and then he took a sip of wine, shaking the tiny bottle for any remnants, then signaling Ximena or another flight attendant for a refill.

Of course, Dinah hadn't told him everything. And she didn't know how to answer his question. Of course, it *was* crazy to follow a man to another country when they had parted with no understanding, no commitment. But Eduardo had implored Dinah to come visit. He'd sounded earnest, even though it could have come from the flush of the moment. But he had said it again, when they lay on the upper deck at two A.M., gazing up at the swirled stars. Eduardo then buried his head under the blanket and kissed Dinah all over, all over again.

"You must come to Iguazú," he'd said, emerging for air

and crooning in her ear. *"Por favor, mi amor,"* he added in a whisper. At the time, Dinah merely smiled and said she'd love to, leaving the rest of the promise hanging in the iced clean air.

Later, after she returned home, she knew she had to go; it was imperative. In the privacy of her bathroom, she had consulted four different home-pregnancy kits, and all of their blue lines pointed in the same direction. But this crucial detail she withheld from her seatmate, who was waiting for the end of the story. Even Dinah had no idea what would happen next.

She flicked off the spotlight over her seat and turned toward the window, leaning against her balled-up sweater. "I'm sorry," she said politely to her companion. "I'm suddenly really tired. Do you mind?"

"Of course not," he said. "I have to say, you sound like you could handle anything. So, good luck to you, young lady."

"Thanks," Dinah murmured as she closed her eyes. Luck had nothing to do with anything, she thought. But faith, she believed, could take her across the Earth.

It is not from above that we watch, as people often think. We see as though through a glass, not darkly, but from a distance we cannot break through or touch. It is like looking through water or the walls of an aquarium. The shapes move about, going their ways, darting here and there. Sometimes they pause, as if they sense they are being watched, but most of the time they carry on with no knowledge or recognition. I try to press closer.

I see my youngest in a seat beside a window high above

the Earth, an old man at her right, close enough to touch her, as I cannot. His elbow grazes hers, but she doesn't notice, or politely pretends not to.

Her hair is still dark, still fine, though I have not felt it since babyhood, when it clung to her skull in silken strands, tiny curls along the whorl of ear, and the indentation at the back of her neck. Her neck is tense now; she twists her head this way and that, still looking away from the old man, other things on her mind. She sits motionless, but inwardly she is rushing toward something—or away, or both. I can see only the present, not the future.

And I left her before I could see anything of the person she would become, though I knew instinctively that Dinah would be the one with the softest heart. There was something in her gaze even at one year that revealed tenderness; an empathy like a tulip bulb nestled deep within her heart, ready to push forth and bloom.

James confirms that she was always acutely attuned to her surroundings and to other people. "And to her faith, preternaturally. In Greece, she spent so much time lingering in the churches, I almost worried—I actually thought it odd—but mostly it made me feel inadequate, as I had doubts that Dinah never seemed to." He laughs. "Oh, me of little faith," he says, waving an arm toward his miraculous surroundings.

"Well, they say there is no real faith without doubt."

"Dinah is having serious doubts—but more about herself and her judgment."

"It was pretty bad judgment," I say, and laugh.

"The Argentinean said all the right things, though," James says. "A real charmer."

Far away from us, Dinah indeed is wide-eyed, pressing a hand to her belly; beneath, a small vibration, a winged heart. Our daughter and her daughter are soaring over the southern hemisphere, toward a destiny written before time was chronicled, or mentioned, or existed.

James looks at me, aglow. We say nothing more.

Dinah sits brimming with a thousand thoughts. And all around her in every seat, the same—a symphony of noise no one hears. Outwardly, there is only the occasional ding of a seat-belt warning, the tiny click of light switches, the metallic snap of a belt released, a polite "Excuse me" on the way toward a restroom. If anyone could truly hear them, the thoughts of a seatmate or a flight attendant would be revelatory.

For instance, the travelers in their seats see only the pressed blouse, printed name—XIMENA—a long braid, and a hand holding a cup of ice. They do not hear underneath the mother's pounding heart; they do not know that her six-year-old, with a gap-toothed smile and pigtails like commas, awaits bone-marrow transplant back home in Buenos Aires. But perhaps it would be too much for them. The concerns of those closest—family, friends, coworkers, lovers—are enough.

For us, a glimpse of our daughter—and granddaughter, two and a quarter inches long, a kidney bean with eyes and translucent skin—is pure elation.

Three

"I think we should call him Dander," Griffin said. He handed the photo to Theo, who took it, rolling his eyes. But then he studied it, trying to seem interested for Griffin's sake. He is so transparent, Griffin thought fondly.

"Very cute," Theo said. "He looks just like you. Same eyes."

"Actually, I think he's a she."

"All the more so."

"Funny—so, what do you think?" Griffin took the photo back and inspected the puppy's face close-up. A friend of a friend had a litter to dispense with. The puppies were six weeks old; it was almost time. The one in the picture had eyes that were dark, wet brown like coffee, almost like Griffin's, as Theo had noted jokingly.

It had always been Griffin's eyes, he'd said, before they'd actually met. Theo had covertly sized him up at a party from across the room, above heads and the lips of martini glasses shimmering in candlelight. A mutual friend had unwittingly invited them both. What were the odds? they often asked each other and themselves. True love appearing in the middle of another boring cocktail party.

"I think . . ." said Theo. He paused. "You know what I think, that's what I think."

"Spoken like a true writer. Don't you get points off for redundancy, though?"

"Grif, I'm not kidding. You know I don't want a dog."

"But it would be good practice, in case things work out."

Theo stared at the ceiling, as if a cloud were descending. Griffin thought that it was—the inevitable soft weight of sorrow, of disappointment. There had been another phone call, a quick message left on the answering machine, as if the caller was afraid someone might pick up midstream: *So sorry, thank you for your application, but we have no options for you at this time.*

"I didn't mean that things *won't* work out," Griffin added quickly.

"But the odds aren't in our favor, are they," Theo said, not a question anymore, but a rhetorical admission of near surrender.

Griffin could think of nothing more to say, and the truth was, he was tired of talking about it. He thought they needed to live in the moment—he'd learned very early that it was all there was to count on—and so why not adopt a dog? It would be tangible, and lovable. And it was far better than wishful thinking.

It had begun a year earlier, Theo hinting like a child in advance of Christmas ("What I'd *really* like . . ."), then actively searching agencies, contacts, anyone who might know how it was done, if it could be done. Knowing, of course, the obvious obstacle—two gay men monogamously, lovingly committed for the past eleven years, but alas, still gay. Gay! Such a happy word, yet so full of defeat.

One agency was coldly blunt, if obtuse: "This isn't that kind of agency." Theo had hung up, and then ranted to Griffin, "Don't they get it? Kids need loving homes. We have a loving home, but no kids. It's a simple, bleeping equation." Theo never swore. Sighing, heartbroken, he added, "I wouldn't even care if the kid was handicapped."

"I think they prefer 'disabled' now," Griffin had said, trying to deflect the rage, the escalating emotion.

Theo looked at him, eyes flaming. "You know what I mean! Disabled, quadriplegic, AIDS-infected, damaged, unloved, abandoned. Anything. I'd take him."

Tears edged out of his eyes, but he blinked them back, defiant. Griffin shifted closer on the sofa, slung an arm around Theo's neck.

"Hey," he said softly. "I know there's one out there with your name on it. On him. Her. Okay, maybe not your name, literally, since it might be confusing. Unless we call him 'Little Theo' and you 'Big Theo.' Big T, Little T! Go, team!"

By then Theo was laughing. No matter if he resisted, Griffin always won him over; it was a gift. It was love.

Later that night, when they were stretched side by side on the bed, flat on their backs like dolls ("We're the Kens," Theo once remarked; "the ones girls never want to play with anyhow"), Theo admitted that he had lied.

"About what?" Griffin asked, instantly perking up. Theo was nothing if not honest; integrity ran through his veins.

He never even fibbed. If he even tried, his ears turned a bright, glowing red, like Rudolph's nose, betraying him.

"About the handicapped thing," Theo said into the darkness. "I thought I meant it. I sort of meant it. And I could do it if I had to; I'd be a heel not to. But the thing is, I always pictured a healthy baby. You know, my own kid to raise from day one. *Our* kid."

"Uh, T? I forgot to tell you—I'm fresh out of ovaries." Griffin held out his hands near his hips in the dark, as if trying to show that his pockets were empty. "But I'll promise you this: We'll work it out somehow. Okay?"

Theo didn't say anything, but a soft sound against his pillow indicated a nod. Then he leaned over and kissed Griffin and went to sleep.

Griffin had lain awake for hours longer, trying to figure things out. He didn't have any idea how they could adopt, and deep down, he didn't want to. Parenthood was something for other couples, or for people like Theo, who were secure in the idea of family. Theo seemed to think it would be so easy—all they had to do was get a child and all the rest would fall into place, as if it were the most natural thing in the world. He never seemed to question their—or rather, Griffin's—qualifications for such a feat.

That was what worried Griffin about being a parent. He hadn't had any example since he was twelve and lost his father, and the years before then had been overshadowed by his lack of a mother. Her absence was a profound presence at the table, on the ride to school, in the auditorium during the school play, at every holiday. Even though Joan had been there—dear old Joan, who had come in from the beginning with her plaid bags and her hugs, taking charge and filling the house with her unintentional humor and love—Griffin had known it wasn't the same. Nothing was ever the same. And when his father succumbed to his defective heart on the street near their apartment in Athens, Griffin succumbed, too—to the notion that families were fragile and prone to collapse.

For years, Griffin had struggled with his double loss, trying to keep some semblance of memory alive, something to hold on to. Now, as an adult, he kept pictures of his parents on a wall in the hallway, but in a spot he rarely passed, and whenever the old grief welled up out of nowhere, he fought it back with lemons and Old Spice. The scents brought his parents close, conjured them, though Griffin never told anyone. Even Theo had no idea, gently mocking the cologne, calling out, "Ahoy, matey!" whenever he caught a whiff. He didn't notice the lemons, though, assuming that Griffin was just trying out a new recipe for work, where he was chef in a restaurant called Paradiso. Griffin would offer Theo a bite of chicken or a slice of cake, preferring to keep him in the dark—or rather, the light, which was what had drawn him in the first place. Theo was the poster child of all the boys Griffin had envied and admired his entire life: sane, happy, and impervious to pain.

When they fell in love, Griffin could only conclude that it was risky, but one had to create a family somehow, odds be damned. And for almost a dozen years, he and Theo had lived a charmed life.

When Griffin met Theo's large clan, the Steins, they welcomed him in so readily, it was like winning the lottery.

They loved that his name was Stenen. "If you talk fast," Theo's father said, "it almost sounds like Stein!" They loved him. Just like that, Griffin had a family.

Griffin had always watched regular families in awe— kids whose parents sat side by side at school band concerts, smiling and taking photos; families at parks, throwing Frisbees and passing around ice-cream sandwiches; couples swinging small children between their strong linked hands. All of them acting as if it were the most normal thing in the world, not thinking or appreciating any of it. Or maybe they did, maybe they thanked God every night for their blessed, enchanted lives.

Theo's family, for one, seemed grateful, as if they knew how special they were and thus clung together at every opportunity. There were so many of them vacationing together at a sprawling nine-bedroom "cottage" on the eastern shore of Lake Michigan, they were like the Kennedys. Winter weekends involved card games, blazing fires, and hours-long snowball fights. Summer was football, lawn bowling, and chairs lined up toward sunset as if at a drive-in movie.

There were generations of Steins—the grandparents, Jeannette and Eugene, both five four, with matching crowns of white hair; and Theo's parents, Jon, a retired lawyer, and Lil, an interior designer. Jon was soft-spoken but deliberate, and he favored complicated jokes that took five minutes to tell. Lil was a somewhat ethereal presence, with silvery curls and slender limbs, but with a commanding voice that could silence a crowd.

Then there were the numerous uncles and aunts and their spouses, and the divorced twin aunts, Kelly and Monica. They were in their late forties, striking and sexy in a tall, high-cheek-boned, swaggering way. They drank gin and tonics and smoked and laughed at private jokes, slightly away from the rest of the crowd—unless football was involved. Then Monica rushed in to play quarterback and Kelly to run long; they had amazing natural athletic grace and could outrun most of their nieces and nephews—a seemingly interchangeable, amorphous mob of kids from third graders to college age to near middle age. And there was a smaller coterie of great-grandchildren, including six-month-old twins, Stella and Paige.

Theo was crazy about the little girls and would gather both on his lap at holidays, tucked into the crook of each arm. Griffin had watched him turn to mush the moment they were born, then at three months, when they'd begun to smile, and then again at the half-year mark, when they were admittedly enthralling, trying to scoot around on all fours. Magnets for attention, just like puppies.

Griffin kept thinking about the mixed-breed retriever-something in the photo. Even if Theo claimed he wasn't interested, Griffin was sure he would be once the ball of fluff was in his arms; it would be like Stella, nuzzling his shoulder. Mainly, it would be a diversion.

Griffin was beginning to doubt they would ever be allowed to adopt. More often, he hoped that they would not. Sometimes he thought it was a battle not of wills but of wishes—he and Theo both vying and praying for opposing outcomes.

So, on a gray, windy afternoon, Griffin decided to take matters into his own hands. He left work early to meet his friends' friends with the dogs in Evanston. He started to remove his shoes at the door, but when he saw there was so much dander rolling like tumbleweed across the mudroom floor, he reconsidered and left them on.

Jonathan, a builder, and his wife, Annie, a dog portraitist, welcomed him with hearty handshakes. Annie told Griffin he was just in time for "the pick of the litter."

"You mean no one's taken any of them yet?" he asked. He'd waited a week longer than intended and thought all of the puppies would be gone.

"No. They're all taken but one," said Annie.

"Oh."

"Don't sound so disappointed! I meant what I said—you get the pick of the litter, the best one, which no one chose." Annie winked. "They didn't know what they were missing."

She led Griffin to the family room, where the mother dog, a midsize golden retriever named Juniper, lay curled on a worn yellowed flokati.

"Hey, we used to have one of those," Griffin said. "I think we left it in Greece," he added quietly, almost to himself. He remembered sitting on the rug in their apartment, tugging tufts of the thick wool through his fingers as if it were dog fur. Sometimes he pretended it was, and called the rug "Fido." In their haste to leave the country, the flokati had been left behind.

"So," Jonathan was saying. "There she is." He knelt down next to a pillow behind Juniper, on which lay a small brownish gold lump of fur.

When Griffin stepped forward to look, the puppy lifted its face to study the intruder. She made a small sound of protest, not quite a yelp, and hid her face in the side of her

54

mother. From what Griffin had seen of the puppy's face, it was nothing like the one in the photograph. The eyes were liquid brown, like the other's, but almost cross-eyed, and the nose was a little squashed, like a boxer's. He didn't know what to say. Was he obliged, by showing up?

Griffin cleared his throat. "It's . . . really cute."

"No, she's *not*!" Annie laughed. "She's a homely little bugger. But that's what's so endearing. That's why she was overlooked. I promise you, this one has personality plus! She won't be a biter, or a rambunctious pest. You won't have to worry about her bothering neighbors or small children."

"And she has heart, you can tell," Jonathan added.

You can? Griffin wanted to ask, but he refrained. He realized suddenly that he knew nothing about dogs, or pets of any kind. He'd acted solely on impulse, and now he was stuck. Perhaps he could stall, with questions and reservations, or maybe mention an allergy he didn't know he possessed until now. He tried a dainty, unconvincing sneeze.

"Maybe I should wait and talk to Theo," he said. "And are you sure she can leave her mother? She looks kind of . . . attached."

"Oh, she's just shy is all," said Annie. "You gather her up, like this, see?" She lifted the pup into her arms, nuzzled its head. "And she'll melt. So will you. Try it." Before Griffin could protest, Annie had dumped the dog into his arms.

It took a minute—he was awkward, and not sure how to hold it, the paws scrambling a little, as if the dog were trying to climb a cliff with no grip—but then they both relaxed. The puppy nudged its nose into the side of Griffin's neck, sniffed, and then licked him—tenderly, it seemed.

Jonathan and Annie laughed. "See?" Annie said. "She loves you already! I think you two were meant to be."

For a moment, Griffin felt suspicion creeping in. What if Annie and Jonathan just wanted to get rid of the dog as soon as possible and had no other takers? But then he glanced around the room and saw that the walls were covered with framed photographs and oil paintings of dogs of every size and breed. On the fireplace mantel perched a bronze dog dish engraved with the name Winkie.

Jonathan grinned. "Yep, she's a keeper. So, do you want her?"

Griffin found himself nodding. He held the dog while Annie went over some papers, tips for new owners and the names of groomers and veterinarians. And then she filled a large grocery bag with "starter" food, a chew toy, and a leash that she admitted wasn't new.

Griffin carried the puppy to his car and set her in the backseat in a cardboard box lined with an old towel. He gently closed the lid and murmured that it wasn't a long trip, as if the puppy could understand. Already, he could see how people humanized their pets. Already, she was his baby, and he started to rack his brain for names. Dander wouldn't do; it seemed a shade unkind now. Perhaps Brownie, or Otto, or Frank, he thought, forgetting for a moment that the pup was a she. As Griffin drove, he smiled. He could hardly wait to show Theo.

As he reached their street in Lincoln Park, the wind was ferocious, blowing from Lake Michigan four blocks away, and Griffin drove for fifteen minutes to find a parking space close enough to home. Then he lugged the box to the door of their brownstone. The puppy, to her credit, didn't protest, holding so still that Griffin worried she had died en route. Once inside the house, he set the box in the entryway and threw open the lid and found the dog was sleeping and content, her squashed face almost charming in repose.

"Theo? T?" Griffin called. He tried to yell in a modified whisper, but when the puppy still didn't budge, he tried again, louder. There was no answer. Though Theo worked from a home office, writing freelance stories for magazines and the *Chicago Tribune*, he often went out on assignment, for interviews and research.

Griffin found a pile of mail tossed hastily on the island in the kitchen, not yet opened, and beside that, a scribbled note: "Gone to check some sources. Be back around nine. Eat without me. Sorry. Love, T."

Griffin sighed and walked back toward the hallway, ears perked for noise from the box, but there was none, so he returned to the mail. Sifting through it, he noticed a postcard. It had to be from Dinah; no one else sent postcards anymore, and he knew she collected them from antique stores and used-book stalls.

The picture was of waterfalls, curving around cliffs, shot through with cinematic rainbows that hardly looked real, though they could be, Griffin supposed. He turned it over. *Cataratas del Iguazú. Argentina.* Below was jotted a cryptic message in ballpoint ink: "Grif and Theo, I'm here on a mission trip—quite an adventure, I expect. I hope you're well. More later! Love you. Di." Griffin noticed with surprise that the stamp and postmark actually were from Argentina, not Washington, D.C. He dropped the card and picked up the phone.

Joan answered on the first ring, as usual, as if primed for disaster. She scarcely said hello; her version of small talk ran along the lines of "Are you sick? Is something wrong?" as if those were the primary reasons for using a telephone.

"So when did Dinah leave?" Griffin asked, after assuring her he was fine.

"It's been about a week, I guess. I haven't heard from her a single time, and that's unusual. I was starting to worry. But she did say there wouldn't be phones in the rooms at the retreat."

"Retreat?"

"Yes, in the Poconos. Something for work—I can't remember exactly what the topic was. It sounded dull, but at least it's a little getaway for her."

There was a lull as Griffin tried to reconcile the opposing destinations. How could his sister be in Pennsylvania and South America the same week? And if the latter, why would she lie to their grandmother? Then he wondered if Joan was starting to get confused; perhaps the radiation and chemotherapy had altered her mind. He always wondered how such treatments could pinpoint a breast, say, and not wander freely throughout the body. His lack of medical comprehension embarrassed him. Thoroughly distracted now, he felt he had to come to some conclusion about Dinah's whereabouts. Joan's next response convinced Griffin that she, in fact, was of very sound mind.

"*Argentina?* She never said any such thing! What is she doing *there*?" A pause. "Why would she tell me she was going to a lodge in the Poconos?"

"I don't know. It's very strange."

"Is there an address or phone number?"

"What? On the card? No, nothing."

"Do you think I did something to drive her away?" Joan asked then, her voice high.

"No, of course not. I don't know why she'd make up a story. Her message says something about 'mission' work."

"Well, if that were the case, why would she hide it?" Joan asked. She seemed to be thinking it through. "It isn't with our church, I know that much. The last three mission trips were to Appalachia, though I kept telling them, 'Enough already'; those people probably just want to be left alone."

"Well, maybe it's something work-related but top secret." Griffin knew he was reaching now.

Joan chuckled a little. "She works for a hardly known Democrat from Portsmouth, sweetheart. It's not exactly the CIA."

"Well, I don't know what to tell you, then. I guess we'll just wait to hear."

"Maybe she'll send *me* a postcard," Joan said, sounding more miffed than alarmed. "I just don't understand how she could go halfway around the world without telling me!"

Griffin didn't know what to say. His grandmother had a point, but after he hung up, it began to dawn on him that maybe Dinah did want to get away from home. She was almost thirty years old, after all. Maybe the good girl finally had had enough.

Griffin was pricked with newfound guilt that he wasn't more involved in his sister's life, even long-distance; that he didn't know anything about how she was feeling or what she was going through. The same was true about Alice. He didn't even know the name of Alice's current play or if she had a starring role. When, exactly, had they all grown apart? They were still a family, weren't they? Yet he knew more about Theo's second cousins than his own sisters.

The door opened and rain blew in, and with it, Theo.

"Hey," Theo said, shaking out of his coat. "I got finished early, thank goodness." He walked right past the box and came over to Griffin, touching both his cheeks as if he were blind and needed to feel his face to truly see him. It was a funny habit, and Griffin was used to it. Theo's fingers were cold and clammy from the rain. He likely had walked; they shared one car, but Theo didn't like to drive. Sometimes he took the el or splurged on cabs, but most often he traveled on foot. His legs were long and muscled, his calves round and firm as oranges.

"So, how are you?" he asked Griffin.

"My sister is missing."

"Missing!" Theo exclaimed. "How? Wait—which one?"

"Dinah," Griffin said. "She's gone to South America, but no one knows why. She didn't even tell Joan, who was completely stunned when I told her. I just got this out of the blue." He handed Theo the postcard.

Theo looked it over, read the message. "Well," he said. "It doesn't sound like a cry for help. I mean, if she were in trouble—"

"I know. It's just weird."

"Yeah, I guess. But people take off and travel all the time for no apparent reason, Grif. Maybe she just needed a change of scenery, an adventure, like she says. And she sent a postcard, so it's not exactly a case of missing, is it?" Theo paused and offered an encouraging smile, rereading the note.

"A 'mission trip' sounds like her anyway. Only Dinah would spend valuable vacation time doing good deeds."

"Maybe you're right," Griffin said, though he still felt something was amiss. He had vague, stereotypical notions about missionaries, picturing pale Midwesterners in polyblend clothes handing out Bibles in the jungle. Even if Dinah was more religious than her siblings, Griffin couldn't imagine her in such a scenario; even she would think it wrongheaded. She was more pragmatic, inclined to handing out food to street people in D.C. But who knew what she'd been up to lately? Griffin couldn't shake the notion that he was partly at fault for being out of the loop.

Theo returned to the entryway to take off his wet shoes. Leaning down, his voice muffled, he asked, "What's in the box?"

Griffin started, having completely forgotten. "Oh! Uh . . ."

"You *didn't*," Theo said then, peering into the box. He shook his head. "Dagnabbit, Griffin."

Griffin wandered over and joined him, sheepishly awaiting the verdict.

Theo stood for a long time, looking down. He didn't reach in to touch the puppy, though. Suddenly roused, she turned lazily to look up at Theo, then she stood up on her little legs and shook herself all over. Standing, her fur fluffed, she looked astonishingly like a chubby bear cub. Griffin smiled, half in love already.

"I don't know why you did this, Grif," Theo said, not looking at him. "It's not— You know how I feel."

"Are you really so opposed to having a pet?"

"No. Yes. I don't really like animals, actually. I thought

you knew that." There was a hint of hurt pride in his tone, and something more. Griffin felt a wash of regret, followed by irritation. He grew defensive.

"Well, I like them," he said. "I've always wanted a dog, and never had one."

"This won't change anything," Theo said warningly.

"I know," said Griffin. "It's not the same. It has nothing to do with that."

As much as he felt wounded himself, and misunderstood, he didn't want to fight. Griffin usually managed to avoid conflict by humoring and placating Theo. But in this case, he didn't want to back down, either.

"I'll take care of her, don't worry," he said a shade testily. He reached down to pet the dog, trying to hide his own emotions.

"Okay, fine. We'll just see how this goes," Theo said, and sighed. "I'm going to take a shower." As he turned to go upstairs, he added, more cheerfully, "Have you eaten? Do you want to go out?"

Griffin shrugged, distracted. "No. I mean I don't want to go out. I'll fix something here."

After Theo left the room, Griffin lifted the puppy out of the box and held its velvet ear against his cheek. He felt that something had begun to unravel. He couldn't put his finger on its source, and he felt a vague panic rising in his chest. He held his nameless dog close, as if his life depended on it.

"We should have gotten him a dog," James muses. "I should have." He sits beside me on a confetti-flowered hill, with soft animals nudging his lap, lapping his ears. When he lies down, they do, too, manes and tails burying him. No fleas, of course, or dander. "But I didn't much like animals back then." He pauses. "I didn't know anything."

"No one does," I note. Wings stir behind me, though whom they belong to, I couldn't say; I don't turn around to look. Small crowds of creatures often gather, disperse. We watch our son holding his dog with its kindly eyes.

The year after I died, James almost relented. How easy it would have been to give in, do anything to fill the void a little. But then Griffin had fallen down the stairs and broken a leg, and all three children came down with chicken pox. Griffin's cast had to be cut away from the swelling of hives, his leg in a plastic splint while he soaked in oatmeal baths. James and Joan had their hands full. The small catastrophes proved to be good distractions, though. Joan dug out a box of marionettes she'd had since her childhood and James came home with a tape recorder. The children filled their hours of quarantine by creating puppet shows and taping songs and jokes.

"For five straight minutes, Griffin told knock-knock jokes," James says. "And we all pretended to laugh like an appreciative audience."

"I wish I could have heard it myself."

"Knock-knock," James says.

"Who's there?"

"Keith."

"Keith who?"

James smiles beatifically and tips toward me. "Keith me and you'll thee."

"Ha! That isn't one of Griffin's, is it?"

He shakes his head; I kiss him.

The dog issue was all but forgotten, James tells me, until Griffin was nearly twelve and a neighbor's mutt produced an irresistible litter—but then James's sabbatical was approved, and the family packed for Greece.

"And then it was too late."

"It's never too late," I say, petting the closest creature into purring, murmuring ecstasy. "Look at him now."

"Too bad Theo is so unhappy."

"It's not about the dog, though."

"I know."

We both have seen the way Griffin tunes out and turns away whenever Theo pores over a catalog of baby products, dog-earing pages featuring maple cribs, fancy strollers, bottle warmers. Theo is stockpiling an imaginary nursery, while Griffin struggles even to accept the idea of one.

"Theo would make a great father," James says.

"So would Griffin," I say, shoving aside a sleeping koala crowding me. But it looks so like a baby, I am momentarily distracted by its velvety nose and squashed little face and I take it into my arms instead.

James smiles. "Probably so. But not wanting to start a family makes him feel like something's wrong with him. That he *should* want it, like Theo does. But it isn't his heart's desire."

"He just wants things to stay the same," I say.

Like all couples, Griffin and Theo make each other happy and unhappy, often at the same time. When they reach an impasse, one or the other will end up aggrieved, even if they are "soul mates." No love is perfect, because no one is perfect. Not even our own children, so hopelessly (and wondrously) human.

"Knock-knock," James says, pulling me away from the menagerie.

"Who's there?"

"Saint Peter."

"Saint Peter who?"

James looks at me. "How ever did you get in here with that attitude?" Then he laughs, darting ahead amid the flap and thump of following admirers.

Four

In an air-conditioned room in the middle of a jungle, Dinah held her face inches from the vent, letting the cold, metallic air assault her skin and just-washed hair. Then she sat down on the spongy bedspread and surveyed her new surroundings. The walls were papered in pink and yellow stripes, and there were two framed prints of tropical flora. On the desk were a phone, a notepad, and a laminated list of hotel amenities in Spanish and in English. And taped to the sliding glass door to the tiny balcony, a sign warned guests not to feed the monkeys if they approached the window. So far, Dinah had seen no trace of monkeys, or any other creature, save some banded dark birds darting through the treetops.

As soon as she arrived, she had stood at the window, astounded by the view, a panoramic wall of waterfalls: Cataratas del Iguazú. They were just as Eduardo had described and guidebooks had concurred: breathtaking. She could scarcely believe she actually was here, that she had come.

Even so, she had convinced herself that her crazy plan made perfect sense.

When Dinah had dropped the final pregnancy kit into the wastebasket, and covered the evidence with wadded tissue in case Joan wandered in later to borrow shampoo or tidy up, as she was wont to do, she'd sat on the edge of the bathtub and thought long and hard. Staring at the same square mint-green tiles she'd stared at nearly her whole life, Dinah decided she had to get out. If not now, when? Obviously, her life had taken an abrupt, lurching turn, and she had to follow her heart. And because it was so sudden and so private, she wasn't prepared to divulge any of it to Joan.

At the congressional office, Dinah had seen a mailing for a weeklong seminar in the Poconos on environmental responsibility and global warming. It suddenly seemed the perfect alibi; she told Joan she was attending for work and that she'd be home in a little over a week. She was vague about the exact timing, but her grandmother didn't seem to take note.

"It sounds lovely," Joan had said. "You should take advantage of the time off and hike in the woods, breathe that mountain air."

"I will!" Dinah said almost too enthusiastically.

"Does the lodge have those heart-shaped bathtubs?" Joan asked.

"What?" said Dinah, bewildered.

"Oh, you know," said Joan. "It's such a big honeymoon destination. I heard all the hotels have them. It would be kind of fun."

"Yes, it would. If there are any, I'll be sure to take a picture," Dinah said, wanting to change the subject. Fortunately, Joan didn't ask any more questions. She rarely did about Dinah's work life, because she admitted that legislative matters bored her, except in the most basic sense of justice. She glazed over if Dinah mentioned a pending bill or resolution.

So Dinah secretly had renewed her passport and made reservations, and requested ten days' leave from work. She told Congressman Elliott that an old friend in Pennsylvania had terminal cancer and needed her to visit, now or never. Her boss readily allowed the time off. Dinah told Touki a version of the same lie, but she left out the cancer and said that the friend was male and she'd dated him in college. Maybe things would rekindle, she suggested.

Touki was as reliably supportive and gullible as always. When they were children, deeply immersed in imaginary life, Dinah would offer little white lies to see how long Touki would buy them—that she had seen a ghost in her room; that Alice could hot-wire a car; that Griffin was really a girl in disguise. Always, she confessed the truth and they laughed, but Touki never seemed to grow warier, even as an adult. It was an endearing quality.

"He lives in the *Poconos*?" Touki asked. "I wonder if he has a heart-shaped bathtub!"

"I hope so!" Dinah exclaimed a little too enthusiastically. She felt guilty deceiving her friend like she had in the old days, even if the lies still were minor and harmless. At the moment, Dinah just needed to go, without explanation.

She decided she would tell her family of the actual trip circuitously, just in case something went terribly wrong, so they would know where to look for her. She sent a message to Griffin from the airport as soon as she landed, finding a kiosk with postcards and a postbox handily nearby. Dinah chose her brother because, unlike Alice, Griffin would read her cryptic note and think nothing of it. Well, he would think it odd, but they each led separate lives; he'd chalk it up to an interesting episode he'd hear more about upon Dinah's return, whenever she called. She figured that mail would be slow from South America, so there was no danger of his calling Joan before her return.

Once she set out on a likely preposterous trail, Dinah focused on the steps needed to fulfill her mission—finding Eduardo.

Apart from the obvious and enormous complication their brief affair had wrought, Dinah had become obsessed with the thought that Eduardo might be the One. The longer they were apart, the more alluring he became. And distance—in miles, culture, and language—could be conquered, one step at a time. If it *were* fate, it would all make sense. It did seem uncanny that their encounter had happened at a time when she was seriously questioning her life with Joan, wondering if it was time to move on. Even if she had never envisioned such a drastic route, perhaps the Alaskan cruise had provided the way out. And Eduardo had begged her to come.

Dinah thought about the old man on her flight asking, "So, you really fell in love, just like that?" She'd dismissed his query as that of someone long out of touch with romance. What did he know of instantaneous attraction? Of finding true love in the unlikeliest of places—a reclining deck chair under a starry sky, a stuffy closet piled with sheets?

After the eleven-hour flight—beside the old man, who

finally fell asleep and left her alone—Dinah arrived in Buenos Aires. She saw the sprawling city mostly in a blur from her taxi window while the cheerful driver proudly pointed out sights in sporadic English, mixed with Spanish he assumed she understood.

Dinah, exhausted and nervous, tried to take note of what she later would read about and wish she'd stayed longer to see for herself up close: the pink presidential palace, once home to Eva Perón; Recoleta Cemetery, current home of Eva Perón—and of thousands of others stacked in coffins in Gothic mausoleums; the parks with palms and banyan trees; and the Teátro Colon, an imposing opera house like a princess in a sooty dress.

When the driver finally deposited Dinah in front of her hotel on Avenida Córdoba, he asked her how long she planned to stay in Buenos Aires.

Sliding out of the backseat, Dinah said in her broken Spanish that she was leaving "*mañana.*" She didn't know how to elaborate, or explain that she had another flight north to Iguazú Falls; she was only leaving the city, not Argentina.

But the driver seemed personally offended, shaking his head as he lifted her suitcase from the trunk. "This no good trip" were his parting words, and Dinah tried hard not to take them to heart, as if they were an omen.

But then a kindly, portly concierge led her into the hotel and over to an elevator, and even pressed the button for her, as if she were a child. In no time, she was prone on a queen-size bed, lying atop the bronze-striped spread. She was too tired to think about where she was (or why), and slept through the entire day, waking at dusk to desperate thirst and raging hunger.

Dinah gamely made her way to the street and ventured a mere three blocks before she found a pizzeria serving single slices and Coca-Colas, as if she'd never left home. She ate two slices and then ordered *empañadas* and *humitas*, which turned out to be cornmeal baked in a crispy husk. The waitress seemed amused that Dinah was ordering so much food, and even more so when the *americana* consumed it all. Dinah thanked her and dropped extra pesos on the Formica table, hoping it was enough.

Dinah walked around the neighborhood, pausing to look into shop windows, killing time. Peering through the glass door of a sporting-goods store, she saw a man helping a teenage boy try out a fishing pole, demonstrating how to cock his wrist; when the boy tried it, they both laughed. A younger sister, perhaps twelve, hung around in blue jeans and leopard-print ballet flats, looking bored. A few doors down, Dinah stopped to watch a young woman in a *lavandería* folding sheets, and she envied her, working on something simple and tangible. Perhaps the woman had troubles of her own, but seen through the steamy glass, she appeared content, white cloth billowing dreamily from her arms.

Dinah tried to fit these scenes into an idea of her future. If she stayed with Eduardo, would they live in Argentina? She imagined her baby babbling in Spanish, and growing up to laugh at her accent. For a panicked moment, Dinah thought of raising their child half the year on a cruise ship—or being left behind as a single mother for six months. But she told herself it was too soon to think of any of it.

When she returned to her hotel room, it was only to wait some more, clicking through seven channels on the television, listening to smiling announcers giving the news and the football scores, or soap-opera actors ranting at one another, or housewives selling something miraculous for cleaning floors or feeding ravenous children after school. Dinah understood none of it.

It was like the first days and weeks she'd lived in Greece; everyone else seemed to be going on with their ordinary lives, while Dinah and her siblings felt they'd come by spaceship to another planet. But after a while, they began to fit in, too. They knew their way around the city, the market aisles, the local customs. They knew which chocolate to buy at the kiosks; which shop owners liked children and which were inclined to scowl. They knew the shortcut to their father's office through a path lined with ivy and clover. They knew the answers to some questions in Greek. By the time they left, they also knew how foreign customs officials and airline security dealt with shocked, bereaved children—very delicately, in softly translated English, accompanied by pats on the head—and how a coffin was loaded onto the plane—with reverence and extra hands to guide it along the way, like a raft up a river.

In the Buenos Aires hotel room, Dinah reminded herself that she could adapt, no matter what. She fell asleep with the television on, the sounds of Spanish lapping at the edge of her dreams.

The next morning, just past dawn, Dinah returned to the airport by cab the same way she'd come, though without the scenic detour. For one thing, it turned out her hotel was suspiciously much closer to the airport than she'd thought, and for another, this cabdriver seemed as tired as she, and disinclined to talk. He kept the radio volume low—tinny tango music that made Dinah feel melancholic, as if she were missing something important.

Once on the plane, however, her excitement began to mount. The cabin seated only sixty, and it wasn't even full. Dinah leaned her head toward the window and watched the city fall behind, giving way to clouds and finally trees, acres and acres of padded green. In the distance, she could just make out the ring of falls, like flowing wedding veils. Suddenly they were obscured by jungle rushing up to meet plane, a hidden runway, and a tumultuous landing that dislodged bags and pillows from overhead bins. Over the speakers, a pilot apologized in three languages.

Dinah had no idea where Eduardo lived, only where he worked, and so she rode a shuttle bus to the hotel that employed him, the one closest to the falls. Eduardo had told her that at the end of the day he always returned to change out of wet clothes before heading home. Dinah had made a reservation at the hotel and thought about the word as she bounced in a rear seat over gravel roads. A "reservation" was to hold a place—and a holding back. With a future that now pinned her to the growing human inside her body, Dinah had definite qualms about her impulse to rush to Eduardo, unprepared. She gripped the door handle and conjured her faith: *It will be fine!*

The desk clerk in the hotel spoke flawless English, and after Dinah accepted her keys, she pretended to be an old acquaintance and casually asked if there was an employee named Eduardo.

"Jimenez?" he asked.

"Yes, Eduardo Jimenez," Dinah said, relieved to have been handed a piece of the puzzle. Then she added, shrugging, "It was a long time ago; he might not remember me."

The man grinned and said, "He probably will remember you. *I* would remember." He looked up at her from his computer screen, his green-gray eyes glinting.

Dinah blushed, unused to blatant flattery; it certainly wasn't common in D.C., where all the men seemed overly conscious of the written and unwritten rules regarding equality between the sexes. Sometimes Dinah wished someone—anyone—would just swivel around and stare at her with unabashed lust. Furthermore, it hadn't helped that she'd grown up in the shadow of a stunning sister. By the time she was fifteen, she realized she was no Alice, yet she consoled herself by thinking that there were the faintest similarities. Dinah thought she was like a chalk outline of the beauty Alice actually was, and that if she waited long enough, she might start to fill in, in the right ways. But, of course, it hadn't happened.

Thus, a handsome desk clerk eyeing her was as flattering as it was disconcerting. Dinah felt as if she were someone else, in every way. She had crossed more than one border, adrift in a foreign country, and in a foreign body. Almost overnight, it seemed, her breasts and hips had begun to swell voluptuously—at the early stage, where one couldn't tell she was pregnant and she could remain in denial a little longer.

She dressed in her favorite A-line skirt and a fitted white top that showed off a hint of brand-new cleavage. Then she slipped out of her room and down the corridor. She felt herself listing a little, as if back on the ship, making her way to Eduardo when she could scarcely wait.

Following arrows and signs helpfully printed in both Spanish and English, Dinah rode the elevator to the basement level of the hotel. She passed a game room with Ping-Pong tables, a claustrophobic weight room, a sauna, and then a door labeled EMPLEADOS. She quickly walked past it, paced, and passed it again. The door swung open, revealing a glimpse of lockers, a table with a coffeepot, and a few plain chairs. A man exiting smiled and nodded, then walked on, smoothing down a cowlick with his palm. There was no one else in the employee lounge.

Dinah next headed to the exit, which opened to a patio and a bright turquoise pool, its surface blinding in the sun. A few turistas in swimsuits and visors lounged in folding chairs, looking especially pale and foreign amid the colorful surroundings. Beyond them, the wall of trees was so thickly, densely green that mist and sunlight skimmed over, rather than through, the branches. Skirting the pool area, Dinah strode across the prickly Bermuda grass toward the falls. Though they were still far off in the distance—a good ten-minute walk, she guessed—she could hear them faintly roaring.

Straggling groups were coming through a clearing in the trees, up the trail from the falls. They all looked hot and damp from the jungle humidity, or the spray, or both. Dinah caught snatches of conversations in German and then in English, uttered in accents that sounded Midwestern.

"Let's go back in the morning. I heard the toucans come out really early."

"Do they migrate?"

"Where to? It's like this year-round. Why would they leave?"

"I thought all birds migrated."

"They fly. That doesn't mean they have to migrate."

"What about monkeys?"

"Uh, monkeys aren't migratory birds, either."

"No, *dummy*—do you think we'll see any?"

And then four dark heads came bobbing up behind the others. Clearly, these were local men, and among them was Eduardo. They all wore damp shirts and rolled-up khakis, and badges that identified them as staff. They were speaking Spanish and laughing about something, but the conversation tapered off when they saw the American woman staring at them. Eduardo seemed slow to recognize her, and when he did, his expression was a mixture of astonishment, delight, and a shadow of (Dinah thought) dismay.

Eduardo muttered something to his friends and broke away, rushing up the sloping lawn to meet her, as she still had not moved.

"Diana! You are here! *¡Caramba!* Why did you not call me?" He paused. "Are you with your *abuela*?"

"It's Dinah," she said, correcting him. She cleared her throat. "And I came alone." She looked into his eyes. They were as deeply brown and animated as she recalled, sparking with life and lust. The lust she suddenly doubted. He had forgotten her *first* name. And he had not thrown his arms around her as she'd imagined. Or kissed her. He was merely holding on to her forearm like a customs official unsure if he should let her pass. He let go and seemed suddenly awkward, as if he'd used up his rusty English.

Dinah said, "I had to see you, Eduardo." She paused, crossed her arms and uncrossed them, not knowing what to do with her hands. "Are you free?" she asked. "I mean, can we go somewhere and talk?"

Eduardo smiled, shifted on the grass, and pulled at his damp shirt. "It is hot, yes?" he said nervously. "Dinah, you come all the way to Iguazú to see me?"

"You told me to come," she said, her voice wavering. "You wanted me to come." She paused then, trying to cover up. It wasn't going at all as she'd imagined; dread seeped through her like the humidity. "But I wanted to anyway," she added lamely. "I've always wanted to see South America."

"I—" Eduardo began. He looked away and then at Dinah. Then his eyes widened and he blurted, "I am going to be a *father*."

Dinah gaped. Was it that obvious? Had she changed so much? Or perhaps her mere arrival signaled the truth—why else would the woman Eduardo had wooed three months earlier suddenly appear before him from thousands of miles away, needing to "talk"?

But then, before she could gauge his reaction, Eduardo added, "I just find out this week, and I am going to be married in two months' time. Before the baby comes—it is the wish of my fiancée, Julieta."

Hooliyeta. Dinah heard the name, felt it bouncing around in her head like a loose balloon. Eduardo was looking away from her again, toward the wall of green and the sound of thundering water beyond.

All at once, it dawned on Dinah: *He never thought I would come.* On the ship, all the kissing and whispering and lovemaking had been just to pass the time—until Eduardo returned home to *Hooliyeta*, who was having his baby. The coincidence was so preposterous and unthinkable that Dinah almost laughed. She thought, *My God, he's right. Why didn't I call first?*

"Wow," Dinah said, her smile frozen in the blazing sun. "You're going to be a father." She perversely enjoyed repeating his news, knowing that he didn't know—would never know—the half of it. "Congratulations."

"Thank you, Dinah. *Gracias,*" Eduardo said, sounding relieved, yet looking chagrined. Finally, he reached out to embrace her, pressing lightly against her newly grown breasts. He quickly let go again, as if he and Dinah were merely acquaintances, which Dinah supposed they were. Deep down, she'd known it had been wrong to let things go so far with a virtual stranger. She once had had higher standards.

As if reading her mind, Eduardo said, "I am sorry about— I liked you very much, as soon as I met you. I couldn't help myself when I was with you! But when I come home, Julieta was here, and we were together once more, and—" He shrugged and looked at Dinah morosely. He murmured something to himself in Spanish and then said, "It is very far for you to come."

Dinah felt her eyes watering, but she blinked away the tears. She put her sunglasses on and started to walk away. "It's very beautiful, just like you said," she managed to utter stupidly. Blindly, she moved toward the path to the waterfalls.

"Dinah!" Eduardo called. She stopped and turned, hoping in some tiny nook of her mind that it all was untrue, that he'd made up a story on the spot in a moment of panic and was coming to tell her so. He sauntered down to where she waited.

"Dinah," he repeated, this time softly, like a lover. He touched her cheek. "I never met someone like you. I thought . . ." He paused, as if searching for the right words in English, or perhaps just the right words. "On cruise ships, there are many women. They flirt. I flirt. No more, I swear this. Until I met you—it seems like something more. But then you go home and I go home, and I think, Well, that is all." He shrugged, but in his eyes was genuine remorse.

"I had never been on a cruise before," Dinah said pointedly, meaning, *I'm not a one-night-stand kind of a person.* Apparently, though, she was.

"I know." He looked at her sorrowfully. There was a long, pained silence between them. Then Dinah, not knowing what else to do, took a step backward.

"Bye, Eddie," she said, trivializing his name. "Adios."

"Wait—"

Dinah turned. One last chance. She held her breath.

"Don't go that way," he said, motioning. "Go the other way, that path there, *derecha*—on the right—it's much better." He had a look of desperation, as if he wanted to offer her something, anything, if only a tourist tip.

Dinah couldn't speak, so she just waved to indicate that she understood, and then she turned again and walked on. When she glanced back, Eduardo was gone, probably running away as fast as he could. She walked and breathed.

She reminded herself that all things happened for a reason. *In thy book were written, every one of them, the days that were formed for me, when as yet there was none of them.* Surely God had a plan larger than Dinah's.

But with each step, new emotions—hostile, bitter, seething—surged. By the time Dinah reached the edge of the falls, where the vista opened up, so that they were nearly all stunningly visible at once, and the sound was deafening, she was ready to scream.

And so she did.

For ten minutes, standing alone just feet from the rushing water spraying her face, Dinah screamed. It took a few moments for her to realize who she was yelling at—not Eduardo Jimenez, but God.

Was this how He treated the ones who truly loved Him? Or was she being punished for her wanton ways?

"It wasn't bad enough that I had to get pregnant?" she demanded. "I had to be an idiot, right? Well, okay, I get it! My mistake! Mea culpa!" The water ran on and on, to infinity, never ceasing or slowing down, a furious symphony accompanying Dinah's shrieks. No one was around to hear, since it was the end of the day (the tourists and their guides now gone for meals and drinks and dry shoes), but her voice might have been drowned out anyway by the thundering falls. Nonetheless, Dinah had business to take care of; she wasn't finished.

"Are You *listening* to me?" she yelled. She looked up at the top of the falls, where the water tumbled over the craggy wall, and to the sky beyond, tinted faintly orange and filled with soft clouds, and to Heaven (she assumed) beyond that. Her voice now barely audible, she implored one last time, sobbing, "I just wanted— Don't You understand? I thought You were supposed to *giveth*, not just taketh away."

The water pounded, the sky pinkened, and the air continued to swell, moist and humid and foreign. But nothing changed. There was no reply. Dinah was completely alone in the darkening jungle, waiting for her life to turn around, waiting for a sign.

Clara Winterthur arrived Here via a waterfall. An Englishwoman from Manchester, she was visiting Niagara Falls when she was thirty-nine, in 1955, and tumbled over a retaining wall, her mouth and ears full of foam and water and pounding noise, falling, falling, falling, limbs churned and yanked and broken. A terrible way to go, yet like me, she remembers no pain, only the arriving.

There are countless ways to get Here: through fire, windshields, unyielding currents, land mines, hearts clenching and thudding to a stop. Also the jaws of lions, cancer cells, the Golden Gate Bridge, bullets, bombs, derailed trains, torn-asunder planes, nursing homes, oven doors, and even mundane pantry shelves. And so on.

Clara says that, given her mode of death, some might think that her love of water is ironic (or vice versa). She loved deep baths, rain showers, canals, and fountains. She was the first one in the sea each spring, the last one still swimming in late fall. When she drowned, no one could believe it. "She was the best swimmer!" her friends remarked. As if one could swim out of thousands of gallons of gushing falls.

As we swim together on the jewel-bright surface of a

pool, Clara tells me that her husband, Hadley, watched with jaw-dropping helplessness as she slipped over the edge, his arm outstretched and useless. She says he still thinks it somehow was his fault, and thus has grown into a scared and cautious old man, rarely going anywhere, taking no risks.

"Someday, he'll see that 'all's well that ends well,'" Clara says cheerfully. She loves old adages. Songs, too. She often sings when she swims, even underwater. The vibrations are lovely.

Clara had no children because her womb was "inhospitable." Nonetheless, Clara had plenty of children to love. She opened a "child-minding" business for mothers who worked or were widowed, especially after the war.

I tell Clara that I don't know which really is worse— not having the children you long for, or leaving them behind too soon. But it's moot now.

From Here, Clara looks in on the grown children she once helped to raise, and sometimes she watches with me when I catch sight of one of my own.

At the moment, Dinah is yelling into a waterfall.

"You don't think she'll jump, do you?" Clara teases.

"Not funny," I say, and splash her.

"The ignorant bloke's a looker. She'll have a beautiful child," Clara says before submerging again, and I follow her.

In spite of her resistance, Dinah already plans to keep the sure-to-be-beautiful child, though she doesn't yet know what that means; the reality is barely sinking in. Screaming is her way of keeping the knowledge at bay. Denial is a very effective human trick. People often tell how a situation was "unbearable," though, clearly, they have borne it. Lived to tell, so to speak.

Clara floats beside me, saying, "I had a mother come to my house once with her baby in tow, a little thing wrapped in a nappy and nothing else. She said to me, 'I can't take it anymore.' Turned out she was a single mum, no husband, just a one-night affair before the fellow went off and got shot through the head at Dunkirk, poor thing.

"Anyway, after a bit—while she drank some beer I gave her and had a little cry—I asked her if she loved him. 'Who?' she said. 'The fellow.' She nodded. Though I suspected it hardly amounted to love, one night and all, I said, 'Well, then. You have to love his baby, too. It's here now. And it's what he left behind for you—isn't that a blessed thing?' And after that, she took better care of the baby, loved him to bits. And he grew up to be a member of Parliament."

"That's a lovely story," I say.

"They're all lovely stories, really," she says. It's true, once you have perspective.

I bob beside Clara for a moment, and then James joins us, diving in and resurfacing agleam, and then sliding onto the shore like an otter. He remarks that Dinah is yelling because she thinks God isn't listening.

"What did I tell you about doubt?" I say. "Now she'll have to shake up her life and change things."

"Things always change," James says.

"Yes, blessedly," Clara says, and then she swims away.

I slip onto shore and recline on a mossy chaise beside James. Suddenly, we spy three toucans zipping over our daughter's head above Iguazú Falls. They are inky black and shocking, their glossy heads and beaks Crayola bright. But Dinah doesn't see them; she is still too preoccupied with her rage, her utter disappointment.

Even so, there is hope. Even she knows deep inside that there is always hope.

Five

"I know you," a voice said merrily.

Alice turned, an accommodating smile pasted in place. Recognition happened now and then in unexpected places, away from the theater, especially since a glowing profile in the Sunday *New York Times* identified her as one of a handful of "actors to watch." The accompanying black-and-white photo was flattering, too. Admittedly, she was pleased.

Now a man in the Midtown Coffee Shop was pointing with a plastic spoon. "You're the woman upstairs!"

"Upstairs?" Alice repeated, confused. The man accosting her kept grinning like an acquaintance she couldn't place. Or maybe he was just a little "off"; such encounters also happened fairly often.

"Yes," he said. "You live one floor up. I moved in a few weeks ago, and I see you sometimes—usually rushing." He laughed. His eyes were very blue and animated.

"Oh, yes, I do that," Alice admitted, trying to be polite.

"I'm often late." She was now late for a script reading for a new play, but she didn't want to dash off after the man's comment, not to mention the fact that she held a very full espresso burbling out of its lid.

"I'm Ian," the man said. "Ian McKay."

"Alice," she replied, not offering her last name.

"In Wonderland?" He smiled. His face was boyish, with a faint fan of wrinkles at the corners, indicating that a smile was a fairly constant expression.

Alice smiled back. "Not usually, though that's who I was named for, actually."

"Really? Hey, isn't it funny we live in the same building and here we are, meeting on the opposite side of town?" He began to sing "It's a Small World After All."

Alice laughed. "I haven't heard that in about a hundred years."

"Really? I wouldn't have thought you that old."

"Ha-ha."

"So, how old are you?"

"That's rather a personal question, isn't it?" Alice teased. Ian's smile had pinned her in place, like a soft spotlight.

"Sorry. I forget sometimes what's appropriate to ask, since I hang out with a three-year-old who blurts out anything he thinks."

"Oh, you're the *dad*," Alice said. "Someone told me about you." She vaguely remembered Mr. Sechenov's remarks about a man with a lot of CDs, and a child.

Ian grinned. "What's that supposed to mean—'Oh, you're the *dad*.' A subtle insult?"

"No, I meant I'd heard that a man with a little boy had moved in."

Ian shifted a little, as if pleased that she'd taken note. "It's much nicer than our last apartment, and we're closer to the park now." His brow furrowed. "But I heard there was a break-in right about the time we moved in."

"Yes," said Alice. "It was my apartment."

"Gosh! Really? Are you okay? I mean, obviously you are; you're here." He looked at her intently. "But it must have been awful."

"Yes, it was."

"Did you lose anything valuable?"

Alice wavered. She had lost her love of solitude, her sense of self-sufficiency, her relative sangfroid. Now she tensed every time she climbed the stairs to her apartment, flinched at ambient neighborhood sounds she'd once ignored, and regarded new faces in the building with suspicion. She'd installed extra locks on the door, requiring two keys. And she occasionally ate dinner with Mr. Sechenov, when she didn't have an evening performance.

Ian was still looking at her, curious, interested.

"No," Alice replied, lying. "It's just stuff, right?"

"Well, if you need to borrow anything, let me know. Or just stop in sometime—when you're running past," Ian said. "I'm sure Adam would love to meet you. We're in Three D."

"Maybe I will," Alice said, turning to go.

"It was nice to meet you, Alice," Ian said, then added, "I like your coat. You look like you should be in a Christmas movie from the forties."

"Thanks," Alice said. The coat had been her mother's—dark red velvet that came to her knees and was trimmed with rabbit fur at the collar and cuffs. Alice always felt lucky when she wore it, as if some essence of her mother's spirit lurked in the satin lining or deep pockets, along with bits of soft lint.

Alice waved to Ian as she pushed her way through the revolving door. Then she rushed across Third Avenue, glancing up as sunlight pinged along the silvery curves of the Chrysler Building. She loved its old-fashioned gleam harking from an earlier era, which seemed somehow safer. It was why she wore the red coat—out of nostalgia for something she hardly knew, and as a talisman that protected her from harm, physical or emotional. She wore it a lot lately. The fact that Ian McKay had noticed it charmed her; everything about him charmed her.

Too bad he has a child, Alice thought. Even if she were interested, it would complicate everything. There likely was an ex-wife somewhere, and furthermore, Alice had no particular interest in small children.

Unlike many of her friends, she did not gravitate to strollers, wanting to peek in and coo, or to cherubic toddlers in tiny patent-leather shoes gripping the strings of balloons in Central Park. When someone she knew had a baby, Alice always sent a gift or a note, but she wasn't inclined to visit right away, and if she did, she had to feign interest in the infant who was placed on her lap.

And now, to drive home the point, a mother with a squalling child, mid-tantrum, blocked her path in front of the theater. The woman rolled her eyes at Alice as she yanked the half-limp moppet back to a standing position and forced her to proceed.

"They're *impossible*," she muttered, as if in general warning against procreation.

Alice smiled with what she hoped wasn't blatant pity. Then she hurried into the theater.

The read-through was already in progress at a table in a small cramped room. The other actors glanced up and acknowledged Alice, but she didn't want to be perceived as a prima donna, waltzing in late, especially after the newspaper profile. She said a soft "Sorry" to the room at large, and to the director, Calvin Heinz, who kindly motioned her to an empty chair.

The room was overheated, and Alice was flushed from running. She shrugged out of her coat as she sat and dug out her script. Fortunately, her character, Gwen, didn't show up until midway through the first act, and when her turn came, Alice read her part as if she had been studying its nuances for months.

The play, called *After This,* was a dark and funny exploration of life and death, with characters offering soliloquies from the afterlife—from various corners of the stage and beams and even audience seats. It had been penned by a talented novice named Imogene Wanamaker.

Imogene was sitting at the head of the conference table, where the actors hunched seriously over their scripts, not as jokey as usual, due to the presence of the author. It didn't help that Imogene was a visibly intense woman, with shorn black hair and dark-framed glasses. Alice typically didn't like to meet the playwrights; they tended to be overprotective and, at readings and rehearsals, were like new parents lurking around the nanny, ready to pass judgment.

Afterward, Imogene stopped Alice near the door. "I saw you in *The Real Thing,*" she told her. "You know, I actually wrote the part of Gwen with you in mind."

Alice was taken aback by this disclosure, since the character was revealed in Act II to have committed suicide. "I'm flattered," she quipped.

"Don't be," Imogene said, either missing the joke or ignoring it. "I'm not sure you'd want to know what I saw in you, what part of you I was tapping into."

Alice wondered if she just had a perverse sense of humor, but there was no way of knowing. Imogene's eyes seemed dark wells of inscrutable thoughts.

"Anyway," Imogene said, removing her glasses to wipe the lenses on her sleeve. Without the frames, she looked suddenly like a teenager, with faint violet circles beneath her eyes. "Just read it—I mean *really* read it on your own—and I'm sure you'll find what I'm looking for. Don't be afraid of the darkness in it, in yourself." She paused, poked her glasses back on her nose, and stared intently at Alice.

Alice felt an impulse to tell Imogene that it wasn't her place to give orders to the actors, though, of course, she had an implicit say in the production. Instead, she turned away, curious and perturbed. She had always managed to present herself as cool and professional, diving into each role on cue, on instinct. Now it was as if a stranger were looming at the edge of the pool, scrutinizing her strokes, watching too closely.

Alice took the subway home and then walked the remaining four blocks. When she neared her building, it was dusk, the October sky closing in earlier every day. The wind swirled bits of trash and dry leaves along the ground like dirty constellations, and Alice blinked away the dust. Seeing a figure seated on the stoop, she tried to steal a look without being too overt. Sometimes a homeless person stopped to rest, and Alice always prepared herself for the mumbled request; she began now to dig in the depths of her oversize handbag for some loose bills, her head bowed in concentration. When she got to the bottom step, however, Alice glanced up and saw that the figure was Dinah, and she was as shocked as if her sister had just fallen out of the sky and landed at her feet.

"I didn't know where else to go," Dinah explained as Alice led the way up to her apartment. Once inside, Dinah set down her duffel, still tagged with international labels.

"Did you come straight here?" Alice asked.

She had heard from a distraught Joan and then a baffled Griffin that Dinah was in Argentina, but no one knew why, or for how long. As she regarded Dinah's unwashed hair and wan face, her disheveled clothes with their faint smell of closed places, she wasn't sure she wanted to know.

"Yes," Dinah said. "I changed my return flight because I didn't want to go home, at least not yet."

"So, what's going on?"

Dinah sat down heavily at the kitchen counter and looked around. "Things look different," she said, instead of answering the question.

"Oh—yeah," said Alice. "I was robbed a couple of weeks ago and weirdly it made me feel like purging. Too much stuff."

Dinah nodded, seeming to miss the mention of a robbery. "Is it okay that I'm here?" she asked, her voice a little higher than usual. "I didn't know where else to go," she repeated.

"Dido, what's going on?" Alice asked again. "What on earth were you doing in Argentina?"

Dinah sighed. "Looking for love in all the wrong places."

"Oh. Well, we all do that," Alice said, attempting to cajole.

"Alice? You know how after Dad died, we all slept together in one bed?"

The abrupt change in topic startled her, but Alice nodded, silent. Of course she remembered; it had happened twenty years before, but also, in a way, yesterday.

It was in the apartment in Athens, for two whole days until their flight back to the States. They had pushed their beds together and tumbled into the starched sheets and flannel blankets like abandoned kittens. They burrowed and wept, keeping the door closed to the murmured voices of their father's friends and colleagues, who were making arrangements on their behalf. It was a nightmare—one Alice tried to forget.

"I felt like that was the only thing keeping me together," Dinah was saying, hugging herself. "Like all my blood and guts and everything would spill out if you and Grif hadn't been on both sides of me. Just having you there made me feel things might be all right." She looked away. "Funny how you can think that the world is ending but still believe things will work out. We always think there's going to be a happy ending out there somewhere."

"Well, some people do," said Alice softly. She thought, but didn't add, *people like you*. She had always thought of Dinah as the Pollyanna of the family, looking on the bright side, taking the higher road, finding the silver lining.

Once, two years after their return to the States, Alice

had taken up the habit of reading their horoscopes, and she'd found uncannily apt descriptions of each of them. Dinah, a Sagittarius, was unfailingly cheerful and optimistic, inclined toward spirituality but also rash decisions. Griffin, a Gemini, showed signs of duality—charming and adaptable, but loathing to be hemmed in. And Alice, a Capricorn, was ambitious, independent, often pessimistic, and controlling. One astrology book included loyalty among her traits, and Alice supposed it was true, to a point.

Now, for instance, she felt a vague panic that her little sister was expecting her to help solve her problems—whatever they were. She was not feeling up to the task.

Alice began to rummage in the fridge for wine, sure that she still had a bottle of white on its side on a lower shelf, but there was none. "How about gin?" she asked.

"I can't," Dinah said, "because I'm pregnant."

Alice turned. As she did, Dinah dropped her head in her hands.

"Oh, *Dido*," Alice said. She walked around the counter and put her arms around her sister.

When Dinah pulled back, her eyes were faintly teary. "I'm a mess, aren't I?"

"Do you want to talk about it?"

"Yeah, but I think I need a shower first," Dinah said.

While she waited, Alice fixed herself a large drink and pondered the implications of her sister's situation. Obviously not too far along, Dinah could still terminate, but she already was eschewing alcohol, a sure sign she was resigned to the pregnancy.

How Alice was going to help, she had no idea. What if Dinah wanted to stay and expected Alice to take charge as she had when they were young, when Alice, the eldest, had to be the strongest? But she reminded herself that Dinah would have Joan as soon as she was ready to return home. The two of them were inseparable, it seemed, and though Alice had tried to talk Dinah into getting her own apartment, and by inference, *life,* now she wished she hadn't. Apparently, Dinah was embracing her own life wholeheartedly, if haphazardly, and was on very shaky ground.

It was starting to make sense to Alice that Dinah hadn't told their grandmother anything about her lover—some mysterious Argentinean—or that she was pregnant. But eventually she would have to tell, and eventually Joan would rise to the occasion, as she always had. Alice had seen Joan several times in the year during and since her bout with breast cancer, and she seemed fine, though perhaps a little diminished. And sometimes she had a slightly startled expression, as if she had just heard something shocking, or expected to. The more Alice thought about it, in fact, the more it seemed preposterous that Joan could (or should) care for a great-grandchild at seventy-five.

She moaned. She felt a headache coming on and poured herself another gin and tonic, squeezed a lime fiercely into her glass, and gulped.

Dinah finally returned to the living room with her dark hair wet and slick against her scalp, like a seal's, her body swathed in Alice's pink kimono, a gift at the beginning of a long-ago romance. Now Alice's gaze went directly to her sister's belly, and indeed she could see a tiny curve of a mound against the slinky fabric.

"Dinah. Dido," she said, feeling the fog of inebriation lurking at the edges of her brain, muffling her sense of judgment. She sank into the sofa. "How could you let this happen? Ever hear of birth control? And aren't you kind of old not to know better?"

"I *know*," Dinah said, sitting down beside her. "We did use it—I mean, mostly. After the first time." She looked away.

"So, who is he?"

"A guy I met on the ship."

"What ship?"

"You know, the cruise I took with Joan, in July."

Alice laughed. "Sorry—you got knocked up on a *cruise*?"

Dinah just stared at her lap. Then she said, "I thought I was in love. I really thought it was different. Like the way they always say 'You'll just know when it's the one.' I thought he was the one."

"On a *cruise*?" Alice repeated.

"I can't help where it happened," Dinah said testily.

"Fair enough. So, what's his name?"

"Eduardo Jimenez," said Dinah, running her fingers around and around along the welting of the sofa cushion. "It doesn't matter now. He's getting married."

Alice gaped. "You didn't know that?"

Dinah shook her head. "And so I went to Argentina, and all the way to Iguazú Falls! To tell him, and to see if— Anyway, I was really, really wrong. And now—" She took a deep breath. "I can't believe this. I can't do this all by myself."

Alice didn't say anything right away, struggling with impatience over her sister's carelessness, and helplessness. Dinah was, and always would be, the baby of the family, all the more so because she'd been the youngest one abandoned.

Finally, Alice asked, "Have you considered not having it?"

"I can't," Dinah snapped. "*Of course* I thought about it, and I don't know why not. I think it's fine if other women make that decision, but I'm having it, Alice, so don't try to lecture me about it. Don't tell me I'm crazy to go through with this, okay?"

"Okay, okay." *You're crazy,* she thought.

"I'm almost thirty. This might be my only chance," Dinah said, though she didn't sound convinced of her own logic. Then she added softly, "I think this was meant to be."

Alice had heard it before, her sister's staunch adherence to the notion of fate, or predestination; God in the details, in the wings, planning everything. *Why bother choosing, then?* Alice wondered. *Why not just sit back and watch life happen?*

Dinah looked at her levelly, as if hearing what Alice was thinking. "I don't expect you to understand."

"It's your life, Di, I'm not going to judge." Though, admittedly, she did. "So, what are you going to do about your job and everything? And what about Joan?"

"I'm still figuring it out," Dinah said. "I just didn't want to go home yet. You know?"

"Yeah."

"She folds my socks," Dinah blurted. "And sorts them by color."

"Wow. That is bad. I sort mine by texture, too; Joan's slacking off."

"It's not funny, Alice. I meant—"

"I know what you meant," Alice said more kindly. "And I've been telling you so for years." She made a snipping gesture with imaginary scissors, but she smiled.

They sat in silence for a few minutes and then Dinah said, "What am I going to tell my child about his father?"

Alice thought, and then it seemed obvious. "Just say he was lost at sea."

Unexpectedly, Dinah burst out laughing. She kept laughing until she began to shake, breathless with mirth, and buried her face in the cushions in an effort to stop. Alice thought her sister finally had cracked.

"Are you all right?" Alice asked.

"Yeah. I could really use a drink," said Dinah, wiping her eyes.

"I thought you said—"

"No, I mean do you have any ginger ale or anything? I feel a little queasy."

Alice got up to look. "Yes. I mean no. I have tonic water."

"Fine," Dinah said. "I don't care. Whatever." She looked away, sober again. She clearly had made her choice, but it was as if she didn't have one. Alice didn't press her anymore.

After a dinner of take-out Thai food delivered to the apartment door, and many cups of green tea, Alice unfolded the sofa bed and adjusted the covers. She gave Dinah an extra blanket and told her to sleep as long as she wanted to; Alice had rehearsal in the morning, but she promised to check in later.

Then she went into her bedroom and picked up the phone.

Joan, of course, answered immediately. "Dinah?" she said expectantly, her voice unnaturally high.

"No, it's me, Alice. But she's here with me, and she's fine."

"She's there? First she said the Poconos! Then Griffin said it was Argentina. And now you're telling me she's in *New York*?"

"Well, she actually was in Argentina, but she just got in, and she's staying with me for a few days. I thought I should let you know. She's just crashed on my sofa, but I'm sure she'll call you in the morning, after she's slept."

"Well, she'd better call!" Joan said irritably. Then, as ice clinked in Alice's glass, she asked, "Are you drinking?"

"*Yesh*, as a matter of fact, and lest you forget, I am of legal drinking age."

There was silence on the other end and then Joan said, "I'm sorry. It's none of my beeswax, right?" She took a deep breath. "No wonder Dinah ran away!"

Alice sighed. Joan had grown more emotional in her old age, and Alice tried to be patient. "She didn't *run away*, Joan. It had nothing whatsoever to do with you. I think she's going through a little bit of a crisis here, the kind of thing people usually have in college or whatever. She's just . . . delayed. You know, things happen, and people go through things we can't always understand, and I hate to be the one to tell you this"—she paused, took a surreptitious sip, away from the mouthpiece—"but the baby of the family is thirty years old. Or will be in a month."

"I do know," Joan snapped. "I just still worry about her, about all of you."

"She's fine, we're all fine. And we love you and always will. You just need to—"

"Let go. Yes, I know."

"Don't be so hard on yourself, Granny," Alice said, using the name they'd all been forbidden to use since childhood. Finally, Joan laughed. Alice assured her again that Dinah would call soon, thinking it was up to Dinah to decide what to tell, and when.

When she hung up, Alice fell back onto her bed. She had had no guests since the robbery, and it was vaguely comforting to have her sister in the next room, though she had no idea how long Dinah intended to stay. When family members visited, they stayed only a night or two at the most; Joan said the sofa bed hurt her back, and Griffin and Theo always just checked into the hotel around the block. When it was Dinah's turn, she seemed to want to treat it like a slumber party, and Alice tried to comply, to please her. They would watch old movies and eat too many cupcakes. Dinah would visit museums or walk around the reservoir, then take the train back to D.C., apparently satisfied.

This was different. Dinah had come truly needing her, and Alice had no idea how to help. But when her bedroom door squeaked open in the middle of the night and Dinah appeared like her nine-year-old self on the threshold, Alice automatically moved over in her bed and made room. The two sisters said nothing, just breathed together in the darkness. And then, when Dinah turned onto her side, Alice tentatively put her arm around her, contemplating the strangeness of another life inside her sister. She couldn't promise Dinah anything or change anything, but she could be there for her—for the moment. It was the least she could do.

Someone once joked, "Hell is other people." But the truth is that connection to other people can be sacred. Why else did God give so many people life? (Adam wasn't enough.) Or more simply, why else would He design hands that so perfectly clasp?

Our daughters are not holding hands. They are not even touching, shifted to opposite sides of the bed. But as they lie together in the dark, their thoughts overlap. The warmth of one sister's body radiates around the other's as they drift off to sleep. I wish I could infiltrate their dreams with messages they need to hear. But of course I can't. Their lives are theirs to live; their dreams are theirs to dream.

"It's heartening to know they're there for each other," James says.

"If only grudgingly," I say, and laugh.

"She's just being . . . Alice."

I nod. "Tired of being the eldest."

People expect a lot of sisters, assuming that they connect on a deeper level than other people, that "sisterhood" constitutes a natural alliance, an innate understanding. Not always true. Sisters can be as different as night and day.

In our ever-night-day-dawn, the mist is rising from a silvery pool, stars are shooting, and fat flowers are popping out all over. Someone sings, or laughs, or chants something sublime. James and I curl up, sleepless, not needing sleep anymore.

Watching our sleeping daughters is captivating now that they are grown women. And yet they are so like their childish selves—personalities pressed into their skin like birthmarks. Alice, the independent one, grudgingly makes room while holding to one half of the bed as if claiming land. Dinah, the youngest, used to and still craving company, keeps trying to encroach on the border, but finally she curls into herself, arms wrapped protectively around her softening belly.

In sleep, they relax, closer to each other than they are in their regular adult lives. In the morning, nothing will change; they will regard each other tentatively, making their silent assessments. Even so, in the midst of this complicated love, there is a holy union.

Six

It had been a hazardous week. On Monday, Griffin sliced open his left thumb (six stitches) chopping basil for a béchamel sauce; Wednesday, he burned his right wrist (second-degree, light bandage) reaching over a leaping flame; and today, Saturday—in a non-work-related mishap—he hit his head on a wrought-iron railing while stooping to scoop up the droppings of his dog. Holly Golightly, as she now was called, needed to be walked and relieved with alarming frequency, and in the early-morning hours Griffin was not alert. This morning, for instance, he was particularly fatigued after a late shift at work, followed by a sleepless night. He hadn't even looked before he bent, and his head cracked hard against the railing. His eyes instantly watered and he swooned. It didn't help, of course, that he already was trying to stave off throbbing in his thumb and wrist.

"Oh, *damn* it all!" he shouted into the dark, cold dawn, startling Holly into yelping.

"Hey!" someone shouted from a street-level window. "We're trying to fucking sleep here!"

"Sorry! I'm just trying to fucking bleed to death here! But don't worry. Go back to bed!" Griffin hollered back before yanking on Holly's leash and stumbling upright. He was surprised at his own sudden rage. Just what was he so mad about? The lump forming on his forehead? The demands of an incontinent pup? The long hours and stress of work? He'd had two anniversary parties of more than twenty people the night before—and all of them had ordered a full menu and dessert; over half their desserts had been crème brûlée, requiring last-minute torching. And Griffin was skittish around flames now.

Or perhaps, just possibly, it had to do with a phone call a few days earlier from an adoption agency. Described in its literature and mission statement as "progressive," it purported to help "forge the bonds of family regardless of race, religion, gender, or sexual orientation." The caller, a woman named Jude, declared with singsong excitement that Theo and Griffin had been selected for the "final round," as if in a game show. They and another gay couple had been singled out by the birth mother, who, for unnamed reasons, wanted her daughter—whose gender had been determined by ultrasound—raised by two men in a stable relationship. All that remained was an interview to determine the "best fit."

"What are we, shoes?" Griffin had joked after Theo hung up and relayed the conversation.

"I can't believe this!" said Theo, clearly lost in his own euphoria. "This could be the one, Grif, I have a good feeling about it."

"What about the other guys?" Griffin asked.

Theo looked at him. "What do they have that we don't?"

"How should I know? I just meant, it's like we're in some weird competition now to see who's better. That's a lot of pressure, if you ask me."

"All we have to do is be ourselves, and the mother will see that we'd be great with a child," Theo said.

Griffin didn't say anything else. While Theo was desperate to win the favor of the adoptive mother and thus permanent custody of her yet-to-be-born daughter, Griffin was terrified. It actually was happening. He and Theo would no longer be just a couple, but parents in charge of another's life. And he still didn't know how to tell Theo how he really felt. It had always seemed important to make his mate happy, to compromise, to keep the peace; wasn't that the basis of true love? Lately, though, Griffin had been lying awake pondering that thought, turned around: If Theo loved *him*, wouldn't he want Griffin to be happy? Wouldn't Theo have to compromise, give up the idea of adoption and parenting—and settle for loving Holly?

After all, Griffin reasoned, Holly was shockingly easy to love, in spite of her urinary demands. She expected nothing more than food, water, and intermittent attention. If Griffin was too busy or tired, Holly would trot off to chew on a chair leg or doormat, or wait patiently at his feet. A human baby needed to be held in the middle of the night, changed and fed all day long, and would require constant supervision. You couldn't put a toddler in a crate for a few hours while you shopped or went to an R-rated movie. You couldn't drop her at a kennel while you drove down the lakeshore for a weekend getaway at a cottage. She would be yours, all the time, and even if you left her with a nanny or babysitter, you would worry about how she was faring, if she missed you, or was unhappy. A dog didn't care whom she was with, as long as someone filled the bowl and rubbed her head now and then.

Furthermore, Holly would always be a mutt with unchanging needs and desires. A baby would grow into a person who talked and argued and demanded and, possibly one day, might break her parents' hearts. Conversely, of course, she might turn into a lovely, generous human being who would light up their predictable lives. Even so, Griffin couldn't quite imagine either version. He couldn't imagine himself the father of a girl—whether an infant, a schoolchild, or a teenager. Theo would be perfect in the role—of that he had no doubt—but Griffin felt more and more detached as the days passed. He dreaded the interview because it would make the situation all the more real, and the vision—Theo's vision—closer to coming true.

Griffin's head ached. He began to trudge through the gray morning light toward home, Holly's reluctant weight pulling the opposite way on the leash.

"Hey," a voice called out.

Griffin turned and saw that Holly was wagging her tail at a man who was standing on the stoop of the building with the cruel wrought-iron railing. No wonder Holly wasn't budging. The man had reached out one hand to pet her head, and in the other he held a small biscuit. He was tall and movie-star handsome, wearing a white T-shirt that nearly glowed in the dawning light, thick gray socks, and a plaid bathrobe loosely tied. When he bent down toward Holly, Griffin caught a glimpse of red boxer shorts covered in *X*s and *O*s. Everything about him looked polished and new, as if he'd stepped out of an advertisement. As Holly nibbled the treat, wagging maniacally, the man looked Griffin over and asked with genuine concern, "You okay?"

Griffin nodded, suddenly mute.

"I heard someone say he was bleeding to death and thought I should come and have a look," he said, standing back upright. "I'm Ray—I live on the second floor." He pointed to a window. "Above the bastard trying to sleep." He laughed.

"Oh, I guess voices really carry, don't they?" Griffin said. "Well, I didn't mean to create a scene. Sorry I got you out of bed. I just . . . whacked it pretty hard, that's all." He gingerly rubbed the spot on his head. Already a plummy lump was forming. "I'm fine, though."

"What about your hands?" Ray inquired.

"Oh." Griffin shrugged, assuming what he must look like. Apart from the bandages and bump, which gave the impression of a klutz, he knew he was disheveled and raccoon-eyed from lack of sleep. "I had an accident at work," he said, deciding there was no point admitting he'd had two.

"Jeez, what line of work are you in?" Ray asked.

Griffin laughed. "I'm a chef."

"Really? That's great! I'm a film editor, but I always wanted to be a chef, or at least be able to bake really good bread," Ray said, smiling. He had his arms folded across his chest now and seemed perfectly relaxed standing on a cold stone step in his sleepwear. "You have a great dog, by the way," he said. "A lot of personality, I can tell."

"Do you have one?" Griffin asked.

"Me? No."

"Oh. You just have dog treats?"

Ray laughed, a deep, throaty laugh. "Well, I thought I was getting one," he explained. "I used to have a sheltie a few years ago, and after she died, I didn't want to 'replace' her, you know. But recently I thought it was time, and I had a breeder lined up and all, but at the last minute it fell through. Some virus or something got the whole litter."

"What was your dog's name?"

"Audrey—after Audrey Hepburn."

Griffin gaped. "You're kidding! This is Holly Golightly." He pointed at his puppy, now sitting obediently at his feet, the picture of perfect loyalty.

Ray's smile turned skeptical. "You just made that up, didn't you?"

"No, I swear. Look." Griffin knelt down, ignoring the pulsing ache in his head, and clutched Holly's collar, from which dangled the engraved ID tag. Griffin had bought it only days earlier and now felt his heart swell with pride and relief that he had. At the same time, he began to feel a deeper unease over his behavior. It had been years since he'd been attracted to anyone but Theo; he hadn't even thought himself capable of flirting anymore.

Ray came down the steps in his socks to inspect the tag. Once he had proof, he grinned. "That *is* uncanny," he said. He was standing close now, and Griffin stood back up, too, not knowing what to do or say. "Mine used to eat tulip bulbs," Ray said.

"Really?" Griffin said, confused.

"Yeah, just like the real Audrey—you know, when she was a starving child during the war, in the Netherlands. That's how her family survived, supposedly."

"I didn't know that," Griffin said. "I just named her Holly because I loved the movie." He felt a little sheepish at his shallowness.

"Who doesn't?" Ray said, smiling. "It's the best." He paused. "Except for *Sabrina*. So, now I know your dog's name, what's yours?"

"Griffin. Griffin Stenen."

The sky was beginning to grow pink over Lake Michigan. Glancing between the buildings, Griffin could see the distant water already turning a brighter blue, like paint being stirred from below the surface. He felt Ray's gaze on him in the golden light, and part of him wanted to bolt for the safety of home and the familiar arms of Theo, but the other part—the part that kept his sneakers planted on the sidewalk—was eager to see what would happen next.

"You know, you have really amazing eyes," Ray said quietly.

Theo scraped the bottom of the pan, where oatmeal stuck in burned scabs. "Sorry," he said, his voice thinly impatient, either with himself or with Griffin; it was hard to tell which. He was wearing his oldest, rattiest T-shirt with flannel pants that dragged at the hem; the edges were frayed and caught underneath his heels when he walked from the stove to the table. "I thought you'd be right back."

"Holly was sort of slow," Griffin said, sitting down and glancing at his bowl. "Plus, I hit my head."

Theo regarded him like a teacher of a chronically disruptive student. "On what?"

"A railing of some brownstone. It was kind of dark out."

"Gee, you're becoming kind of accident-prone."

Griffin said nothing, letting the silence speak his defense. If Theo was inferring that it was his own fault he'd gotten hurt, there was nothing Griffin could—or would—say. Things between the two of them had been tense lately, and Griffin was weary of the source, which for once remained blessedly unspoken. He didn't want to hear Theo mention a baby or birth mother or adoption agency—or Jude, whom Theo seemed to consider a fairy godmother, ready to grant the greatest of wishes. "Jude says," or "Jude thinks," or "When I called Jude this morning," Theo often reported, revealing how much time he was investing in trying to gain an advantage; it seemed he was becoming fast friends with the social worker, who was supposed to be a neutral go-between.

Griffin poked around the charred chunks and added extra raisins to sweeten the remaining oatmeal, which he then didn't touch. He drank three cups of coffee, instead of his usual one and a half, and pretended to read the front page of the *Tribune* so he wouldn't have to meet Theo's eyes. He was feeling vaguely guilty about his encounter with Ray, though nothing had happened, aside from Ray's casual invitation to "drop by anytime." Yet if Griffin really allowed himself to think about it, something had happened, and it wasn't casual. He'd felt a magnetic tug emanating from Ray, who—Griffin had learned during the thirty minutes they'd spent on the sidewalk—was currently single, in addition to being dogless. On top of that, he was an orphan, too.

Ray's parents had been killed in a car accident one icy January night when he was a senior in high school. He'd delayed college to tend to his younger sister, Carrie, who was fourteen at the time. As Griffin had listened to Ray— and told his own story—he'd felt a strange buzzing between them, something that made the hairs on his neck rise a little in recognition. It was as though they were both alien abductees who'd just found out that they had been through the same terrifying experience, and until now, no one else had understood what it was like.

It was almost as if they'd been destined to meet.

It was the same thing Theo believed about the cocktail party where he and Griffin had met. "Neither of us wanted to go, but for some reason we both went anyway," Theo always began when stories of "how we met" went around a table at a dinner with friends.

Now Theo and Griffin sat in silence for a few minutes, each with a section of the newspaper. Griffin kept one hand on Holly's head. He was becoming used to her amiable presence, her warm nose nudging his leg or her whole head flopping onto his lap.

"I don't think she should eat at the table," Theo remarked.

"She's not eating," Griffin said. "She's sitting. I'm eating."

"I just meant— Never mind." Theo sighed. Then he brightened. "Oh, I talked to Jude—"

"I wouldn't mind if she were more obscure."

"What?"

"*Jude.*"

"Are you making some bad joke I'm not getting?"

"Thomas Hardy? I thought you were the English major,"

Griffin said. "Forget it." He reached into the box of raisins and ate a handful.

"Oh. Ha-ha," Theo said mirthlessly. "Why don't you like Jude?"

"I don't like or dislike her; I've never even *met* her," Griffin said. Then he looked at Theo. "Why don't you like Holly?"

"What do you mean? She's a dog," Theo said, laughing a little.

"So?"

"So? So, it's not a matter of *liking* her. I mean, I guess it is, if you're either a dog person or you're not."

"You're not," Griffin stated, as if for clarification, though his tone was accusatory.

"No, Grif, I'm not. And you knew that all along and you still went ahead and brought her into our home—completely disregarding how *I* felt."

Griffin felt himself balk, tempted to throw it right back. Shouldn't he be honest?

But then Theo said, "I'm sorry. I don't know why we're fighting. I don't care if you have a dog. It's no big deal, really. I mean, I miss sleeping in, but maybe that will change when she's housebroken. And she's probably great with kids. Kids love dogs, right?"

Griffin watched him with a growing sense of sorrow. He wanted to stand up and pull Theo into his arms, to smooth away all the knots in their recent past. To remember—and to remind Theo—why they'd fallen in love in the first place. But then, Theo went on.

"Anyway, Jude said the interview was moved to tomorrow afternoon, and all we have to do is answer some questions. Like, um . . ." He fished around on the counter-top for a piece of paper. He turned back, reading, " 'What are your basic philosophies about parenting? Do you have a name picked out for your child? Does it have any familial or cultural significance? What traditions do you celebrate—religious or other? Did you have a happy childhood?' "

At the last question, Griffin almost wanted to laugh. But then he sobered and said softly, "I can't do this. I'll fail."

"It's not a test."

"Yes, it is. And I'll fail." He paused, feeling for the words. "I could lie—or I could try to explain to some desperate birth mother what it feels like not to have parents, and how you cope with that as a kid, and how it affects every-thing in your life. You obsess about death. You think about how nothing lasts—it would be the last thing she would want to hear."

Theo started to interrupt, but Griffin went on.

"*You* don't even understand, Theo, even though I know you try. But you have a family—a huge, happy family. You still have both of your parents. You even have all your grandparents, for Pete's sake, and all the rest. And they're great. You're great. I know you would be an outstanding father. But I wouldn't be. I can't."

After a long, painful silence, Theo said quietly, "So, I should cancel the interview with the mother. And just . . . drop the whole idea of being a parent." He wasn't asking a question, Griffin knew. He was saying for Griffin what Griffin had been thinking but not saying himself all along.

Griffin felt terrible, and yet, almost relieved. The truth was out now; he didn't have to pretend otherwise. Maybe they would get through it. They got through everything else.

Theo set the papers down and silently turned to the sink to start cleaning up. He seemed to be ignoring Griffin now; the clatter of plates, the harsh scraping of the saucepan, even the vigorous spray of the faucet all rebuked him.

Griffin stood up and started to walk upstairs, with Holly following clumsily at his heels, still unused to stairs. When the phone rang, he waited for Theo to pick up, and when he didn't, Griffin sighed and lifted the receiver in the bedroom.

"Griffin!" exclaimed a woman's throaty voice. Kelly. Or Monica? Griffin never could tell the twin aunts apart over the phone.

"Yes?" he said flatly.

"Jeez, buddy, don't sound so excited," she laughed. "Listen, Mon and I are planning a big bash for Thanksgiving—"

"Sorry, Kelly," Griffin said, cutting in. "We can't. You know we always have Thanksgiving with Joan, with my family."

"I know, I know. I just thought maybe you could make an exception, because we have these friends who are amazing musicians—and they're having a concert at Andy's Jazz Club that weekend, and we thought it would be great to get everyone together to go hear them after we eat ourselves to near death." She paused. "We really want you and Theo there."

Suddenly, Griffin felt anger rising. Why did the Steins always think their plans took priority? Who did they think they were, anyway?

"Well, maybe Theo can be there," Griffin said finally.

"Griffin?" Kelly said. "Did you lovebirds have a fight or something? You sound . . . odd."

"Well, maybe I am odd."

"Grif—"

"I'll tell him you called," Griffin said, and hung up.

He went to the bathroom mirror and pushed aside his hair to inspect his latest wound. It had swelled to the size of a robin's egg, pressing against his skin like it wanted to hatch. He touched it carefully and recoiled at the pain. Then his gaze dropped to his own eyes. He blinked and then stared at himself for a full minute, thinking about how he appeared. His eyes—wide, deep brown, and thickly lashed— were indeed his best feature, though he had to admit the rest of him wasn't bad, either. Griffin knew that in certain circles, he was known to turn heads. He hadn't turned Theo's lately, but Ray definitely had noticed him, in a way no one had in a long while—or maybe ever. It was as if Ray really *saw* him, not just the exterior but all the internal turmoil and history, too.

It seemed that Theo wouldn't ever understand. And it was partly Griffin's own fault, for keeping up the facade that he was fine, that his past was past. He had done it to protect Theo from the weight of tragedy that haunted Griffin, and to keep that weight at bay for his own survival. It was all he could do to take care of himself (and a dog).

The phone rang again. This time, Theo picked up first. Griffin assumed it was Kelly calling back. Theo would fill her in; he had no boundaries, it seemed, when it came to telling family members everything. For instance, the Steins all knew about the various adoption trials and sorrows. And now, Griffin thought, they would know how he really felt about it. He almost wished he hadn't told Theo the truth, but it had been so much easier just skimming along when it seemed the baby issue was moot, when no one was letting them adopt.

"Damn," he said ruefully to his reflection in the mirror.

And then he heard a crash, the distinct sound of breaking glass. Griffin ran back downstairs, heart pounding.

When he got to the kitchen, Theo was leaning calmly against the counter, gazing vacantly at the wall. On the floor was Griffin's blue coffee cup, in tiny shards.

Griffin stared for a moment at the mess, then at Theo. "What happened?"

"I dropped it," Theo said. "No, that's not true. Actually, I threw it. Against the wall, there." He pointed. A triangle of missing plaster indicated the spot.

"Why?" Griffin asked, though he knew the answer. Or thought he did.

"Jude just called," Theo said. He looked pointedly at Griffin. "Yes, your favorite person. She called to say the interview is off. The whole process is off. It seems the mother-to-be went into early labor this morning, and lo and behold, she changed her mind. She's keeping it—her. She's keeping the baby. So we aren't needed anymore."

"Theo—"

"No, don't say you're sorry, because I know you're not."

Griffin said nothing. The phone rang once more, and Griffin hesitated, but when Theo didn't move, he reached for it. This time, he was surprised to hear his elder sister's voice. He welcomed the distraction, and pulled the long phone cord with him around the corner to the hallway.

"It's about Dinah," Alice said.

"Is she okay?"

"Fine, don't worry, it's not something bad."

Griffin relaxed, then remembered the postcard. "What's she doing in Argentina?"

"Well, she's back now," said Alice. And then she explained as Griffin tried to comprehend: the Alaskan cruise, a crew member, a misguided trip to Buenos Aires and some resort near a waterfall.

"Wait—" Griffin said. "She's pregnant? *Dinah?*"

"I know," said Alice. "It's so unlike her. But in a way, it's exactly like her—she thinks it was 'meant to be,' all part of God's plan. Except He forgot to tell her what to do next." She laughed a little. "The thing is—I think she needs a complete change of scenery, to get out of the family homestead, you know? It's high time."

Little bells of alarm were jingling in his head ("The thing is . . ."), and Griffin feared what Alice would say next. What she did say next.

"I was wondering if she could stay with you and Theo for a little while? While she gets on her feet."

"With us? When?" Griffin asked, trying not to sound discouraging.

"After the holidays. She thinks it's a good idea, too, but I think she's just afraid to ask you herself. She doesn't want to impose." Alice paused. "So, is it okay?"

Inwardly, Griffin started to protest; the timing couldn't be worse. But for the first time in a long time, his sisters needed him, and for better or worse, he knew he had to comply. He also knew, without asking, why Alice couldn't keep Dinah with her. It was a matter of space, and lifestyle, and, well, just Alice. And they both knew Dinah; under normal circumstances, she probably would have embarked on her own path long ago. If Griffin now had to be a stopping point along her way to independence, he would do it. And in a way, he thought, her arrival might be a good diversion, considering the mounting tension in his own household.

After he consented and hung up, Griffin stood still for a long moment. Theo was crouched on the linoleum, sweeping up the shattered cup with a whisk broom and a used envelope.

"Guess what?" Griffin said to his curved back. Maybe the news would lighten things up.

"What?"

"Dinah is having a baby!"

Theo craned around to look at him. He shook his head and made a strange sound, a small, choked laugh.

"Lucky girl," he finally said. "That's just . . . swell." He stood and shook the shards into the trash can. *"Lucky, fucking girl."*

It was the first time Griffin had ever heard Theo curse. What was more alarming, however, was the edge in his voice—of condemnation and bitter jealousy. Griffin felt the room shrinking around them. He looked at Theo and thought he saw a complete stranger.

Behind him was the chalkboard on which they made daily lists or left each other messages. Two had been there for weeks: "T, you hog, you ate all the Rice Chex," and "We need paper towels (4-pack)." Below that, their coats were tossed atop each other on a bench, sleeves companionably entwined. The cupboards held matching plates they'd bought or been given; upstairs, their razors and toothbrushes lined the sink; and folded over the rack were twin hand towels embroidered HIS and HIS. The entire house was a testament to a shared life, to a union of common tastes and property, to settled, domestic bliss.

But now it seemed to belong to someone else, to another life. Perhaps more than a cup had been broken, and Griffin didn't know how—or if—they could reassemble the pieces. At the moment, he didn't even care. He felt as detached as Theo seemed to be, though he suspected they would make up later, as they always did. Until then, Griffin didn't dare mention the additional news of Dinah coming to live with them.

"I think I'm going to take Holly for a walk," he said. "We can talk later—if you're in the mood." Without looking back, he pushed his way out the door, pulling on his jacket as he went.

The wind from the lake was picking up and the sun was submerged in clouds that pressed low on rooftops and shoreline; after a promising start, it almost looked like an early snow was on the way. Huddling into his collar, Griffin plowed on, frustrated, angry, fed up.

The more he brooded, the more he wondered what exactly had gone wrong and when; perhaps it had been happening for a long time and he just hadn't been paying attention. He was six blocks from home—and dangerously near a brownstone with a wrought-iron gate—before he realized he'd completely forgotten his dog.

"For affliction does not come from the dust, nor does trouble sprout from the ground, but man is born to trouble as the sparks fly upward," someone says, then flies off with a merry little wave.

"What was that about?" I ask. I know the speaker is familiar: I'm sure we've met. He's been here a lot longer than we have, I know that much. Not that I'm keeping track of time.

"That was Job," says James.

"*The* Job?"

"Yes. He was quoting from his own words, chapter and verse. It's a little surreal, isn't it?"

"He's nothing like I'd expect," I say. Of course, no one is. We're all different selves here.

"He's right, though," James says as we see Griffin struggling with his warring desires. "Trouble in Paradiso."

"Funny how things are going along pretty well, and then out of the blue comes a stranger with dog treats."

James smiles. "I think people just respond to novelty, in every form. And Griffin likes Ray's form."

"*Men,*" I say. And we both laugh.

We know things will change now; a current is stirring through the household. Griffin doesn't know where to turn, so he turns to the nearest, the newest.

James grows reflective. "If I had been around longer for Griffin when he was growing up, I'm sure I would have been awkward, but I like to think I would have been there for him."

"You would have been," I say.

"Awkward?"

I laugh. As a magical snow begins to fall, James and I fall quiet, sweeping up memories of life There. We lie together buried in snow, though not cold. And then the snow dissolves and the air around us fills anew with sparking lights, like fireflies on a summer night. We can hear the whole kingdom breathing.

It is no different from the way it is on Earth, if one is paying attention. If only people would pay closer attention, to everything. Then they would know what mattered without stumbling blindly (albeit at times willingly) in the wrong direction.

Man may be born to trouble, but he doesn't have to stay there.

PART II

Adam, Eva, What's-His-Name

Seven

Alice was ready to hang up her wings. *After This* had played to a packed house five nights a week, plus a matinee, for almost five months. For Alice, that was long enough to inhabit Gwen, the mercurial suicide victim; she was ready for something else, someone else. For one thing, she had to spend fifty minutes every night perched on a rafter under a glowing pink spotlight, from whence she delivered her character's meditations on life, death, and the afterlife. Gwen had hanged herself from the rafter a few years earlier, and that was where she remained, hovering, whenever she visited from Beyond.

"*I died,*" Alice/Gwen solemnly said. "I'm dead. What you see is the shadow of the person I used to be. A shadow, but also much more."

Each night, Alice spun the same story, leaning down conspiratorially toward the audience, seeming to risk falling, but not, an expert trapeze artist. As she spoke, she could hear periodic gasps and sighs, laughter, and an occasional sniffle.

It was steady work and well received, and Alice had to agree with the critics that the play was beautifully written; that the sets and lighting were magical; even, proudly, that the acting was "top-notch." Still, more than any play she'd done before, it was exhausting, and a little perilous. Once, during an early rehearsal, Alice slipped off the ledge and was caught by her safety wires halfway down, narrowly missing a wall but wrenching her shoulder. On another night, all the lights went out during a storm in the first act, and, plunged into darkness for several minutes, Alice suffered an attack of vertigo. The audience's murmurings and her cumbersome papier-mâché wings only added to her anxiety.

Alice blamed it on Imogene's interference with the play's production. With the director's blessing, Imogene had continued to tinker, rewriting lines and expecting cast members to learn them moments before going onstage because she considered the play "organic." She also seemed to enjoy keeping actors on edge, alert. Thus, Alice couldn't relax into Gwen's skin, into the role, with her usual aplomb. She began to think how she preferred dead scribes—Ibsen and Chekhov and Tennessee Williams and others—whose words remained burned onto the page, always the same, but coming to life anew in the interpretations of directors and actors. Alice didn't wish Imogene dead, but she wished she would step out of the limelight, out of the way, and let her do her job.

Furthermore, Imogene had taken to badgering Alice like a pushy therapist, trying to get her to go deeper into her character's anguish by tapping into her own.

"That isn't how I work," Alice declared. "I'm not into 'Method'; I don't use my own pain to act, and my own pain, if I have any, isn't anyone's business." *Especially yours,* she thought.

Imogene had stared at Alice for a long moment. "I know," she said. "I don't have to know what it is. But if you'd only have the guts to use it, your acting would rise to another level. You have a lot of talent, Alice, but you have something else that would lead to even greater things if you wouldn't hold back."

Like any ambitious person, Alice wavered between believing she was capable of being the best and fearing that she might not come close—or come just close enough to look through the glass at what might have been. She was well into her thirties, and it wouldn't be long before she'd be relegated to certain roles, of women of a "certain age." Stardom had a short shelf life. Not that she cared about the fame, Alice told herself; she just wanted the work.

And though Imogene's comments had gotten under her skin, Alice would not heed her plea to give more of herself— not personally anyway. Containment was her forte and also her armor. And it had served her well this long; she wasn't about to let someone like Imogene push her around. Alice would simply push back, or dig in her heels.

Offstage, however, someone else had successfully toppled her.

Since December, two months after their coffee shop encounter, Alice had been seeing Ian McKay so regularly—and exclusively—she'd broken her own long-standing rule: She'd given a lover a key.

"To your heart?" Ian had asked sweetly, eyes crinkling.

Alice laughed. "To my door, for now." She paused. "But maybe."

It wasn't exactly *I love you*, but close enough. To her great surprise, she was falling in love—with Adam, Ian's three-year-old son.

It wasn't at first sight, nor was it immediately mutual. Adam McKay was particular about the people he invited into his life, and, specifically, his "lair." That was his comical term for his tiny bedroom, which held a futon, assorted pillows, a collection of wild animals (hard, molded plastic; none soft or stuffed), and a shelf of books. A star-patterned curtain provided a door, and that, along with a strand of fairy lights pinned around the perimeter, created a magical hideaway.

One night in January, after Alice had visited their apartment several times, Adam finally asked Alice if she wanted to come in. With a serious expression and one small hand clutching the curtain, he stood like an undersize usher waiting to seat her.

To her credit, Ian later noted, Alice did not laugh. "Even though it sounded like something a porn star would say," Ian said, "but with a lisp: 'Come thee my lair.'" Then Alice did laugh, but only because Adam was out of earshot, sound asleep, with one fist gripping a yawning hippo.

When she stepped beyond the starry curtain and knelt down, while Adam gave her the tour of his most treasured possessions, Alice was enthralled. In spite of her habitual indifference, she was aware that children could be lovely, surprisingly adaptable, and entertaining—about which their parents liked to brag to anyone who would listen. Due to the latter, Alice had grown weary of child worship, in which everything the offspring uttered or did seemed akin to holy. She never had understood it.

Yet when Adam sat on the edge of his futon, one hand idly fingering the orange quilt as he spoke, everything changed. Alice was converted. Adam's cheeks were round and pale, and his gray eyes were like smoked glass. His feet, in striped blue socks, softly rubbed back and forth on the slippery space of wood floor. He seemed full of important thoughts.

Listening to Adam's lilting monologue ("I like this one because his horns, thee, they're kind of fuzzy, but oh, they're called 'ant-leers,' and I don't know if that's like in real life or they just made it like that, but I hope they're fuzzy, because if I was a elk, I would want fuzzy ant-leers"), Alice felt herself slipping into the skin of the three-year-old. She could feel his small, steady heartbeat underneath his silken muscles and his little bowl of rib cage as if it were her own. Alice didn't want to move. Even when Ian came to the doorway, smiling down on both of them and asking if they were ready for dinner, Alice didn't want to leave the lair. She'd been lured and pleasantly trapped. She wished Ian would leave them alone awhile longer.

But she stood and thanked Adam for showing her his things and letting her come inside—which had meant far more to her than she could explain. Ian took her hand and led her to the table, where he'd poured wine, and they talked and drank until Adam joined them. He hopped up into a booster seat and merrily ate ziti with his fingers, humming between bites. When he was finished, he dashed off again to play. The apartment felt cozy and safe, secured by the presence of other people, even though one of them was only three. It was an entirely new feeling for Alice, like entering another climate.

"I can tell he likes you," Ian said. "And he's usually a tough customer."

Alice smiled. She knew what was happening, and she wanted all of it, for the moment at least: this apartment, this man, this child, this mismatched set of plates atop this scratched teak table, even this little clot of spilled pasta. She was teetering on the edge, but afraid to let herself fall; there was too much at stake. One didn't casually get involved with children's lives and then leave.

Well, apparently Adam's mother had. Or rather, she had left before getting involved at all. From the abbreviated version Ian had shared, Alice learned that his ex-wife was devastated when she got pregnant. And she wasn't sure Ian was the father.

Clearly, he hated to talk about it, about her; he never even used her name. All Ian would tell Alice was that shortly after that awful admission, his wife learned that her lover was sterile. When Ian found out, he pleaded with his wife to keep the baby; he secretly ("stupidly") thought it might change things between them, bond them back together. In spite of everything, Ian was elated by the prospect of a child, his child. Amazingly, his wife agreed. But upon giving birth, she demanded a divorce—and then relinquished entire custody of the baby to Ian. A child did not fit into her plans, she said. Her last words to Ian were, "Don't try to find me." And then, according to Ian, she disappeared in search of herself.

Alice marveled over this story, and that Ian so capably

had taken on solo parenting. But she supposed Ian was no different from a single woman, like her sister, who wanted to keep and raise her own child. Alice believed that Ian and Dinah were cut from different, perhaps stronger cloth than she was. Or perhaps it wasn't a matter of strength so much as pliability, a willingness to let life become unpredictable and sometimes even unravel. Alice didn't mind surprises, but she prized her independence.

For all of her adult life, she'd plotted her own course. She enjoyed working nights in the theater. She often ate out, on the run, or at the edge of the stage during rehearsals while someone nearby sang or recited their lines or random Shakespeare for fun. At the end of the day, she took long baths, and sometimes smoked cigarettes and drank gin, alone. She knew her limits, but most of all she liked not having anyone else's limits.

Thus, Alice knew she was not the ideal wife or mother. In addition to her inexperience with children, she changed personalities like overcoats, and lovers nearly as easily (though not really, and not lately). Actors she knew rarely married unless it was to other actors.

Ian had a "real" job as a broker for an auction house, though he said he personally disliked antiques, no matter how supposedly valuable. His work seemed to involve a lot of paper, reams of it, requiring signatures and initials, and phone calls that sometimes sounded like modern matchmaking ("Richard, she said it's not her type, and believe me, I know her type by now"). Alice marveled at the way Ian jostled work and home life, seemingly content in both. She wondered what it would be like to live like that, to form a family out of what life handed over.

An hour after the kitchen was clean and Adam was asleep in his glowing cave, Ian led Alice into his bedroom for the first time. The sheets smelled freshly laundered, and the only light came from a small lamp in the hallway. When Ian gently pushed Alice onto his bed, her head landing squarely on his pillow, she let herself pretend that tonight she *was* the wife and mother. After they undressed, Ian began slowly kissing her and running his hands along her hips; Alice got lost in imagining that they finally had a night alone, their child asleep in his bed.

Then Ian jerked away and flung the sheet over Alice like a sail, saying sweetly, "Hey, buddy, what's up?"

"I lost my hippo," Adam said from the doorway.

"He's probably right there in your bed."

"He's not."

"Go look again. Okay? It's pretty late, madman."

"Okay." There followed a long pause. "Daddy, can you look?"

"Sure."

Through the scrim of sheet, Alice could see Ian, with a towel hastily tied around his waist, guiding his small boy down the hallway. She waited, motionless, just in case.

When he returned, he closed the door quietly, tiptoed to the bed, and peeled back the sheet covering Alice, looking her over. And then he slid down beside her once more, tugging her close.

He said, "Just so you know, this doesn't happen every day. Or really, ever, lately."

"The interruption?"

"No. A woman in my bed."

It scared Alice a little, this confession, but the thought of Ian's arms around her while his small boy slept down the hall made her feel something brand-new; maybe it wasn't just a fantasy. Maybe this was where she was meant to be. It sounded like something her sister would say.

"What are you thinking?" Ian whispered.

"Nothing."

"Liar," Ian teased. "I know what I'm thinking."

Then, while they lay silently in the dark, Ian pressed his hand between her legs. She started to move toward him, but he nudged her gently down. "Just let me," he said quietly. And he distracted her with his touch, her nerve endings rising to meet his fingers, gently exploring. She caught her breath, and then she came, collapsing into his hand. It was the sweetest thing a man had ever done, just for her, just that quietly. And then he whispered, "Sweet dreams," and kept his arms wrapped around her until she fell asleep.

At dawn, Alice woke, disoriented. Then she looked around and panicked that they would be discovered intertwined. As Ian slept on, Alice slid away to dress and escape before Adam came in, as undoubtedly he would. She moved quickly, pulling on her clothes. As she turned to go, she felt a presence at her side. She looked down.

Adam's face was a little moon floating in the semidarkness, lit by some intangible quality.

"Hey," Alice said quietly. "You're awake early."

"Mm-hm."

"Are you hungry?" Alice asked, hoping for diversion; it seemed unseemly, her still being here. However, Adam simply took her hand and led her to the kitchen.

"I like Eggos," he said, "but these guys like Cheerios." Alice saw that he was clutching a menagerie, hooves and bristled tails sticking between his fingers. He set the animals on the table. "They're *really* hungry."

Alice opened cupboards and found the cereal and a bowl, which she filled to the brim.

"That's too many," Adam said, giggling. He plucked out a small handful and lined up individual Cheerios, one for each animal. He guided the horse's nose toward one, making nibbling sounds, and then did the same with the hippo and the elk and something that looked like a rat but might have been a mongoose; his collection veered toward the exotic. Alice had noticed a peacock and a manatee, as well as an albino pony. Or perhaps a unicorn? There was a nub where a horn might have broken off.

"Where do you get these?" Alice asked, picking up one to inspect it. The details were impressive: lidded eyes, hollowed ears, striated fur, and tiny, tiny fangs.

"They just come," Adam said, eyes wide.

"Really?"

He nodded. "Sometimes there's one on my pillow! And one time, I found a"—he paused, scanning the table, before pointing to an orca—"killer whale right in my *shoe.* Isn't that funny? Whales *have* to have water. But I put him in my bath and he was okay."

Alice didn't remark on the fact that said whale now lingered on the tabletop, its gaping pink mouth tipped toward a piece of dry cereal. She thought of the mysterious appearance of toy animals, and the forethought on Ian's part to obtain and then hide them, to foster a sense of magic. It was the trait she recalled most tenderly about her mother. She admired Ian all the more, yet reminded herself not to be swayed by what was probably normal parental attentiveness.

Also, Alice knew she should leave; she had errands to run before the matinee performance, and she hadn't showered yet. She should have been itching to go, but Adam pinned her in place.

So she stayed, hunting for frozen waffles, then syrup ("You can put on lots, my dad won't mind"), then milk in the right cup ("I can drink from a big cup, you know"), followed by a paper towel to swab spills, and then a damp one to wipe the sticky mouth.

When he finished, Adam slid away from the table, slowly curling off the chair like a serpent, purposefully clunking his head and dramatically rubbing it, all the while watching Alice—showing off, yet utterly guileless. It was something to observe, a winning performance. Alice laughed and Adam grinned, all of his tiny teeth showing like little pebbles.

When he ran off to use the bathroom, Alice tiptoed back to the bedroom. Ian was buried facedown, and she pulled back the covers, looking him over this time. As she leaned in and kissed him softly on the shoulder, inhaling his warm skin, he jerked around and pulled her on top of him.

"Whoa!" she said, startled. "Adam's up, you know."

"Adam who?" Ian said, grinning. He ran a hand underneath her sweater. "And where do you think you're going, missy, all dressed and everything?"

"To work," she said, holding his hand in place on her waist, though she let it drift upward. "We have a matinee."

"You know, you're amazing," Ian said, fondling her. "I

can't get over it, every time I see you onstage. It's you, but it's not you."

"Every time? Like how often?"

He thought. "Six times."

"Are you kidding? *When?*" Alice gaped at him, pulling away and dislodging his hand from her breast.

Ian sat back against the pillows, looking sheepish. "Opening night, and then a couple of Wednesday matinees, and two Fridays, and, uh, last Saturday."

"That's insane," Alice said, and laughed. "How can you stand it?"

"Well, you do it night after night, right?"

"Yes, but I get paid—you're paying."

"*Tu es qui en vaut la peine.*"

"I don't speak French," Alice said. "Translate, *s'il vous plaît.*"

"You are worth it," Ian said softly. "You're worth every dime."

Alice was used to flattery; it was the currency of every relationship she'd had. But this somehow was different. Ian was so earnest, she didn't know what to say.

She stood up and then Ian rolled out of bed and pulled on a pair of jeans from a small pile on the floor. He turned to look at Alice. "I know. I need to do laundry."

"I'm not judging," she said, and laughed. "But I really do have to go. Thanks for—you know."

"Yeah, it was wonderful."

"Not for you, though."

"That's what you think, *ma chérie*," Ian said, smiling sweetly as he sidled up to her, pressing close. "I could do it again," he whispered. "How about right now?"

"Dad," said Adam, suddenly appearing at their sides, brushing like a cat against Alice's legs. "What are you gonna do?"

"Uh, nothing, little man," Ian said, recovering without a beat. "We were just talking about doing our laundry together, you know, since Alice lives upstairs?"

"Good! Can I put in the quarters?"

They laughed, and Alice kissed Ian on the cheek and then bent to kiss Adam on the top of his head. He didn't pull away or protest, but leaned into her side.

"Bye, guys," Alice said.

And as she walked down the hallway and through the door, she almost believed that this was her life.

"I like him," I say. "I think he's the one."

"Really?" James says.

"But, alas, he's only three."

James chuckles.

There is no shortage of little ones around us, running with dogs and any kind of furred creature, climbing nimbly up trees, dangling from their limbs, or flitting overhead now and then. Sometimes we join them. They are irresistible.

"The attraction is obvious; she's smitten," I say, climbing high. The view is stunning, golden light tinting every-colored leaves.

"Getting involved isn't simple, though," James says, following me.

"Especially for someone with an aversion to children," I say as we settle on soft, thick branches, bobbing gently.

"I wouldn't say *aversion*."

However, I recall how utterly disinterested Alice seemed when Dinah arrived, a tiny, adorable bundle. She had reacted the same way with Griffin. It was as if Alice assumed she herself had arrived fully formed, skipping over the stages of infancy and toddlerhood. But I didn't consider it a character flaw. I liked that each of the children was distinctly different, true to themselves from early on.

"But children do change everything," I say. "For better or for worse."

They make life fuller, but also more complicated, and, at times, unhappier, depending on the child or the parent. Some people are meant to be mothers or fathers; it's like a thread drawn through their bodies that naturally wants to twine to the generation coming next—offspring or adopted. Others don't feel that pull but have children anyway, to their detriment—or delighted surprise. And some, like Alice, don't feel the pull at all, and stay contentedly solo.

Until a certain someone comes along, draws back the curtain, and pulls her inside.

Eight

Dinah was living in denial. She supposed it was simply a stage of unplanned gestation perversely akin to the stages of dying, and perhaps one day soon she would move into acceptance.

Meanwhile, she felt the irrefutable truth dawning each morning in the folds of Theo and Griffin's cushy guest bed, with Holly Golightly licking her face; in the sounds of trucks rattling down Armitage; in the yeasty smell of warm ciabatta rising from the nearby deli; in the muted burble of water through pipes as Griffin prepared for an early shift. Then Dinah would remember. She had severed her regular life and set herself adrift in the midst of her brother's life in Chicago—and behold, she was great with child.

Everything now was leading to the arrival of the alien form that turned in her womb, ran its salamander limbs along the inside walls, and sometimes shook her like a tiny earthquake. Late at night, when time mercifully seemed to slow down, Dinah lay cocooned in the darkness, swaying on the languid hours, trying not to think about what was ahead. She clung to the hope that a mystical kind of clarity would accompany the birth; that things would fall into place and she would know what to do. She would know how to reshape her life, after ripping it wide open like a badly knit sweater.

Months earlier, when Dinah finally had told Joan that she was pregnant, her grandmother was predictably surprised, though at first subdued. Dinah had always appreciated that Joan didn't criticize her or her siblings for their choices; when they were young, she only harped on little things like manners and grammar, laziness or unwashed hair. Joan rarely lost her cool. Maybe she figured that, given what they had survived early on, the rest was merely incidental. For instance, Dinah had no idea how Joan felt about Griffin's homosexuality; if she had any issues with it, she kept them to herself. And when Alice once claimed she wasn't sure she believed in marriage, or maybe even absolute fidelity, Joan disputed the latter point, but she didn't belabor it. ("You make your bed, you have to lie in it," she'd said.)

Thus, Joan had listened to Dinah's abridged explanation for her condition, and then grew practical, as if it were merely a diversion on their normal domestic path.

"So, which room should we set up as a nursery?" Joan asked a little too brightly. She was sitting across the kitchen table from Dinah, wearing the "lucky" cable sweater she always wore on Tuesdays to play bridge. She looked, thankfully, healthy and robust.

Dinah met her grandmother's eyes. "I'm not going to have the baby here."

"Well, where—" Joan broke off. "Have you found another place to live? Are you sure this is good timing? I mean, you're going to need help," she said, adding a shade ominously, "You have no idea, sweetheart, doing this alone."

"No," Dinah said. "I mean I don't have another place exactly, but I already talked to Griffin and Theo, and I'm going to move out there and stay with them for a while, till I get settled." She took a deep breath, realizing she'd been holding her ribs clamped together. "I know it's all a lot to take in at once. But Joan, when this happened, it was a shock, but then I realized I've really needed a change for a long time. I think it's time for me to get out of D.C., away from—well, everything that's familiar and the *same*."

Joan said nothing, then: "Was this by any chance Alice's idea?"

"No. Why?"

"Well, she's made no secret of the fact that she thinks I've coddled you too much, and that I need to let you go." She paused. "As if I were holding you captive! Is that how you feel?" As she studied Dinah, her eyes began to water.

Dinah reached over to clasp her grandmother's hand. "No, *never*. I love living with you, I always have." She let go, clearing the emotion from her throat. "But it's time I tried to be on my own—"

"With your brother? And Theo?"

Dinah shrugged. It did sound contradictory, and though she wouldn't admit it to Joan, she knew she couldn't jump ship without a little life ring to hold on to. Theo and Griffin were the most stable couple she knew, and they had told her that of course she should come.

"I think I've found a job in Chicago," she told Joan, "working in a homeless shelter, which I've always wanted to do. I'm just going to stay with the guys until I can find my own place."

"But you're having a *baby*."

"I know, but I think it will all work out. Women have babies on their own all the time."

Joan looked at her for a long moment, and Dinah suspected she was thinking that Dinah was being utterly naïve. And while she knew that it probably was true, in that moment, in that look, Dinah felt certain she had to leave. She couldn't have her grandmother—essentially her mother—standing by to watch her fail, or even, possibly, succeed. Most of all, she didn't want Joan to feel obligated to help raise her child. She'd already reared two generations.

"You just have to let me do what I need to do," Dinah said finally.

When she told her boss and coworkers in late November that she was moving to Chicago—and was pregnant (obviously)—they all wished her luck and smiled too hard. Dinah could tell that they were regarding her slightly askance, as if they wondered if they had ever really known her, like an A student with a secret life.

She spent her last few days forging the congressman's signature on House of Representative calendars to be sent to his constituents, and drafting letters to Boy Scouts who had metamorphosed into Eagle Scouts. "Congratulations, James! As your congressman, I applaud this outstanding accomplishment." These were usually the duties of the receptionist or college interns, but Dinah had finished all of her legislative work, as well as a backlog of correspondence, and had contacted lobbyists she'd befriended to let them know of her departure. She had even cleaned out her desk; the surface shone, empty of papers. Finally, Vera, the office manager, cornered Dinah in her cubicle and told her that she could leave early. Her expression read, *should*.

"You don't have to do busywork, you know," Vera said. "And to be honest, you seem like you're not really 'all here.'" Vera was two years younger than Dinah, but she seemed more sophisticated. She wore her hair in a chignon and dressed in elegant suits, with shoes that always matched. Dinah looked down at Vera's shoes, gleaming patent leather the color of cream against the cherry red of the carpet.

"I think I might throw up," Dinah said, lunging for her wastebasket.

Vera kindly went into the tiny office kitchen to fetch wet paper towels for her. Watching Dinah blot her mouth, Vera said in a hush, "I hope you really want this kid, Dinah. I mean, not that it's any of my business. It just seems like—I can't really imagine, actually."

"Neither can I," Dinah said. She stood up to take the wastebasket down the hall to rinse it out in the ladies' room. It was not, she knew, an auspicious conclusion to her eight-year career in government.

More significant things were coming to an end. After the holidays, Dinah helped Joan take down the decorations, and began to pack. The night before she was to leave for Chicago, Dinah stayed up until Joan was asleep. Then she wandered through the rooms of the Takoma Park house she'd known since birth.

She paused outside the room that had been her parents' bedroom, long ago turned into a sewing room piled with remnants and cotton batting for the quilts Joan started but never finished. Dinah passed her siblings' rooms, empty and silent, with teenage posters still tacked to the walls. Downstairs in the kitchen, she ran her fingers over the yellow-flecked Formica and studied the familiar shadows cast by an elm outside the window. She glanced for the thousandth time at the pantry where her mother had died, no longer spooked by the thought. The house felt like a living thing to Dinah, pulsating with the personalities of the whole family, living and dead. It was comforting—and, at times, suffocating.

It occurred to Dinah for the first time that perhaps she had stayed so long not for Joan's sake, as she had convinced herself, but because she didn't want to let go of the only place that felt like home. Since she possessed fewer memories than did her sister or brother, she'd clung the hardest to the ones she had. But with her pregnancy, the past was fading in the mist; she could only go forward to the equally obscure shore on the other side, where a future loomed. And she was ready—or not; either way, Dinah was going.

The next morning, dark and threatening snow, she and Joan shared their last breakfast and then a tearful but stoic farewell. Dinah told Joan she appreciated everything she'd done for her. Joan kissed her and told her that she only wanted her to be happy. Then she cleared their plates and cups and told Dinah to go, before they both got "too mushy."

When her friend Touki arrived to drive her to the airport, Dinah waved to Joan on the steps, then turned around to face the road in all its literal and figurative forms. *Less trav-*

eled, she thought. *To perdition.* For a while she and Touki rode in silence, feeling the weight of farewell between them.

"Shit!" Touki said.

"What?" Dinah asked, startled. "Did you miss the turn?"

They were on Rock Creek Parkway, and Touki sometimes forgot to merge or exit; in general, she was a bad driver, but Dinah was grateful she was willing to take her to the airport. She had been watching the scenery whip past— the archways of barren branches and stone bridges high overhead, the zoo and the winding bike paths—thinking this was the last time, et cetera.

"You're leaving, that's what!" Touki said angrily. Her eyes blazed, and even her tidy Afro seemed to bristle.

"You just got that?"

Touki glared at her for too long, her eyes off the road. Dinah's heart beat faster at the threat of vehicular disaster and her friend's apparent wrath. "I just can't believe you're doing this," Touki said. "After all we've been through together!" Now she was crying, one hand loosely grasping the wheel, the other wiping her eyes. A driver in the next lane honked to alert her to her weaving, and she jerked the car back in line.

Dinah teared up, too, feeling like she and Touki were still nine, when Dinah was preparing to move to Greece for a year. "A whole *year*!" Touki had moaned. And when they applied to different colleges, they'd parted in the same way, heartbroken.

"But you have George," Dinah said, wiping her nose on a fast-food napkin she found on the floorboard. "You guys are practically married—I hardly ever see you as it is."

"But he's . . . *George*," Touki said. "Who am I going to complain to about him?"

"You can still call me," Dinah said, and then laughed. "But you know you never complain about him except to say he's too perfect to be true."

Touki smiled then. "Damn it, girl. You really are doing this, aren't you?"

"I am."

"Well, you better stay in touch. And take care of yourself, you hear me?"

Dinah promised. It began gently to snow, fat, sporadic flakes that stuck to the windshield, and they both *oohed* a little at the sight.

And then, everything seemed to speed up. Dinah was at the airport gate, and then on the plane. And suddenly she was walking through O'Hare, dragging her luggage like an oversize pet, pausing to vomit in the ladies' room.

After helping Dinah settle into the guest room—adorned with plumped pillows and fresh-cut flowers—Griffin fixed her snacks at odd hours and Theo rubbed her feet, or wedged a cushion into the small of her back. Even more than her brother, Theo doted. Coming from a large family with numerous children and recently arrived twin nieces, he seemed a bit of an expert. He noted with satisfaction the incremental changes in Dinah's body: the weight gain and altered gait, the glossy thickening of her hair, the glow of her skin, the fatigue shadowing her eyes. If she'd let him see, Theo likely would have exclaimed about her swelling pubis, growing areolas, and even the alarming tiny hairs sprouting around them. Griffin, thankfully, was less interested, though he cheerfully accepted Dinah's presence and didn't press her about getting an apartment, though she had begun to look.

As the weeks dragged on, however, without her finding a suitable place to live, Dinah felt she had to keep reminding the two men that her stay was only "temporary."

"Don't worry, Di," Theo said over dinner one night. "We love having you here." He smiled. "You can even stay when you have the baby, you know—winter is a hard time to try to find an apartment. Plus, you might need us."

"Yeah, he's right," Griffin said. "Besides, on your income, I don't think you're going to find anything that isn't roach-infested or underneath the el."

Dinah laughed. He was right. The job at the homeless shelter turned out to be currently unavailable; she was told that an employee would not be leaving until summer after all, and that she could come back then for another interview. So, apart from her savings, Dinah's income consisted of her hourly wage at Cupcake Heaven, a nearby bakery, where she was working merely two days a week.

Making scones and sugaring snickerdoodles wasn't what she'd hoped for, but it was something to do, and a welcome alternative to the brisk chaos of a congressional office. And Dinah liked the apparent contentedness of Midwesterners; they didn't seem to need up-to-the-minute accounts of politics or world events as Washingtonians did. While they walked as briskly, it was as likely due to the cold as to a sense of professional urgency. It was almost a relief to stop worrying about bills or budget crises. Now Dinah cared about frosting density and how many customers could fit inside the bakery when the lines grew long.

Also, instead of packing sandwiches from home, she was able to take the bakery's day-old pastries and "blunders"— muffins that broke, misshapen éclairs, badly iced cupcakes— and distribute them to homeless men and women she passed on her daily walks.

When she talked to Joan, usually twice a week, Dinah assured her grandmother that she was doing fine. "Of course, I miss you," she always added, though it wasn't entirely true. She was busy and preoccupied, and loved living with her brother and Theo. Unlike Joan, they were attuned to popular culture, to current movies and books and fashion. It was like being back in college with roommates who shared her youthful interests. They never discussed strategies for bridge or lamented the caloric count of Cool Whip. And they smelled of men's cologne, a welcome change.

The only drawback was her place as the third party, skirting the edges of a confirmed, virtually married couple. Griffin and Theo spoke in long-practiced shorthand, shared inside jokes, and flirted when they thought Dinah wasn't listening. If she were brutally honest, until she lived with them, she had never thought too much about the physical intimacy they shared. While she considered herself enlightened and open-minded, not in the least homophobic, picturing Griffin and Theo making love was as disconcerting as a child imagining his or her parents in the act. Maybe a little more so.

Some nights, Dinah lay awake, trying to find a comfortable position with her burgeoning belly, and heard faint moaning coming from the master bedroom. At first, she froze, both curious and repelled, thinking of what, exactly, might be taking place on the other side of the wall. But then one of them—usually Griffin—would mumble, "You're dreaming. Wake up." Then, after another moan: "*C'mon*. Stop." And then there would be silence, or soft snoring. After that, it occurred to Dinah that either her brother and his lover were very, very quiet or they weren't having a lot of sex.

And then, after their initial welcome, the pampering and fussing over her, Dinah began to notice a palpable tension between the two men. She heard Griffin coming and going at odd hours and worried that he was straying from home, from Theo.

One morning in February, Dinah walked into the kitchen after hearing Theo slam the back door on his way out. She found her brother muttering and fuming as he plowed from table to sink, rattling dishes. Then he abandoned them altogether and turned to yank the dog leash from a hook.

"What's going on?" Dinah asked.

Griffin sighed, glancing at her. "Ups and downs, peaks and valleys—the maladies of married life."

"So, you're just going through a rough patch," Dinah said sympathetically. "But did something happen? Of course, it's none of my business."

Griffin shrugged. "Nothing happened. Or, actually, as far as Theo is concerned, nothing happening is the problem.

You know we were trying to adopt. Well, he was, and I was just sort of keeping my mouth shut, hoping for the worst. Probably I jinxed it."

"What does that mean?"

"I don't want a kid, Di. He does. It's a simple conundrum." Griffin paused and knelt to fasten the leash to Holly's collar. "That might be an oxymoron."

"Why don't you?" Dinah asked her brother as her hand went to her belly defensively. She was in her final weeks, a walking billboard for procreation.

"I don't know. I just don't see myself as a parent. Maybe it sounds selfish, but I really can't imagine it." He stood and looked at her then. "No offense."

"I know." Dinah didn't say anything else, just bent over to pet Holly Golightly behind the ears and stroke her ridged spine. She felt tender toward the dog, and was beginning to understand Griffin's attachment to Holly, as well as to observe Theo's lack of it. Dog hair, wafting about like tiny tumbleweed, was a particular vexation—as was the dog it was attached to. Theo complained about the yelping, and the smell of dog food, and the latest chewed shoes. But clearly, there was more going on.

"Griffin," Dinah asked. "Is there someone else?"

Her brother seemed to bristle, but he maintained his composure. "Someone else what?"

"You know—another guy?"

"Theo and I have been together a long time, Di," Griffin said. "It's—I can't explain. I could never imagine being with anyone else, but all of a sudden, I sort of can. Imagine it, I mean. Not that I would—" He stopped. "I can't talk about this right now. I have to get Holly outside before she does some serious damage."

"Want me to come along?" Dinah asked.

Griffin smiled. "Uh, sorry, but we're going to run, and you're a little slow these days." He paused. "There's some spinach frittata in the fridge I brought home from work, if you're hungry."

Dinah watched her brother head out the door, and in the pensive tilt of his head, she saw him at thirteen. That was the year after Greece, after Joan had settled them back home. They'd had to adjust all over again to the loss when they walked through the rooms filled with the scent of their father's Old Spice and his belongings—his coats and shoes and books and replicas of Greek pottery and ruins. Their father had had a tiny plaster Parthenon—bought long before their trip—which he'd kept on top of his dresser. Griffin took it and hid it in his own room, along with the cologne and a tweed jacket. Dinah never said anything about his acquisitions, because she kept some things, too—a clay lamp that looked like a genie might live inside, and a plaid scarf she wore each winter. It no longer smelled like her father, but she felt some part of him was trapped within its fibers; she'd never washed it. And Alice still wore their mother's red coat trimmed with rabbit fur.

That first year home from Greece, Griffin had developed a way of walking that seemed faintly crooked, his head at a tilt, as if he couldn't quite lift it, couldn't face life directly. Over time, he learned to stand erect, but Dinah noticed that whenever he was sad or brooding, his neck would bend like a flower stem. Like it did now.

After Griffin was gone, Dinah tugged on her coat, shoved her feet into slip-on boots, and headed out the door for what had become her daily rounds. Even on her days off, she stopped at Cupcake Heaven, filling her bags with the cast-off goods. One of the men on her route ate only cheese Danish, and another begged her, half jokingly, to "stop with the sweet cakes and bring me some beer." Sometimes she brought him coffee, and once, against her better judgment (but the weather was so bitterly cold), a tiny bottle of schnapps.

During the winter months, the windchill skimming over Lake Michigan could be subzero, and sometimes the daily high reached only the single digits. It was bad enough for Dinah to have to adjust after a lifetime of milder winters in Maryland; she couldn't imagine how the people camped over sidewalk grates could bear it.

She knew that her small mission was partly self-serving. Anyone who helped "those less fortunate" often did it to assuage the guilt of privilege, to feel more worthy, or secretly to laud himself for good behavior. Dinah did it because she believed she had a responsibility to do something meaningful. To Dinah, befriending the most destitute seemed as logical a task as any, even though she knew some of them wouldn't remember her from one day to the next, and one man in particular was openly hostile. But all she could do was try.

Thankfully, today the sun shone with promise, shimmering across the lake and turning windows of skyscrapers silvery as new coins. And the bakery warmed Dinah, filled as it was with good cheer and the scent of chocolate and yeast. The shelves behind glass fairly sparkled with sugar-sprinkled cupcakes, swirled butterscotch icings, and jam like dark jewels in the center of each Danish. Customers milled about, trying to choose.

"Hey, Dinah," said Belinda, the manager, who, as usual, was a vision in white—apron, shirt, "nurse shoes," and platinum hair spiked into swirls like meringue. She dropped her voice to a whisper. "There's a whole tray of just *slightly* burned molasses cookies. If you want them."

"Thanks," Dinah said, coming around the counter to the kitchen. She inspected the cookies, scraped a few of the dark edges with the side of an icing knife. "They're fine, I think."

Mario, one of the bakers wearing headphones, nodded hello, then went back to bobbing to his private sound track while shoveling dough out of a massive mixer. Nearby, Kitty, a teenager who had dropped out of high school, was arranging heart-shaped cookies on trays. She was wiry, with razor-edged hair streaked a different color every week. Today, the swaths were blue, "for Valentine's Day," she said without irony.

Once, Dinah had asked her if she ever considered going back to school, and Kitty had shrugged, glancing at Dinah's protruding belly.

"I don't know. Do you think about going back to being unpregnant? I mean, sometimes you make a decision and there's kind of no going back."

"Right," Dinah said, chagrined.

"I mean, no offense," Kitty hastened to add. "I just didn't belong in school. I like working, I like making money, I like making cookies." She grinned coyly. "And I like having sex with my boyfriend in the middle of the afternoon, instead of, like, studying the periodic table. Life's short, baby."

"That's true," Dinah said. Suddenly she felt very old. And she half wanted to warn Kitty about the dangers of sex with her boyfriend ("Look at *me*"), but she thought it none of her business.

Now Kitty turned and smiled at her, holding out a pink cookie dotted with silver dragées. "Here," she said. "Maybe you can give it to one of your sweeties."

Dinah laughed as she accepted the gift. "How many do you think I have?"

She shrugged. "I meant, those guys on the street you feed. I think it's cool, by the way."

"Oh. Well," Dinah said. "Thanks, Kitty."

Balancing her paper bags full of warm baked goods, she proceeded south on Halsted and almost immediately met the white-bearded man who called himself Merlin. He claimed it was his given name, and Dinah believed him until he began to regale her with tales of the dark forest and sea nymphs and black magic. He always spoke in a mixture of Old English and an odd sort of brogue, and peppered his speech with names and terms clearly gleaned from fairy tales and fables. However, when Dinah once asked him if he was familiar with the Knights of the Round Table, he scoffed at her and said, "What are you thinking about? That's Dorothy Parker, you silly bitch."

Today, Merlin approached Dinah with what seemed like recognition.

But then he barked, "Stay away from me! You wilt bewitch me." Up close, his eyes looked rheumy and unfocused. Dinah had guessed his age to be around fifty, but he might well have been twenty years older.

She stood still, a few feet back, only faintly apprehensive. She'd never thought Merlin was any threat; he was just lost.

"Hi, Merlin," she said calmly. "It's me, Dinah, your friend. I brought you an apple tart." She looked into the bag. "And a Valentine cookie."

"You tell lies and falsehoods," he snarled. "You are *the Lady of the Lake.*"

Dinah remembered that there was a Catholic church in the neighborhood called Our Blessed Lady of the Lake, but Merlin more likely was referring to Arthurian legend.

She suspected that if she handed Merlin the food, he would deem it poison and throw it at the curb. Dinah worried about his health—he was painfully thin, even with layers of clothing—but she couldn't force him to eat. And she knew that he received one meal a day at least from a soup kitchen and spent most nights in a shelter—or so he had said in lucid moments. And while he might need medication, as did many on the streets, Merlin seemed content to wander about the roads of his elaborate fantasy world. Dinah decided that it was best to leave him there for now.

Without another word, Dinah turned and disappeared around the corner, imagining that Merlin was breathing a sigh of relief that he was safe from her wiles.

She walked for a few more blocks before she found the familiar cluster of men who took turns panhandling and then gathered to share food and conversation. They had an easy camaraderie and nicknames for each other like "Choirboy" and "Crackhead." The only one with a real name, Sam, appeared blind, clutching a white-tipped cane and staring straight ahead, but if Dinah talked to him directly, he seemed to focus his gaze on her, so she never could tell if it was a ruse. The whole group claimed to be Vietnam War veterans, though two of them clearly were too young.

"Hi, baby," several said at once when Dinah approached.

"Her name's *Diana*," the one named Kansas said. "Just like Princess Diana. Show some respect!"

Dinah didn't bother to correct him. Suddenly, she felt desperately hungry, on the verge of swoony. After passing out the muffins and Danish, she reached in the bag and broke off a piece of the pink cookie and stuffed it in her mouth.

"You all right, miss?" one of the men asked. He was someone Dinah didn't recognize. Sometimes the group shifted and gained or lost members.

She nodded. "Just a bit hungry." Almost immediately after swallowing, she felt better. She glanced down at her belly, which ludicrously seemed to have grown instantly, the skin tauter, more constricting beneath her coat.

"Well, you're eating for two, princess," Kansas said. "You shouldn't be out walking around here by yourself, messing with this nasty crowd." He laughed. The others laughed, too.

"You're not all bad," she said, leaving them to laugh harder as they debated about whether she meant it inclusively or was singling out one or more of them. Dinah grinned. "See you guys tomorrow," she said.

In an hour, she had emptied her bags and bought coffee for various people who looked particularly cold. She knew that for every cupcake and sandwich she handed out, or for every dollar someone stuffed into a paper cup held out, there were dozens, hundreds more who were not receiving a thing.

Griffin and Alice sometimes called her "Pollyanna,"

but what they failed to understand was that Dinah wasn't Pollyanna so much as the Grimm maiden spinning the endless mound of straw, hoping not that it would turn to gold but that she could finally be free from the burden of trying so hard. She could never do enough. Even so, making her rounds gave Dinah a sense of purpose that just waiting for her baby could not; at least it helped keep her mind off the impending event.

What a concept! A tiny personal cake with swirled sugared icing that can fit in a palm. When I was a child, I thought that cupcakes should grow on trees, like apples or oranges, so I could stroll through an orchard and pluck them at will. It turns out, happily, that they do. And I can.

I am licking a little of the frosting from my forearms when James appears. "Where have you been?" I ask. "I haven't seen you in about a million years."

He smiles and twinkles at me. "Actually, I've been just over there," he says, pointing to a row of trees I haven't reached yet. I'm taking my sweet time. "I was getting caught up on Joan."

"Oh?" I say. Since she and Dinah parted when Dinah moved out, we have waited for a glimpse. "Is she lonely?"

"No," James says, and smiles. "I've heard she's got a secret."

I squint at him in the candy-colored light. "Heard from whom?"

He looks at someone I can't see from where I sit. "Edgar."

"Oh, your father! Of course!" I turn and spy him across the orchard, his arms laden with cake. I wave and he grins.

I only met him Here, as he died long before James and I fell in love. "What a lovely surprise."

"I know. I haven't bumped into him in ages. But he looks in on Joan now and then. The secret is that she has a little friend."

"How little?"

James laughs. "A hair over five feet, like Joan. His name is Peter, a retired professor of economics, an ace at bridge, and a widower. They're just friends, but it's a good start."

"Yes, better late than never."

Joan had been a widow already for twenty years, and had been dating, but she put all that aside for the sake of our children after my death—and then James's. It was saintly, though not all that healthy. Everyone needs love that isn't merely filial.

The Greeks have numerous definitions for love, all of them necessary. *Agape,* which can be a love of the Divine, is also known as deep, unconditional affection for another person (sometimes James called me *"agape mou"* when we were married), and which sometimes, but not always, leads to *eros.* That, of course, is the heart-palpitating love that encompasses desire and lust—and just wanting to be close enough to smell the object's hair. All the time. True love is a wonderful melding of both *agape* and *eros.*

Philia, or charity, is the love for one's family, friends, community. For years, Joan put most of herself into *philia,* including her church, volunteer work, and bridge club. Then, when tragedy struck, she focused on her grandchildren. She gave them stability and affection and a sense of normal family life—while suppressing her own needs. The Greeks have another word, *storge*, which is a kind of long-suffering love, putting up with a situation, or difficult people.

James took the sabbatical to Athens as much for Joan's sake as his own; he wanted to free his mother from caring for the children—for a year at least—so she could see her own friends, and even boyfriends.

"And then I had to go and die, too," James says, sighing. Then he smiles. "I'm glad for her now. Peter sounds like a swell guy."

I laugh. We all lapse into the jargon we knew There; it dates us, I suppose. But it's also delightful to hear all of the others' idioms from countless eras, countless cultures; more amazing still is the ability to communicate without barriers. Even with belugas and sloths. The kind of divine love we know Here defies definition, by the sage Greeks or anyone else. It is all-encompassing—a light, a warmth, a color all at once, seeping into and out of our lovely thin skins.

Thinking about human life, and watching Dinah bumbling along, I can't help wondering if she will find true love.

"So do I," James says, mind reading, reaching over to swipe a little swirl of icing from my nose. "If things were different, I know who would be perfect for Dinah."

"Who?"

"Theo."

I smile. "But that's clearly not meant to be."

There is plenty of filial love between them, but of course, no *eros*. Not that *eros*, or the lack of it, is always a problem—but the former gets people into more trouble than the latter. Look at how Dinah got into her situation in the first place.

Eduardo was nothing but *eros*. Even Dinah knew that, but she chose to ignore it.

Love is so much more complicated There. We watch Dinah unconsciously splaying a hand over her large belly, lost in her thoughts, in her good deeds, a lot like Joan (though she is less pragmatic than her grandmother, more given to flights of fancy). She is trying not to think about the only thing she can think about.

I know how she feels; I felt the same way with each pregnancy, and was astounded each time by the shock when the baby arrived—the kind of shock upon first seeing someone who before didn't exist, someone brand-new, original.

Dinah may not find true love just yet, but she will have many loves, and the forms they take will surprise her, I'm sure of that.

I reach up to the lowest hanging branch and pluck another treat. Someone nearby is singing sweetly "There Will Never Be Another You," accompanied by strings and bells.

"So true," say James and I in unison, smiling at each other.

Nine

Griffin's shirt was damp with sweat and steam, and he plucked the fabric away from his skin. It was the end of his lunch shift, and he was staying to take inventory. First, though, he needed a cold drink. He yanked his apron from his waist, wadded it into a ball, and threw it across the kitchen, where it landed two feet outside the laundry bin.

"O for six, Griffin," teased Sol, a waiter, bending to pick it up.

"Well, I had my eyes shut this time."

"Very funny. You just suck."

Griffin laughed and pushed his way through the swinging door to the restaurant and rounded the bar. Immediately, Darlene, the bartender, handed him a glass.

"Help yourself," she said, "as long as it's just carbonated. Management's been nosing around and checking."

"Dar, you know I never drink on duty," Griffin said. He

filled his glass with ice and a mixture of three kinds of colas, one of them a toxic yellow.

Darlene laughed. "That's disgusting. You're such a child."

"Yes, ma'am." Griffin grinned.

"Don't you goddamn dare 'ma'am' me, mister."

"Yes, sir," Griffin said, and Darlene gently slugged him.

Darlene's age had been a source of debate among the staff for some time. She could be fifty, or thirty-six, or even closer to sixty. No one knew. She was trim, with light, coarse hair that changed hue every six weeks. A self-described "devout smoker," her voice, skin, and teeth all bore evidence of the damage. Griffin once asked Darlene when her birthday was and she guffawed. "Like I'd tell you," she said.

"I wasn't asking the *year*," he'd said. "Just the day, so I can bake you a cake."

"Honey, you can bake me a cake any damn time you like. But you'll just have to keep wondering. I know what you're up to, all of you." Then she'd smiled and stepped out for her fourth of six cigarette breaks.

Now she said slyly, "Someone's watching you, darlin'." She nodded toward a table in the corner.

It was a large, raucous group, lingering over dessert and drinks, their plates bare, napkins rumpled on the floor or tossed on the table. They were a good-looking, well-groomed lot; Griffin knew instantly that half of them were gay. The two women could be, too, but one leaned toward the man beside her and smiled adoringly. And then Griffin saw the someone Darlene had picked out of the crowd.

It was Ray, beaming back at him.

Ray stood and excused himself from his friends. He

glided across the floor, skirting empty tables without looking, like a dancer at ease in his sleek muscles. His sweater was a tight black rib, clinging to his broad, taut chest, and he put one hand over his heart as he approached.

Griffin felt his own heart skip a beat as he stepped around the bar. For a moment, he felt as shy as a kid at a junior high dance, embarrassed that he'd worn the wrong thing (how wet *was* his shirt?), or that he wouldn't know what to say.

"I have you to blame," Ray said as he came close.

"Really? What for?" Griffin asked.

"I've gained about five pounds, and nearly gone broke because of you." He smiled. "You see, I've been eating out every meal for the past few weeks, just hoping I'd find out where you worked, since I forgot to ask. And finally, Cinderella, here you are!"

Griffin laughed, sure he was blushing. Behind him he could hear Darlene chortling.

"*Paradiso,*" Ray said. "I should have known. It's so perfect."

Griffin glanced around nervously, as if someone (besides Darlene) might be watching or listening. His stomach gurgled with too much soda, and guilt mixed with desire, making him feel faintly ill.

"So, how late are you working?" Ray was asking.

"I'm finished in the kitchen for now," Griffin said. "But I have about two hours' worth of inventory to do."

"Oh," Ray said, sounding disappointed. "I'm off for the afternoon." Then he brightened. "Hey, I could help with inventory!"

"Um . . ."

"Oh. There are probably rules and regulations, right?"

"Yes and no," Griffin said. Then he shrugged. "Sure, why not."

"Do I have to wear a hairnet?"

Griffin laughed. "No, it's not a hospital. And we're not going to be working with the food. Just counting supplies."

"I'll be right back." Ray strode over to his table, leaned down, and said something that made all of his friends turn around. They grinned and several waved at Griffin, who waved back sheepishly. Then Ray returned and touched Griffin's arm, saying, "Okay. Just tell me what to do."

The way he said it was arousing. It was all Griffin could do to walk in a straight line back to the kitchen with Ray at his heels. Thankfully, everyone else was on break, and the walk-in fridge was empty. Griffin headed there, knowing full well it was deep, secret, and very dimly lit when the door was closed. Once inside, he didn't let himself think before he pressed his damp, sticky shirt against Ray's flawless, sweatered chest, wrapped his arms around him, and kissed him. Ray's lips were soft, fuller than Theo's. He tasted like wine and also faintly of garlic and goat cheese. Besides that, he tasted simply new.

All along, Griffin had entertained the thought that if anything happened, it wouldn't be his fault; it would be an accident—Ray making a pass, making the first move. Somehow, the idea of being taken eliminated any culpability. Yet Griffin was the one lunging forward, grabbing and seizing. Ray was too beautiful, the attraction too powerful; the moment unfolded like a gift. How could he resist?

The heavy door swung open, and Sol was there, standing for a moment before he saw the two men in the dim corner and said, "Oh! Wow. Sorry," and then backed out, letting the door slam behind him.

"We can't stay here," Griffin said, pulling away.

"Is there somewhere—"

"I can't," Griffin said sorrowfully.

"Too fast?" Ray asked as vapor escaped his lips. He looked cold, and Griffin wanted to pull him close again.

"Too everything," Griffin said.

"Too bad, I was just getting warmed up," Ray joked.

Griffin cleared his throat. "You do know I'm kind of married, don't you?" He wondered when he had started to think imprecisely; in spite of the lack of a formal ceremony, he and Theo long ago had declared themselves wed.

"I suspected that, and I shouldn't be so pushy," Ray said. "But I sensed something between us that day, when you showed up with your dog—Holly. Was I wrong?"

Griffin shook his head. "No. But—"

"I understand," whispered Ray, his eyes dark and full of longing. "But can I just kiss you one more time?" Then he rephrased it. "I need you to kiss me like that one more time."

Griffin said nothing, thinking, *I can't.* But then, he could.

"Well, if it isn't the prodigal son," Theo said, as Griffin walked in. Griffin stopped in his tracks, but then he saw that Theo was smiling. "I thought you finished at two."

"I had inventory," Griffin said, feeling sheepish, as if he were lying, though it was (mostly) the truth. He realized he needed to act normal, as if nothing had changed. Perhaps it hadn't; a kiss was just a kiss, wasn't it?

Dinah was across from Theo at the table, filling in a

crossword puzzle with a red pen. "What's an eight-letter word for *slow*?" she asked.

"Got any of the letters?" Theo asked.

"I think it starts with an *r*."

"Retarded," Griffin said, reaching into the fridge for a beer. He unscrewed the cap and took a deep swig.

"That's not very nice," Dinah said, looking up and scowling. With her belly obscured by the table, her hair in its dark, short bob, she looked like she could be fifteen. "No one uses that word anymore."

Griffin laughed. "It's an actual word! It means *slow*, you know, as in 'retarded cell growth'? Not as in calling someone a retard, retard."

"Ha-ha," Dinah said, filling in the word without admitting he was right.

Theo turned to look up at Griffin. "You're drinking early."

"It's four-fifteen!" Griffin said, and laughed. "Does it have to be five on the dot? Are you keeping track?"

Theo looked taken aback. "No. And you don't have to get so defensive. It's just—you never drink until dinner. I mean, you know, like seven. It's unusual, that's the only reason I commented."

"I didn't think I was being defensive," Griffin said defensively. "Or unusual."

Dinah bowed over her newspaper, apparently not wanting to get involved in a discussion turning testy. Her presence had shifted the dynamic in the house, and in some ways it was welcome. She acted as a buffer at times like this; neither Theo nor Griffin wanted to pull off the gloves in her midst. And her gravid state had seemed to take Theo's mind off his adoption obsession, at least for the time being. Now he was simply obsessed with Dinah's pregnancy; baby paraphernalia was fast filling the house, much of it purchased by Theo in impulsive bursts ("Look what I found on sale at Marshall Field's!" and "I know we'll be throwing you a shower, Dinah, but I can't help it—this stuff was so cute I had to get it now").

But it wasn't just the addition of Dinah to the household. Something else was changing, and the tipping point was Ray, coming out of his apartment that dark morning, a harbinger of something new. And today in Paradiso, there he was again out of the blue—except that he had been looking for Griffin. It both exhilarated and scared him.

He stood against the countertop, his beer bottle resting against his thigh, and closed his eyes. He pictured Ray in the dim light of the walk-in refrigerator, the softness of his lips, the warmth of his muscled body in the cold room.

"We need to talk about Lamaze," Theo was saying.

"Who?" Griffin asked, startled.

Dinah laughed. "It's a class—you know, for childbirth. *Who-who* and *hee-hee* and all that."

Griffin looked at her, baffled.

"There're breathing techniques," Theo said. "I'm sure you've heard of *Lamaze*?"

"Oh, yeah," Griffin said. "It's that seventies thing, right?"

"I guess," Dinah said. "But they still do it. It's supposed to help." She didn't look convinced. She stared down at her belly, which was wedged against the table. "I wish there was an easier way. I'd like to just lift this whole thing off and pull the kid out."

"They do do that, Dinah," Theo said. "It's called a C-section, but you probably want to avoid it."

"No, I meant like setting it"—Dinah made a motion encompassing her entire mound—"on a table and pulling it out, like a raisin out of a muffin. Not surgery."

Theo laughed. "You're so funny. Listen, it will be *fine*. And we'll be with you." He looked at Griffin and said, "She had to get signed up for classes—it's already pretty late—and I think we should be her coaches."

Griffin looked from Theo to Dinah. "Both of us? I mean, won't it be all couples? We'd look like some kind of love triangle."

Dinah said, "Maybe he's right, Theo. Maybe it would be . . . crowded. Couldn't you just do it? It would be kind of weird with my brother."

"Sure. Yes," Theo said. He smiled. "I'd love to."

Griffin looked at him, at his beatific face, and realized that Theo was falling in love, too—with the yet-unborn baby, as if it were his own. He wondered if Dinah knew what she was in for, then he wondered what *he* was in for. It seemed that everything was shifting beyond his control.

He couldn't even control himself.

"You look really good," Theo said when they were alone in the bedroom one night.

"Really?" Griffin said, glancing at himself in the long mirror. He knew that he did. Since Ray had stopped by Paradiso a few weeks before, Griffin had gotten his hair cut, and had cut back on bread and fries, thus dropping five pounds.

Theo looked him over again from the edge of the bed,

where he was pulling on his shoes. "Yeah, I've been noticing. You know, we haven't exactly been—"

"I know," Griffin said, catching Theo's eye in the reflection. Then he turned around. "But I think it's normal, after so many years."

"What, we're just going through a dry spell? The seven-year itch, a little late?"

Griffin shrugged. "I guess."

Theo stood and came to Griffin, wrapping his arms around him. "I wish I didn't have Lamaze tonight," he said. "And it's more than two hours long."

Griffin laughed. "I thought you were really into it."

"Oh, I am. I love the whole process—it's amazing. But right now I have other things on my mind." He kissed Griffin's ear.

Griffin jerked his head a little. "That tickles," he said. Just then, Dinah called from downstairs that it was time to go. Griffin hid his relief.

Theo sighed and pulled away. He walked to the doorway and yelled, "Coming, Di." Then he turned back. "I just want you to know I miss you."

I miss Ray, Griffin thought after Theo left, immediately stricken with guilt.

It made no sense. He had a happy life, a partner who loved him for better and for worse, in sickness and in health, in lust and in boredom. How could he turn his back on all of that? Yet, for a long time, Theo had been turning away from Griffin, toward the single-minded notion of parenthood. Now all he seemed to care about was Dinah's impending delivery.

And what would happen then? Griffin wondered. Did

Theo think they would be one big happy, unconventional family? What about when Dinah moved out, or fell in love, or in other ways moved on with her life? Then they would be right back where they'd started: Theo wanting a child, and Griffin happy with a dog, with life as it was.

But life never remained as it was, Griffin reminded himself; he should know that by now. People changed. Or died. They fell in and out of love all the time. What one wanted changed from year to year, or even day to day. And right now, Griffin just wanted to kiss someone new, much as it shamed him.

Before they parted at the restaurant, Ray had given Griffin his phone number. "Call me anytime, if you just want to talk. No pressure, I promise. The last thing I want to be is a home wrecker." He smiled. "But you know, if things ever change . . ."

Griffin looked at the phone and then at the clock. Two hours. *No.* His fingers rapped on the bedside table, *yes, no, yes, no, yes, no. No, no, no, no.*

In ten minutes, Griffin was seated, waiting, at the neighborhood Irish pub called the Little Leprechaun, which he and Theo never visited, though they joked about how gay it sounded. Clearly, it was not. When Griffin looked around, he saw that it was frequented by very straight-looking blue-collar patrons, either just off work or out of work; he guessed the latter from an overheard conversation between two men at the end of the bar.

"Anything?"

"Nope."

"Sucks."

"Yep."

The first man put his arm amiably around the other's shoulder, giving it a consoling squeeze before letting go. Griffin thought that if he and Theo—or he and Ray—made the same gesture, all eyes would be upon them; people could tell. He wondered if it had been a mistake to meet here, but then, it was just a drink. He and Ray could be colleagues from work, or old college pals catching up after years apart. How would anyone know?

But then Ray walked in, wearing a too-tight leather jacket with too many zippers, and fitted jeans, and Griffin imagined he felt the entire bar population swivel and gawk.

Ray sat down on the stool beside him, lightly touching Griffin's back. He unzipped the main zipper of his jacket, revealing a very tight gray T-shirt. "Nice ambience," he whispered to Griffin, grinning.

"Just don't order anything with fruit," Griffin whispered. "And stop whispering to me. It's queer."

Ray smirked, then called out to the bartender, "Whatcha got on tap?"

Griffin moaned inwardly. The bartender cocked an eyebrow in what appeared to be derision. He was a smallish man, with a few extra pounds, which on first glance made him appear burly, on closer inspection merely paunchy.

"Guinness, Harp, Bud, Bud Lite, Heineken," he said.

"Which would you recommend?" Ray asked.

"You serious?" the bartender scoffed.

"Uh, no. I'll have a Guinness."

"And for you?" the bartender asked Griffin.

"Same," Griffin said.

The bartender slapped down two coasters with the cartoon image of a buxom woman holding up frothy steins of beer, foam spilling into her cleavage. When he turned around to get the drinks, Griffin shook his head at Ray, laughing.

"You're such a dork," he said. "Have you never had a beer before?"

Ray shrugged. "I don't drink much, actually."

"Oh. Sorry. I only suggested this place because it was about halfway between us, but we could have met for coffee or something."

"No, no, this is fine," Ray said, spinning around on his stool like a child unused to such novelties. "I didn't care where we met. I was just so glad you finally called."

"I just feel like . . ." Griffin paused, growing serious, and Ray stopped spinning to face him. "It's like my life has been taken over. My sister's living with us, and she's having a baby in about two months, more or less, and everything revolves around that now, and—" He lowered his voice. "I mean, it didn't *just* happen. Theo's been obsessed with the idea of having kids for a long time now."

"You don't want kids?" Ray asked.

"I don't know. I just don't think I'm cut out for it." He paused. "Do you want kids?"

"No. I have nothing against them. I just don't see myself guiding one into the world."

"*Exactly!*" Griffin said. "That's a good way to put it."

The bartender interrupted with their drinks, setting them down heavily. Both men ignored him. They sat so that their knees were pressed together tightly; Ray caressed Griffin's leg. The bartender cleared his throat, and when they looked up, he glared.

Ray turned to the bartender and demanded, "What? You have a problem?"

"*I* don't," he said, continuing to glower at the two of them.

"*Ah,*" Ray said. Griffin felt the hairs on his neck prickle. Ray pulled out his wallet. He set a ten-dollar bill on the bar for the beer they hadn't touched, then stood up. "C'mon, baby, let's go."

Griffin was shocked that Ray would meekly accept a barely veiled insult and just leave—though he wasn't exactly protesting himself. He just wanted to leave, too.

Then Ray suddenly pulled Griffin toward him and kissed him hard on the mouth. The bartender watched but said nothing, just shook his head in disgust as Ray, laughing, tugged Griffin out the door. Someone in the back of the bar applauded, and Griffin wondered if it was for the kiss or for their departure.

Once on the sidewalk, Ray said, "Well, that was fun, wasn't it?"

"Not really," Griffin said warily. He had always lived his life quietly, for the most part, and people who knew him accepted him. He realized he tended to avoid situations that would place him in the open. Or make him feel degraded.

"Sorry," Ray said. "If they want us to feel ashamed, I figure why not give them something to talk about." He fiddled agitatedly with one of the zippers on his jacket.

They walked in silence for two blocks. When they got to an alley, Ray suddenly steered Griffin into it. Griffin, confused by his emotions, hesitated but then succumbed.

He couldn't help being drawn to Ray, though he hardly knew him. Maybe because he hardly knew him. In many ways, Ray was the polar opposite of Theo. For one thing, he was tougher—even if that wasn't necessarily a good thing. He even kissed harder, though at the moment, that *was* a good thing.

"I have to go," Griffin finally said, sensing Ray wanted more than kissing. It was tempting, though not in an alley a stone's throw from a homophobic bartender. Or a few blocks from home.

"I know," Ray said.

"But—"

"You'll call."

"I'll try."

"You'll *try*," Ray said. Then he whispered, "I live alone, you know. So you could just come over. We don't have to meet in public bars and risk life and limb."

Griffin chuckled. "Well, the Little Leprechaun probably was a bad idea." Then they both started laughing.

"I don't know," Ray said. "It was kind of exciting." He kissed Griffin again and said, "I know it's not very Catholic of me, but I would have beaten the shit out of that guy for you, if I had to."

Theo was holding a giant stuffed bear in front of his face. It was as tall as he was, honey colored, with shining black eyes the size of golf balls. "Don't you love it?" Theo asked.

"Yeah," Griffin said from the sofa where he sprawled. He had just come home from work, and his back ached from leaning over the stove. "It's really . . . big."

"I know, and you won't believe how much I paid for it," Theo said, eyes twinkling. "Guess."

"I don't know. Ten dollars?"

"Be serious," Theo said. He set the bear down on a chair and it flopped over like a drunk. "It was only a hundred."

Griffin gaped at him. *Only?*

"It *was* twice that! I thought it was a bargain." Theo looked a little deflated.

"T, don't you know they overprice everything and then 'slash' prices so you think you're getting a deal? And if you ask me, I wouldn't have paid more than ten bucks for an obese teddy bear."

"He's not obese," Theo said in a feigned wounded tone. "He's just fluffy."

Griffin laughed and closed his eyes. "How do you know it's a he?"

"His name's Walter," Theo said. "Anyway, I think Dinah will love him, even if you don't."

"I didn't say I don't love him," Griffin said. "I hardly know him."

"Stop that!" Theo said sharply. Griffin opened his eyes and saw Holly trying to tug the bear with her teeth. Theo tried to shove her away, but she had latched on to a paw and clearly had no intention of letting go of such a big toy. "Grif—" Theo pleaded, irritated.

Griffin sat up and sighed. "Holly," he called firmly. "Go lightly." At the sound of her name, the dog stopped in her tracks and obediently turned to Griffin. And when Griffin motioned to her with one hand, Holly bounded over and wagged her tail.

"See?" Griffin said to Theo. "If you just bothered to get

to know her, and learned a few simple commands, you wouldn't have to yell at her."

Theo righted the bear back on the chair and sat on top of it, guarding it bodily. "I don't know how," he said, frowning. "I don't know how to train a dog."

"And you won't try," Griffin said, holding Holly gently by her collar and stroking her head and ears as she continued to wag.

"I didn't ask—"

"I know," Griffin said, interrupting. "You didn't ask for a dog. Just like I didn't ask for my sister to descend on us, and to have a baby under our roof, or for you to drop everything in our life for her. But I'm adapting. I'm *trying*."

Theo looked at him. "You're trying," he repeated. "Huh. You could have fooled me." Then he stood up and walked out of the room without saying another word, leaving the bear behind.

Griffin lay back down, moaning, and Holly jumped up on top of him, licking his face, before settling down into the crook of his arm. Across the room, Walter, with his stitched-on Mona Lisa smile, stared at Griffin with his round, cold eyes.

❦

I fold myself into the soft wooly side of a compliant polar bear. One day, they will be extinct, when ice floes melt and they can't swim to shore. Their enormous muscular limbs will flail and then sink. Naturalists and environmentalists will lament the loss, but by then, so much will have been "lost," it will seem inevitable. And life will go on. Of course, it goes on. Here and There.

There, the troubles seem aplenty, when one is in the midst of them, which is as it must be. And (most) human beings embrace each day, for better or for worse, struggling to make sense of it all, making the best of things, trying to adapt.

"Griffin is trying," James says, though I know in some ways he is fooling himself. Griffin, that is.

"Human nature is getting in his way," I say. "And as my grandmother used to say, 'He's got a lot of human in him.'"

James laughs. But we don't laugh, really, about what is happening between Griffin and Theo, the rift that we watch growing wider—the way a tiny tear in a long-worn and loved shirt can shred if you keep putting your fingers into it and tugging mindlessly. Or not so mindlessly.

"I see the allure of this new one," I say. "Ray."

"Griffin is blinded by the light," James quips.

"Theo is more . . . subtle," I say. But the kind of light he emits spreads farther, and burns longer, faithfully. If only Griffin could see that. We are rooting for Theo; how could we not? He's family, though he doesn't know us.

"I love how Theo dotes in odd little ways," James says. "Have you noticed how he folds Griffin's T-shirts, running his hands over them and smiling to himself? Or keeps track of herbs and spices running low and replaces them?"

I have noticed. I have also noticed that Griffin does not. He obliviously wears the shirts and seems to think that thyme just never runs out.

Our son is beset on all sides by life and love and temptation. He knows what he wants, and what he should want, but I'm not sure he knows the difference, nor how much the two overlap.

And he thinks a kiss is just a kiss.

I've seen a lot of kisses. Good ones, lazy ones, sloppy ones, ones that take a person's breath away, ones that portend the beginning of something—and the end. Right now, someone's kisses are delectable, irresistible. They are sweet crumbs on the path through the woods, and it is up to Griffin to decide if he will follow them. Sometimes, there is not a clear right or wrong path; but there is always a choice. And an outcome.

"That really is one big bear," James is saying as Griffin slumps in his living room before fading once more from our view.

"Walter?"

"Is that his name?" James asks, looking over. "Hi, Walter." The polar bear nudges him cheerfully with a giant white paw and I laugh and laugh.

Ten

Alice took a surreptitious sip of her wine when Joan's back was turned. She'd put her grandmother to work folding napkins into swans, the way Griffin once taught her. There were going to be ten guests, including one Alice had never met, and she was a little nervous about adding Joan to the mix. But Joan had come to New York to see Alice's play in its final week, and planned to stay an extra night. The dinner party at Ian's had been planned far in advance.

When Alice lamented Joan's timing the day before her arrival, Ian said, "It will be fun having her here; people love other people's grandparents."

"Yes, but that's because they don't have to worry about drinking too much in front of them, or being scrutinized."

Ian looked down at the sweater he wore, his favorite, pilling along the seams. "Should I change?"

Alice laughed. "No, she'll love you."

And Joan seemed to. When she arrived at Grand Central, looking tiny and lost in the crowd, Alice and Ian had rushed over and greeted her, and Ian had gently taken Joan's luggage for her and then offered his arm. Alice knew he'd passed the "gentleman test."

However, that night Joan had attended the play with Ian, who later told Alice that her grandmother seemed disturbed throughout. Ian thought it was seeing Alice perched precariously on high, so he leaned over and whispered, "Don't worry; she's wearing a harness. You just can't see it." But Joan looked at him quizzically and said, "I know that." Afterward, she told Alice how proud she was, how much she loved the play, but Joan was pensive when they returned home to Alice's apartment. She said she was just tired from the trip, the long night.

Now, fortified by her second glass of wine, Alice decided to prod her. "So, Joan? I was wondering—what do you think of Ian?"

"He seems perfectly nice," Joan said, then turned back to the pile of linens. "These would look more like swans if they were actually white, you know."

"That's all Ian had in the drawer," Alice explained. The napkins were green-and-red plaid, perhaps a long-ago Christmas present. "I guess I should have bought some. I didn't really think of it, but our friends aren't the kind to care about things like that."

"Maybe I should redo them," Joan said, collapsing one of the swans. "I can make the little sleeping bag fold so you can tuck the silverware into them. The spoons look like little heads then."

"*Joan,*" Alice said impatiently. "Forget the napkins. I'm asking you a serious question." Distractedly, she refolded the napkins herself into simple neat triangles and moved them out of Joan's reach.

"Fine," Joan said. "If you must know, I resent the fact that you think you can fool me."

Alice balked. "Fool you?"

"Yes, you act like I'm some dotty old woman from the eighteenth century. I lived through the sixties, you know. I know a thing or two. And I know that you and Ian are living together and you only moved back to your apartment when I arrived. It doesn't take a detective to notice things like dried-up soap in the shower and curdled milk in the fridge. I mean, *really*." She shook her head.

Alice laughed. "Is that what's bothering you?"

"Well, yes. The deceit more than the shacking up—which I'm pretty used to by now, concerning all of you. I tried to bring you up the right way, the godly way, but, well, there's only so much I can do." She sighed. "But I hope you know what you're doing."

"I *am* thirty-six," Alice said.

"Why are you always reminding me how old you all are? It just makes *me* feel ancient! Anyway, age has nothing to do with it. I'm talking about Adam. You've gotten involved with a man who has a child; there are boundaries. I just hope you're thinking about long-term repercussions."

"I *am*," Alice said. "I adore Adam. I would never do anything to hurt him."

"I know, darling," Joan said, her tone softening. "It's just that, with what Dinah is doing—I just hope you girls understand how serious it is having a child. Especially you. It isn't something you can enter into lightly."

Ian walked into the apartment then with an armload

of fresh baguettes and a plastic grocery bag slung from his arm.

"Hello!" he called cheerfully. "I got the last ones, thank goodness. And the garlic *and* the Dijon we forgot. And Adam's down the hall at Miriam's till bedtime, overjoyed. . . ." He paused. "So, how are you two doing?"

"Great," Alice said tersely. "How much time do we have? I don't want the appetizers to overbake." She turned and went into the kitchen. Ian followed with his bags.

"You all right?" he whispered.

"Yes," she said, sighing. "It's just going to be a challenging evening."

"It will be fine," said Ian, kissing her. Alice kissed him back, passionately.

At seven, the guests began to appear: Alice's friends from the theater—Beth and Janine; Janine's boyfriend, Hayden, an out-of-work drummer; and the director Calvin and his wife, Collette; and then Wanda and James, a couple Ian had introduced Alice to a few weeks earlier, colleagues from work; and Billy and Nico, two of his closest friends since high school, who had come together, without dates. The only one who had not yet arrived was an Englishman named Neil Lovelace, an old friend Ian had met when his company sent him to their London office for six months, a year before Adam was born. Neil was retired from the company, and divided his time between London and New York. Since he had stayed in touch with Ian over the years, Neil had heard about and wanted to meet Alice.

With this in mind, and Joan's unexpected presence, Alice felt doubly in the spotlight.

While guests were shedding coats and getting drinks,

she excused herself for a few minutes to hide in the bathroom and take a deep breath. She fussed over her hair, loose and unruly, clipping it up and then letting it fall back down; put on red lipstick, then wiped it off in favor of clear gloss, but her mouth and cheeks remained flushed. She stood for a moment longer, wondering if her dress was too tight or too low-cut. Joan had said nothing, but she'd glanced at the bodice pointedly, making Alice want to plunge it even lower, as if she were sixteen. Finally, she emerged, looking no different from the way she had before, but resolved to put on a game face, no matter what.

"Alice," Ian was calling. "I want you to meet someone."

She strode toward him and saw the man behind him, almost a full head taller, and startlingly handsome for an older man (Alice guessed sixty), the only guest in a suit and tie. He had graying hair and a chiseled face, and Alice recognized him immediately, as if he'd stepped out of the black-and-white movies she'd seen growing up. Of course, he wasn't actually Cary Grant, but close enough, a dark-eyed facsimile.

"So *this* is Alice," Neil said, his accent warm and honeyed. "Ian told me you were something special. I can see why." He glanced at her cleavage, the curves of her dress. Since eating in more regularly with Ian and Adam, Alice had put on a few pounds; she'd lamented them, but Ian had assured her he loved her that way. "All men do," he'd said.

"Okay, okay," said Ian, smirking now. "You can turn down the charm, Casanova. She's not buying."

Alice pretended to ignore the flattery and guided Neil to the tiny bar set up in the living room. "Let me guess," she said. "You're a martini man. Am I right?"

"Sure. I'll be any kind of man you like." When Alice gave him a sidelong glance, he smiled. "I'm joking. Ian would have you think I'm a bit of a rake, but I assure you I'm no such thing. It's just nice to get out and socialize with young people again. I just came back from a tour of Tuscany and it was all gray-hairs." He glanced around, then whispered, "I hope she's not here as a setup." He nodded toward Joan, who was across the room.

Alice laughed. "That's my grandmother! She's just visiting for a couple of days. You're in no danger, I promise." She passed Neil a glass, then held up a curled lemon peel and a spear of olives. "Take your pick," she said.

"Olives," Neil said, accepting them. "Cheers." His eyes twinkled.

Alice smiled back, charmed. "Come on, I'll introduce you around." She guided Neil to the cluster of actors, where she then left him, rushing to the kitchen to retrieve a tray of stuffed mushroom caps.

As the evening progressed, the group grew warm and congenial, the talk lively and at times bawdy, the theater group outdone by the comic duo of Billy and Nico, who delighted in embarrassing Ian with tales of his "geek-thug" youth on Long Island.

"Did you hear about the time Ian tried to shoplift a box of condoms?" Nico asked. "And he came out of the store with a security guard, holding up the stolen box of Kotex?"

"I wasn't stealing them!" Ian said over the laughter. "They fell off the shelf as I was running out and I stopped to pick them up."

"That's even better," Billy said. "Such a thoughtful thief."

"And then," Nico added, "Ian tried to offer cash to pay for them, but the cop thought it was a bribe."

"Yeah, it's amazing he's not in jail to this day."

Everyone laughed, Joan the hardest.

After dinner, while the others abandoned the table and gathered in the other end of the living room, Neil helped Alice clear the dishes and stack them in the tiny kitchen.

"You don't have to—"

"I want to," Neil said. "So, your friends tell me you're the star of the play."

"Oh, they're just being sweet—or sucking up," Alice said, laughing. "Anyway, it's the last week, thankfully."

"Then I'd better hurry and get a ticket," Neil said. "I would love to see you as an angel."

Alice laughed. "I'm no angel. Trust me," she said, thinking of the character.

"Even better," Neil replied.

Alice looked at him quickly, but Neil smiled innocently and glided back to the group, sitting beside Ian with one arm slung over the back of the sofa, his tie loosened. Alice busied herself making coffee and wondering if she was reading too much into everything. She'd known plenty of men like Neil, such practiced flirts that they didn't even realize what they were doing half the time. *She* was just out of practice, she reasoned.

After the last guest finally thanked them and bid farewell, Alice gave Joan the key to her apartment and told her she would follow shortly, after they'd cleaned up.

"No rush," Joan said, kissing Alice's cheek. Then she whispered, "I know you want to stay here, and that's okay. I'll be fine alone."

Alice laughed a little. "You really are something, Granny."

After Joan had gone upstairs, Ian went down the hall to collect Adam from the neighbor's. He returned with a squalling, kicking boy who bore no resemblance to the sweet child Alice knew so well. Adam usually ran directly to her, winding his arms around her waist or jumping onto the bed to wedge beside her. Alice had begun to take his affection for granted.

"Well, somebody got up on the wrong side of the sofa, apparently," Ian said through clenched teeth, wrestling Adam through the door. "It's just way too late."

"I don't *want* to sleep here!" Adam screamed. "I want to stay at Miriam's!"

Alice reached out, attempting to help placate. "Hey, c'mon, buddy—"

"*No!*" he said, aiming a kick toward her knee. "I don't want you, either!"

"Don't bother; there's no reasoning," Ian said to Alice over the shouting.

Leaving Ian to deal with his feral son, Alice went into the kitchen to sort the dishes. They were piled all over the countertops, and suddenly it all seemed too much; wearily, she retreated.

Hearing Adam sobbing in the bathroom, where Ian presumably was trying to get him to brush or pee before bed, Alice knocked lightly on the door.

When Ian opened it, Alice blurted, "I have to go upstairs. Joan doesn't want to stay alone."

"Oh, okay," said Ian with a beleaguered smile. "See you tomorrow, then."

"I'll come back to help you clean up in the morning," Alice said lamely.

"Don't worry about it," Ian said. "Good night." He kissed her lightly, then turned back to scold Adam sharply. "Stop it, *now*! This has gone on long enough."

Smitten with guilt, Alice stole out of the apartment and up the stairs to her own. She had to rap loudly before Joan heard her and let her in.

"What happened?" Joan asked, swathed in her familiar white Pond's cream.

"Oh, nothing. I just wanted to be with you," Alice said, collapsing into a chair.

"Well, that's sweet, but I'm so tired, I don't think I'll be much company," Joan said as she walked toward the bathroom. She called back, "It was a fun party. I really enjoyed myself—such a lively group!"

"Yeah," Alice said absently.

After Joan was asleep in her bed, Alice stretched out on the sagging pullout sofa, unable to rest. She knew she was cowardly and selfish, leaving Ian to deal with Adam's tantrum. As long as she retained her apartment one flight up, she would have an easy way out when things got rough or she had had enough. But what was wrong with just wanting to be alone now and then? After all, between the rehearsals and performances and living with Ian and Adam, Alice never had any time to herself anymore. She never had time just to think.

But now that she did, the thoughts plagued her. She wanted to be with Ian, and Adam, but she wondered if things had happened too fast, if she'd dived into the role without thinking about how deep and wide the water of commitment might be, how much *treading* was involved in domesticity. Yet when she thought of Adam haloed by his tiny Christmas lights, tugging her into his lair and trapping her in the sweet syrup of child love, she ached with longing—and also anxiety. Joan had planted doubts with her well-meant advice. There *were* boundaries, all kinds of walls to keep families in and interlopers out.

Many times over the years, Joan had tried to instill the traditional notion of "First comes love; then comes marriage," et cetera, and warned her grandchildren to choose carefully and to choose well. None of them had heeded the advice, except perhaps Griffin.

It seemed to Alice that she and Ian were playing house, while still trying to gauge how strong the other's feelings were before admitting their own. Ian often told Alice she was "wonderful" or that he "adored" her, but never "I love you." Alice pressed the words against her own teeth like hard candy.

Alice had to admit that sometimes in the whirl of their life, she didn't actually know how she felt. Her doubt was intensified tonight, not just because Adam had thrown a fit and Ian was irate—the pair of them locked in parent-child conflict, in which Alice really had no part—but also because she'd felt another man's eyes on her, which hadn't happened offstage in a long, long time.

The boat pond was murky, clotted with dead, soggy leaves, and the Wollman rink had turned to slush. Alice wasn't in the mood for the zoo, either, since it seemed especially bleak to her in late winter, the animals curled into dens and the visitors hunched into grubby coats. But she was determined to have fun. And she had promised Adam a day—or at least a couple of hours—at the park. Ian was at work, but Alice had the entire day off. She had suggested that Adam stay home from day care.

"I just want to hang out with him by myself," she'd told Ian. She wanted to prove something to herself, or to Ian, or both.

"That's a great idea. Just be careful—he moves fast."

"Don't you trust me?" Alice asked, a little hurt.

"Of course I do," Ian said, kissing her. "He's just a maniac when he gets outside."

Ian was right. At every intersection, Alice had to grab hold of Adam's hand and remind him to wait for the red light, and for her. As soon as they were across the street, he would be off again on his sturdy little legs.

Riverside Park was closer to their apartment, but Adam was "bored of it." Central Park beckoned, as always, as the land of wonders: playgrounds, lakes, boulders, and even polar bears. Sometimes Alice imagined they were in Paris, wandering Tuileries (which she'd yet to see but had heard about), with its tree-lined paths and carousel. Adam wasn't interested in the carousel, though, as his tastes of late ran to the more physical.

"Chase me, Alice!" he called, darting on ahead of her over an arched stone bridge. She ran after him, relieved that swings were in sight, and monkey bars; perhaps she could just watch him play for a few minutes. Adam didn't want to pause there, however. Umpire Rock still lay ahead, a Mount Everest to small city-bound children.

Of course, he wanted to climb. Alice sighed but then smiled and gamely followed. The day, while cold, was intermittently sunny, and the melting snow revealed patches of dark, damp earth that smelled like spring awakening. Alice wanted to lie on the ground as she had as a child in her backyard, face to the soil, inhaling and listening, expecting the underground world to be alive with sound. It had always surprised her that it was so densely quiet, but she had liked that, too.

While Adam struggled up the side of the boulder, Alice kept careful watch a few steps behind. He was growing fiercely independent, and she respected his efforts. He looked comically tiny against the waxy rock, wedging his sneakered toes into grooves like a seasoned climber. Once atop, he hopped up and down triumphantly.

"I did it!" he exclaimed.

"You did," Alice said, laughing, patting his head. "Good job, buddy."

"I want to climb another one," he said, scanning the horizon for new challenges.

"Okay," Alice said. "Then I think we should go find some lunch. Okay?"

"I'm not hungry."

"You will be," Alice said, realizing she sounded like a mother. When they descended, Alice insisted on holding Adam by the wrist so he wouldn't slip. He tried to tug free, but she was firm. "If you fall, it will hurt; it's a long way down."

"I won't fall," he said.

"I know, but if you did—"

"C'mon!" he said breathlessly, impatient to proceed. Alice was beginning to regret her ambitious plan for a whole day together. It was only eleven A.M. and already she was tired. Young mothers and nannies passed by, languidly pushing strollers, looking relaxed and, Alice thought, enviably in control.

She coaxed Adam to slow down enough for a snack. A vendor was parked near a redbrick arch, selling roasted peanuts, so Alice bought a waxed-paper bagful, and a bottle of juice. Then she turned to offer Adam a drink, bending a little to where he was standing—but he wasn't. She bolted back upright and looked around. He was gone.

"Adam?" she called. She rushed through the arch, but he wasn't on the other side. She ran back to the vendor, breathless with alarm.

"Did you see a little boy right here?"

The man, who was Cambodian, shook his head. "No see."

"He was just right here!" Alice insisted indignantly, but then she realized that, of course, the short man on the other side of the cart could easily have overlooked Adam, scarcely visible from where he stood. Besides, the man had been preoccupied with steaming her peanuts and counting her change.

"Oh, God," Alice said under her breath. "*Adam!*" she yelled now, rushing around the vicinity of the cart, the arch. He can't have gone far, she thought desperately; she'd turned her back for mere seconds. But he moved fast, as Ian had warned and Adam himself had proved all morning. And what if he hadn't run off, but been taken—just as her attention was diverted—by someone half hidden in the shadows of the archway, the density of trees?

Alice's heart pounded, and she broke out in a prickly sweat. It was just as Joan had warned and Alice secretly feared, secretly *knew*—that children were too great a risk; there was too much at stake; the responsibility life-altering. How did anyone do this, waking and sleeping, with the chance of loss hovering around the edges, ready to snatch?

She wanted to scream for help, she wanted to turn back the clock just two minutes, she wanted—

"Alice?" said Adam, suddenly looking up at her with his round gray eyes.

"Adam!" she snapped, swooping down to his side, dropping the bag and the bottle, which exploded on the sidewalk, spraying orange juice. She grabbed his shoulders. "Where did you go? Why did you run away? You can't *ever* do that! Do you understand?" She was almost crying with anger and relief.

"I had to pee," Adam said in a nervous voice, pointing vaguely toward a clump of bristly bushes in the opposite direction from the archway.

"I don't care!" Alice shouted at him.

Now Adam was crying softly, his shoulders shaking beneath her fingers. Alice pulled him into her arms then and held him close. He felt small and fragile; she was ashamed that she'd yelled at him—and that she'd thought she was up to the task of caring for him. What if he hadn't reappeared? How would she have told Ian? How would she ever have been able to get up and face another day of her life?

She had to feign calm, she knew, so she stood, forcing a smile and lifting Adam into her arms. "I'm *so* sorry I yelled," she whispered into his ear, his cheek damp against hers. "I was just scared I'd lost you." Adam buried his face into her neck and didn't respond. They stayed that way for a long moment, Alice wondering what was going through the child's mind; she could only guess.

"Let's go home," she finally said.

As she walked, Alice felt a powerful gratitude for the weight in her arms, and also a throbbing sense of terror that she had come so close to the unbearable loss of it.

Once inside the apartment, Adam disappeared into his tiny room, pulling the curtain closed. When Alice peeked in, he was on his bed, playing listlessly with a handful of toy animals. And a little while later, after she had fixed a grilled cheese sandwich, she opened the curtain to tell him it was ready, but Adam was sound asleep, curled on his side. Alice crouched down, unlaced and tugged off his shoes, and covered him with a blanket. Then she went to the living room and sank into the sofa.

When Ian came home a few hours later, he found them both sulkily silent, Adam drawing in the living room and Alice in the kitchen, stirring risotto in a pot. As she mindlessly tossed in some steamed vegetables and leftover chicken, Alice explained in a low voice what had happened at the park. She didn't minimize her own culpability.

"Well, he shouldn't have gone off without telling you," Ian said judiciously.

"But I shouldn't have yelled at him," she said. "I don't know if he'll forgive me."

"Don't be silly," Ian said, reaching over to take a sip from Alice's very full wineglass. "He's too little to hold grudges. I'm sure he's over it already."

"Look at him," Alice insisted, motioning toward the living room. "He won't even talk to me."

After dinner, however, Adam seemed to perk up, his old self. He prepared for bed without protest and hugged Alice without any sign of reproach. Still, the whole event had left her with the uneasy sense that she was standing on a pond, the ice cracking beneath her in every direction.

Alice prepared for the end. The other actors privately joked about there not being "life *After This*." At the same time, they grudgingly admitted that, despite Imogene's quirky demands, the play had been a boon for all of them, bringing notice and new roles. And Alice knew that Imogene indeed had pushed her to do her best work.

She found that she could adapt to the unexpected, could dig into her character's darkness a little deeper every night and still find something light within it. Talking about death over and over—with laughs written into the script—seemed to diminish its horror somehow. Alice felt not only that she had shrugged off some of its long-standing weight but also that perhaps she'd given audience members a kind of gift.

Alice waited while a costume attendant adjusted her wings one last time, tightening the elastic bands underneath her arms and across her back, and the makeup artist, Sandra, brushed glittery blush across her cheeks and nose. At times like this, Alice often felt like a small girl preparing for a beauty pageant or ballet recital, her stomach fluttering in anticipation while she was aware of the soft caressing sensation of someone's hands combing her hair or dabbing foundation on her face.

She knew that tonight Ian wouldn't be in the audience,

since he didn't have a babysitter, and it was something of a relief. She could just act, and then, when it was over, go home to her own bed. Alice had explained to Ian that it was because she had a cast party after the final curtain. Truthfully, she just thought it might be nice to be alone.

Now, lifted by steel wires onto her beam, she slid out of her own life and into that of suicidal Gwen. As the pink lights warmed her shoulders and scalp, softened the skin of her bare arms and made her glow, Alice/Gwen smiled into the darkness that was a sea of rapt faces.

"When the rope tightened," she said sweetly, miming with her fingers about her own neck, "the world grew dark and darker—and then light. You've heard all about the lights, the tunnel, the myth of the world beyond." She paused. "But maybe it's all true. Maybe life goes on; otherwise, how could I be gone but also here with you?"

In the months since the first readings and rehearsals, and then during all the subsequent performances, Alice had pondered the notion of an afterlife. She couldn't help it, of course, having spent most of her life wondering about the whereabouts of her parents. If indeed they were Somewhere Else, were they watching her even now? Did they care?

As she sat on her beam in the dark above the stage, Alice shivered a little, half convinced she felt something in the air nearby. She turned to see, but it was just the wires, the edges of her papier-mâché wings.

At the final curtain, the applause was deafening, and Alice and her friends grinned and bowed and sighed collectively. Backstage, Beth threw her arms around Alice and then yanked off her own and Alice's wings.

"Let's burn them!" she cried.

Alice laughed but bent to retrieve hers, strangely melancholic. "I think I want to keep mine," she said as they headed to the dressing room to change. A moment later, an usher poked his head around the door.

"Are you decent?" he asked.

"Never," Alice joked.

"Uh," the young man said, sounding embarrassed, "there's someone here to see Alice Stone."

"Is it a stalker?" Beth asked.

Alice gave her a little shove and went to the door, wondering if Ian had come after all to surprise her. But when the door opened wider, she was surprised to find not Ian, but Neil.

He was as dashing as she'd remembered, and holding a bouquet of pink tulips against his jet-black coat. The coat, Alice could tell, was cashmere.

Neil handed her the flowers. "You were absolutely wonderful, Alice, just as I'd heard. Not that I had any doubts."

"Thank you," she said.

It occurred to her that Ian had never brought flowers, not once in all the times he'd come to see her backstage and lauded her performance. It shouldn't have mattered, but Alice admittedly was touched that Neil *had* brought flowers. It was old habit, she chided herself—being drawn to the admirers, especially those well dressed and groomed, the ones who thought to bear gifts. And it was unfair, she knew, to equate superficial signs of attention with superior traits. Just because Ian didn't buy her things didn't mean he didn't love her. Even if he never said it.

"How about dinner?" Neil was asking.

"What?" Alice asked, distracted but covering it by pre-tending to struggle with the armload of tulips and wings.

"Oh, allow me," Neil said automatically, stepping forward to relieve her of the bouquet, glancing around the cluttered dressing room. There were flowers everywhere, for Alice and other cast members, from their director, Calvin, and various admirers. Alice reached underneath a cupboard and pulled out a dusty ceramic vase the color of Band-Aids.

"It's pretty awful," she noted. "But it'll do for now." Neil tucked the bouquet into the vase and took it to a sink to fill it with water.

"So—dinner?" he said again softly. "Could I take you out?"

Before Alice could respond, the rest of the actresses tumbled into the dressing room, shrieking and hugging. They swept Alice into their arms, and the room filled with the mingled scent of sweat, melted makeup, sticky hair-spray, and warm female skin.

"Just give me five minutes," Alice told Neil above the noise. "And I'll be ready to go."

"Go?" someone asked. "Aren't you coming to Calvin's party?"

"Later," Alice said calmly. "Tell him I'll be a little late."

"Imogene will be so insulted if you don't come," Beth said. "You're her pet, you know."

Several actresses laughed, and one said, "*Awww*" in an exaggerated tone. Alice rolled her eyes.

"Ah, of course!" Neil said. "Closing night. You should go with them."

Alice had been to dozens of cast parties, after dozens of closing nights. It would be as it always was, noisy and lively, and bubbling over with praise and too much champagne, going on till dawn. "No, it's fine," she said. "I can catch up with them later."

"Sure?" Neil asked, and when Alice nodded, he smiled. "I'll wait for you in the lobby."

Don't, Alice warned herself, even as she pulled on the sexier of the two dresses she kept in her locker, even as she washed and remade her face—her eyes smoky now and her lips deep red—knowing full well that Ian preferred her without makeup, and that it was the act of a woman preparing for a first date.

Don't, she told herself as she walked beside Neil toward a waiting cab, where he held the door for her. But then she relaxed. She reminded herself it was just dinner. They made amiable small talk on the ride down Seventh toward TriBeCa, where Neil knew of a new place he'd heard was "swell."

The restaurant was darkly paneled and decorated with thin urbanites smoking cigarettes and posing, shifting angular limbs around the mahogany bar. Though older than most of the crowd, Neil fit right into the glamorous decor. Alice's gaze flickered to his warm, dark eyes as he handed her a martini and silently toasted her above the din. And when they finally were seated in a booth, she noticed how long and strong his legs appeared beneath the flawless drape of his flannel trousers, and that his body language was like that of a seasoned actor embodying a character with the smallest of gestures.

"So, is Alice Stone your given name or a stage name?" Neil asked her after they'd ordered dinner and a bottle of red wine.

"Yes and no," she said. "My real last name means 'stones' in Dutch."

Neil smiled. "Are you going to reveal the Dutch word, or do I have to look it up later?"

"It's Stenen," Alice said. "I just liked the solidity of Stone."

"Your secret's safe," Neil said. "Let's toast to self-made identities, the best kind." He lifted his glass and Alice followed. She gulped deeply. Then she let the conversation unfold. It felt good, just being with someone new; she was at ease but also alert.

"I get the impression that you and Ian are quite serious," Neil suddenly said.

"I think so."

"You think so? You aren't sure?" Neil prodded. "He seems sure."

Alice considered how much to reveal, especially to a friend of Ian's. "We spend a lot of time together, and I adore Adam. We've become kind of a threesome the past few months." She didn't mention almost losing Adam in the park, and her recent doubts.

Neil was watching her as she spoke. "And what about the twosome part?"

"Well, you know how it is, with a kid around all the time. It's a little complicated."

"Yes, of course. They take priority. So much for romance, eh?" Neil smiled, his eyes crinkling, and Alice wondered if he was toying with her. "So, what are you going to do now?"

"About what?"

Neil laughed. "I mean next. Now that the play is finished."

"Oh. I start rehearsals in two weeks for *Cat on a Hot Tin*

Roof," Alice said. "I get to play Maggie, and I can't wait. It's a juicy part." She paused, then said aloud what had just occurred to her. "But I'm going to Chicago first, since my sister's about to have a baby and I could use a change of scenery."

The waiter interrupted with the check, and after insisting on paying, Neil stood and helped Alice with her coat.

"Don't forget your wings," he said, lifting them from the booth. Light penetrated the thin edges, causing them to glow gold. Alice felt suddenly like a terrible fraud, far from angelic. And she didn't know anymore when she was acting; or rather, why, when she was around Neil, she kept reaching for her old self.

On the street, Neil hailed a cab for Alice, and again he held the door open for her. "We should do this again sometime, when you return from Chicago, or when I get back from London—I'm leaving next week for a while."

Alice smiled faintly, neither agreeing nor disagreeing. "Thank you for coming to the play, and for dinner. It was very generous of you."

"Generosity had nothing to do with it," Neil said. Then he lightly lifted and kissed her hand. "Thank *you*, Alice Stenen."

Alice sat back in the taxi as it drove off. She felt a faint buzzing in her head, an undercurrent, as if something were plugged into the wrong socket. She attributed it to the wine and the emotion of the play's finale, and the undeniable pleasure of flirtation. She felt herself flung against the deep seat of the cab, trying to hold on in more ways than one.

It is no wonder human beings love life lived onstage. Love and loss, betrayal, misunderstandings, sorrow and death! All neatly explained, tidied up. How comforting to nestle into worn mohair seats and watch the heavy velvet curtains part; to hear the truth in poetry that real life often lacks.

Thus, behold, there is our daughter, aloft with childlike wings and with her strong, clear voice and beautiful face, drawing in the masses, so that all eyes are on her, all ears perked to hear her story. A bedtime story for grown-ups all dressed up yet nonetheless lulled in their seats, moved and frightened and entertained all at once.

James and I, and a few other onlookers, silently watch the show unfolding from our special vantage point.

In orchestra row fifteen, a woman in pearls is watching Alice as her husband of thirty-one years—who is betraying her with his young assistant (though he doesn't know she knows)—reaches for the opera glasses in her hands to take a look for himself. While Alice sways on a high beam, telling how she took her own life, the woman feels real grief, and a slow-growing murderous rage that has nothing to do with the theatrics onstage. She jerks the opera glasses back from her husband's grip and presses them to her own eyes, blurry with tears. Her oblivious husband, thinking she is moved by the play, digs in his pocket for a handkerchief and, after inspecting it for cleanliness, hands it to her. The tenderness of his gesture, coupled with his duplicity, makes the woman weep all the harder.

A few seats over, a young man is aware only of the silent jangle of a diamond ring in his right pocket, and the pale, slender hand on his left thigh. He can hardly concentrate on the play. He wishes he and his girl were strolling through Central Park, or even riding in one of those cheesy horse-drawn carriages with the dingy lap blankets. He thinks it will be like a fairy tale, and he the prince, kneeling (well, hard to do in a moving carriage) to offer his hand and his heart to his angelic girl. But she has taken her hand from his leg to dig in her purse for a mint, which she hands to him, leaving him to wonder if his breath is bad. And the talking onstage goes on and on and the young man's confidence recedes, as does the imagined luster of the ring in his pocket.

And, two rows back, there is another, older man, whose eyes never once leave Alice's face until the lights dim, causing her to vanish. Already he is planning to find her backstage, already he is thinking of ways to pin her in place, to inspect her up close. His motives are not necessarily corrupt, but he knows he is taking a chance. Someone could get hurt. Nonetheless, a bouquet of tulips sits on the floor at his feet.

After the curtain falls, the others drift away, but James and I watch the show that continues backstage, and in a romantic restaurant. We watch Alice move through these new scenes, feeling her way, rightly or wrongly. It is how everyone goes through life—on faith, or instinct, or by ignoring both.

" 'All the world's a stage, and all the men and women merely players,' " James quotes.

" 'They have their exits and their entrances,' " I add.

"No one wants to think about that," James says.

But eventually, it will be time. After the show comes the inevitable exit. And then another kind of entrance.

In fact, a new arrival from Spain settles in beside us, curious. Coincidentally, she is—or was—an actress, just emerged from a fatal car accident in Madrid.

"Aqui, e pues andato," she says, smiling at us, still awestruck. *Here, and then gone.*

We should know.

Eleven

Gripping the handrail, Dinah made her way down the hallway to the stairs, pausing every few steps to take deep breaths. *Oh Lord. Oh no oh no oh no,* she thought with each pang, an invented Lamaze mantra that seemed to help, but only for a few seconds. *Not yet,* she pleaded. Dinah needed more time, but it was as if she'd gotten into a car with no brakes and was careening downhill. She came to halt at the door of the kitchen, where she arrived, unwittingly, in the middle of a domestic explosion.

It was a marital breakdown the likes of which Dinah had never witnessed before, not including the random viewing of daytime soap operas. Even those couldn't compare, and if she thought about it, one of the parties involved usually had mascara streaming down rouged cheeks. Fortunately, neither Theo nor Griffin wore makeup. Theo, however, seemed on the verge of tears.

The two men stood at opposite sides of the table, their

expressions flushed with rage and pain. Theo was in tattered pajamas and Griffin wore black pants and a pressed blue-striped shirt with the shirttails hanging loose. He still had on his shoes, either because he'd only just come in or was on his way out. Dinah suspected it was both.

She didn't want to be here, a voyeur at an intimate spectacle, but she'd stumbled downstairs to announce that it was time, that "it" was happening, two weeks earlier than she'd expected. And the baby seemed to be twisting around with monumental force, trying to find a way out. Dinah needed help, but neither Griffin nor Theo even acknowledged her presence. They were far too preoccupied.

"*I saw you!*" Theo shouted. "I saw you—so you can stop pretending your work schedule is 'erratic.' It's been 'erratic' for weeks. I'm not an idiot."

"T—"

"Just shut up. Just. Shut. Up." Theo paused, bowed his head. "I don't even care," he said, his ears reddening with the lie. Then he looked up at Griffin across the table and asked in a low voice, "So, what's his name?"

Griffin froze in the cold, hard gaze of his longtime mate. Dinah saw that her brother's expression was anguished.

"Ray," Griffin said. "He's—"

"I don't want to know anything else," Theo said, interrupting tears brimming. "I don't want to know what he does or who he is or what he likes or anything at all about him. I know what he looks like; he's gorgeous. And I know what you look like with him—I could see that plain as day. I saw—" He broke off, now openly weeping.

Griffin started to circle around the table toward Theo, but just then, Dinah's water broke with a small gush, and although it was nearly noiseless, both men jerked their heads in her direction as if she'd fired a gun.

Everything stopped then—the fight, the tension, the tears, normal life, time itself—and then everything sped up.

Griffin and Theo snapped to attention, assigning each other tasks, their voices overlapping: "Call nine one one. . . . Never mind, get my keys. . . . Does she have a bag or anything? Dinah, do you have a bag, anything you want to take? What do you need? Get her some water. . . . No, forget it. . . . Get a towel—not for the floor, dummy! For her legs. She's covered in—what is that, anyway? . . . We better just go; she looks pale. Is it coming *right* now?"

Griffin put an arm around Dinah, who was doubled over, and Theo deftly gathered coats and keys and wallets. Somehow, in the intervening moments, he also must have raced up to the guest room and jammed a small overnight bag with Dinah's things; he listed these on the way out the door: "I got your toothbrush and your little makeup bag—not that you'll need it, but I mean, you never know—and a clean shirt and some socks, because hospitals are always cold—"

Dinah couldn't hear anymore. All she heard was the pain; it actually seemed to have a sound, a throbbing, rushing, whooshing, clamoring sound that thrummed through her body. The earlier contractions were polite jabs, nothing in comparison. Dinah felt like an overstuffed sack about to split wide open, and she wrapped her arms around her massive middle. What if she broke? What if she actually shattered? Her pelvic bones, her spine?

"It's happening too fast," she gasped as the men rushed her into the car, tripping and dropping things in their haste.

Griffin took the wheel and backed out of the parking space and into traffic, much too slowly, Dinah thought. Beside her in the backseat, Theo was holding her hand and tenderly murmuring reassurance. "You're going to be fine. Just breathe, remember? Slow, deep breaths. You can do this."

"Yeah, just breathe," Griffin added uselessly.

Why don't you *fucking breathe?* Dinah thought hostilely, but she breathed anyway.

"Good," Theo said, then paused to call out directions to Griffin. "Wait—why are you turning here? Don't take Halsted; take Dayton—I know it seems like you're backtracking, but it's faster."

"What are you talking about?" Griffin asked. "You never drive."

"Trust me. It's faster, I swear. You won't hit all the red lights—plus, you can turn at that alley about four blocks up."

"Okay, okay," said Griffin under his breath. Griffin looked in his rearview mirror to ask Dinah if she was all right, but his gaze rested on Theo.

"Just hurry up!" Dinah barked. And Griffin obeyed.

Outside the hospital entrance, an orderly who looked like a teenager greeted them with a wheelchair. Theo jumped out of the car to help.

"Ease on in. Here we go," the orderly said as he guided Dinah into the chair and planted her feet on the footrests. She managed to smile tersely. "Are you the dad?" he asked Theo, then glanced at Griffin, who was still behind the wheel, preparing to drive off and park.

"Uh, no," Theo said. "I'm a relative—friend. We're—he's her brother and I'm—" Theo was stammering, apparently confused about his current status. Dinah looked up from the wheelchair and grasped his sleeve.

"He's my coach," she said. "Can we just go now?"

The orderly laughed. "Follow me, coach." He took Dinah into the hospital, Theo at his heels. Theo turned back once to look toward the glass doors, obviously to see if Griffin was coming, and then he faced forward, jaw set, as if he didn't care one way or the other.

In the hallway near the elevators, Theo put a hand on Dinah's shoulder and said, "We made it—you're going to be fine."

"You're staying, right?" she asked nervously, but just then a woman in a white coat approached and Theo stepped out of the way.

Dinah looked up, tried to meet his eyes. She wanted to will him to stay, to forgive her brother, to do whatever was necessary to make things work. She'd heard enough to know things were dire, and that Griffin most likely was in the wrong. But then, who was she to intervene or judge? She was having a stranger's baby, thousands of miles from the oblivious father. Eduardo's face flickered in Dinah's mind, and she wondered what he would think, and if he already was cradling his other child.

And all at once, Eduardo vanished, as did Theo and everything else as the baby made its presence keenly known.

"It's coming!" Dinah yelped, almost lurching out of the chair.

"How far apart?" a woman was asking. "Your contractions—have you been able to time them, Dinah?" Whoever she was, she seemed to know who Dinah was. She had flawlessly bobbed and highlighted hair, and beneath her unbuttoned white coat was a trim ivory suit. She even wore pearl earrings and lipstick, which seemed vaguely insulting to Dinah in her disheveled state.

She asked the question again, patiently, as Dinah hadn't responded.

"Four minutes? I don't know—six?" Dinah ventured, like a recalcitrant math student.

"Hmm," the doctor said, her tone implying *Guess again.* "Let's take a look."

"I haven't called my doctor yet. It's Melbourne—" Dinah managed to protest.

"He's out of town, I'm sorry. I'm Dr. Janowitz. I'm taking his call this week."

"Where's Theo—he's supposed to coach—"

"Your husband?"

"No," Dinah snapped. "Never mind." She felt lost and irritable and terrified. How could Theo have failed her now? She bit her lip, tasting blood, realizing for the first time that she really was on her own.

She felt that she was stranded in the middle of a road, which had seemed familiar and now was all wrong. Perhaps it had been the wrong one for a long time. When Dinah became pregnant, even after she knew Eduardo wouldn't be there, she had imagined herself in a normal life with an adoring husband (but who?) and a house with a small garden—she'd even pictured tomato plants and a swath of cut lawn and her small, as-yet-faceless child running through a sprinkler. It had seemed such a predictable, attainable dream; now it seemed impossible, silly, even. At what point could it have happened? Dinah wondered. She was on a different road altogether. And now it was as if a detour had risen up out of nowhere and the imaginary husband and home had fallen off a cliff.

Without warning—or any say on her part—Dinah was wheeled to a birthing room, painted dove-gray, with crisp white blinds and fake leather wing-back chairs tucked in a corner. For the viewing guests, Dinah supposed—for those lucky enough to have any.

The doctor's hands, warm in latex gloves, were nudging Dinah's knees apart. She tried not to squirm; it seemed imperative, as she gazed at the perfectly made-up face looming over her, that she should behave with decorum.

However, when two nurses, male and female, appeared out of nowhere like angels flanking Dinah's bed, Dr. Janowitz said matter-of-factly, "Dinah, it's all right if you yell, you know. You should do whatever you feel like doing—this is going to be hard work and fast, I expect. You're already ten centimeters, so you're going to be pushing soon. Don't hold it in—yell like the dickens if you want. It will help." She chuckled and added, "They always tell you to *breathe,* but by this point I say, to hell with that—just scream."

The nurses laughed, too, but demurely, as if well trained in birthing etiquette. The female one stroked Dinah's hair; the male adjusted her sheets and poked an ice cube between her parched lips.

And then, without even meaning to, Dinah let out a feral guttural sound that she'd never made before in her life. It alarmed her, yet she did it again. The pain was excruciating; she was soaring off its edge, prepared to crash against the rocks.

Then the male nurse said excitedly, as if were the first time it had ever happened, "I can see it! I can see the—"

Dr. Janowitz interrupted. "Wait a minute. We have a breech."

Dinah heard voices. She imagined they were just around a corner, or a few rooms over; the sound was like muffled cocktail chatter. Perhaps she had died and these were souls coming to greet her. She had gone in and out at various times, her eyes fluttering to lights and blurred faces hovering over her. Her body ached, yet it felt disconnected; she wasn't sure she had survived. Then someone had asked her a question, someone else commented about her pupils, and then the first voice told her that her baby was fine: "She's perfect." As the astonishing news sank in—*a girl!*—Dinah sank back into unconsciousness.

Now she opened her eyes, startled to find herself surrounded by loving, familiar faces: Griffin and Alice, and Joan.

"When did you get here?" Dinah asked, looking from one to the next.

Joan bent to kiss her forehead as she always had when Dinah was a child. "About an hour ago. Griffin called us last night, as soon as you were admitted, and miraculously, we both got flights this morning, and then took cabs right over." Joan's gray hair looked freshly coiffed and she was dressed in a pale pink cardigan over a paler pink blouse with a fine plaid skirt. She looked like she'd just come from church, though a shade more glamorous. She even wore shiny lipstick, which she'd never done before. "It's so good to see you, sweetheart," Joan added softly.

"You, too," Dinah said, squeezing her hand. She was

glad to see that Joan looked robust, as if she had been taking better care of herself in Dinah's absence. Looking more closely, she saw that Joan's hairstyle was new, with little feathered layers; and she wore a silver necklace strung with natural pearls that Dinah had never seen before. If Dinah didn't know better, she would have thought that her grandmother had a lover.

Alice leaned over Dinah, beaming. "Congratulations, Dido," she said.

"We heard it was rough going, sweetheart," Joan said.

"I know," Dinah said. "They said it was unusual that close to the end, for a baby to flip."

She still could feel a faint throbbing in her abdomen, but it was nothing like before. Turning her head to the right, she looked at the clear acrylic bassinette, and, inside, her sleeping daughter, with her swirl of dark hair and her ruddy scrunched face like a little fruit. Dinah's eyes welled up and she wiped them with her left hand, which was attached to a monitor, a needle taped into her skin. She focused on the tiny face, still trying to take it all in.

When she didn't speak, Alice said softly, uncharacteristically emotional, "She really is gorgeous, Di."

"Perfect," Joan agreed, lifting the baby out of the crib and handing her to Dinah. The impossibly minute weight of her—six pounds and three ounces of skin and bones and organs and newly minted soul—sank against Dinah's chest. Dinah inspected her. There was no sign of Eduardo, but for the dark hair (though so was hers), and her eyes, when they opened a slit, were navy blue. Dinah ran a finger along the velvet cheek. Her baby *was* perfect, more perfect than anything she'd ever laid eyes on. She looked up at her family.

"I'm so glad you're all here," she said. Then: "Where's Theo?"

There was an uncomfortable silence, and Dinah saw that her brother was looking at the floor. She knew then that Theo hadn't just stepped out; he was gone. In the drama of the past twenty-four hours, she'd forgotten the fight and what it likely had meant. And selfishly, as it sank in, she felt worse for herself than for Griffin. She needed Theo. He was her ally, her coach, the one she could count on, did count on. It hurt her to think he wouldn't have thought of *her*—and the baby—after all this.

Griffin cleared his throat and changed the subject. "So, what are you going to call her?"

Dinah looked away and swallowed, trying to adjust to all the change. What would she do now? Where would she live? How could she do any of this? But then she took a breath and inwardly prayed. All she had to do was cope with this moment. *Fear not,* she heard from afar.

"Any ideas?" Joan gently prodded. "For a name?"

Any names Dinah might have entertained, she'd shoved away in the last weeks, like bills she couldn't pay. She was afraid to think about them, about *her*—but here she was, in stunning, minute perfection, and she needed a name. Dinah's own name meant "judged, vindicated." Aside from being named for a fictional cat, the Hebrew origin seemed most prescient. Names mattered, and she had to choose well; she had stored away the one that seemed to fit, and she said it out loud for the first time now.

"Eva," Dinah announced. "I'm going to call her Eva Moses Stenen."

There was a respectful silence, followed by little waves of laughter. "Moses?" Griffin asked.

"Was that the father's name?" Joan whispered to Alice.

"I don't think so," Alice stage-whispered back. "But she won't say." Of course, she knew the truth, and Dinah was relieved she didn't tell.

"I just like the name," Dinah said, keeping the reasons to herself. "It fits."

Eva (Eve) was the first, and her name meant "life-giving." It was the name Dinah had had in mind all along for a girl. As for Moses, she remembered a story she'd first heard in a basement Sunday school room with gray linoleum floors and immaculate blackboards. The story was about the Egyptian mother hiding her child in a basket of bulrushes "daubed with pitch," and shoving it downriver, where Pharaoh's daughter found it. She pulled him out and held him up and named him Moses, which meant, "drawn from the water."

Dinah's baby had been conceived in the middle of the ocean, and Dinah had been feeling lost at sea the past months, unsure what to do about the impending birth. But now it seemed she was on dry land, with her child safe in her arms, her family having surfaced with her, for the moment at least. Tomorrow would come soon enough, and like Scarlett O'Hara, she would think about that later.

"*Oh*" is all we can say as we watch her slip newly into the world, our happiness bubbling over, so that anyone around us could scoop it up, and they do.

Twelve

Griffin woke, disoriented, vaguely guilty, wondering where he was. It was a feeling reminiscent of a brief, regrettable period in his younger years of strange beds. Indeed, he was in a strange bed, but it was a futon on his own living room floor, beside a snow-white bassinette, wheeled in from Dinah's room at three A.M. The disorientation, he realized, was mostly due to abject lack of sleep.

He remembered pacing most of the previous night with Eva in his arms, squalling in his ears. It amazed him that such a small bundle, no bigger than a wadded towel, could emit such noise. And that Dinah could sleep through it. Of course, Dinah had been up, too, feeding her infant three times in six hours, and was understandably exhausted. And Joan, seventy-six, and scheduled for an early flight home, couldn't be expected to take the night shift. Griffin felt compelled to help; he wasn't sleeping anyway.

In the past three weeks, everything had changed.

Griffin had moved out of the house on Orchard Street that he and Theo had shared for the past eleven years. He couldn't very well stay, or ask Theo to leave, as he legally owned it. The day after Eva was born, Griffin had gone to the house to pack his and Dinah's belongings, and Theo had not tried to stop him, though he had grown close to Dinah in the previous months. Theo even stuffed the giant bear, Walter, into the backseat of the car. Then he went inside without looking back and shut the door. Griffin, heartsick, had driven away.

His new home was a small loft farther south, and closer to Paradiso. Griffin told Dinah that she and Eva could stay with him. He hoped it was temporary, but he hadn't broached the topic; his sister had enough on her mind now that she was about to be alone with a baby.

Initially, she had had a lot of help. Alice had stayed on for a week and Joan another two, but Alice had a new play about to begin rehearsals, and Joan needed to return to Takoma Park to care for her friend, Letty, who had broken a leg and needed surgery. Torn between crises like a triage nurse, Joan fretted about leaving so soon.

In fact, she was leaving in a matter of hours, so Griffin stumbled out of the twisted sheets. After checking on his niece—sleeping with her fists curled adorably beside her dark head—he tiptoed toward the kitchen for coffee.

The apartment was a third the size of the house he'd just vacated, but seemingly vast, as the ceilings were high and there wasn't much furniture. Griffin had told himself he had been suffocating from Theo's penchant for overstuffing chairs with pillows, and beds with too many coverlets. But while he did enjoy the relative starkness of his new apartment, the truth was, Griffin felt adrift, almost like a refugee waiting to be told where to go next.

"Hi, darling," Joan said when he walked into the kitchen. She was seated across from Dinah at the little foldout table beside a window with a view of an ivy-covered wall. Dinah was slouched in her pajamas, staring vacantly at the wall, while Joan was sitting up, fully dressed, with her luggage packed on the floor beside her. "I just made some orange pekoe tea," Joan said. "Would you like some?"

Griffin grunted, startled at hearing his fifteen-year-old self emerge. He cleared his throat and tried again. "No, thanks. I'm just having coffee."

"I think we're out," Dinah said wearily.

Two thoughts collided—the absence of caffeine, and the harbinger of the word *we*. Both caused Griffin to hang his head and groan. His days and nights might be filled in perpetuity with soggy, wadded diapers, dangling bras drying in the bathroom, and the mingled scents of Eva's Ivory Snow and Dinah's coconut conditioner. After today, the only difference would be the absence of Pond's face cream.

"Well, I guess I can get some on the way back from the airport," Griffin said. He checked the wall clock. "We probably should go, Joan, if your flight's at nine. You always worry about being late and everything."

"I'm not worried," Joan said, "except about Petey."

"Who's Petey?"

"I meant Letty," Joan said quickly.

Griffin glanced at her. "Joan, who's Petey?" he asked again, eyes twinkling.

Joan rolled her eyes. "*Peter*. Just a friend from bridge club. Are you going to change your clothes?" she asked, her tone reminding Griffin of school days: "Are you wearing that?" "An iron might be a good idea, just a quick once-over." "Don't forget your gloves."

Griffin was wearing the jeans and T-shirt he'd fallen asleep in. "No time," he said. "We're going to hit rush hour as it is." Holly bounded to his side and Griffin stroked her back, crouched down to attach her leash. "I'll take Holly along, Di, so you don't have to worry about her. In fact, I'll probably just take her to work with me, so I can tie her up outside the kitchen." The dog liked the tiny enclosure behind the restaurant where scraps of food sometimes got tossed, and where she could bark at birds.

Dinah said nothing, still staring out—or rather at—the window. Joan stood and wrapped her seated granddaughter in her embrace.

"You take care of yourself, sweetheart," Joan said softly but insistently. "Take naps whenever Eva does, okay? Sleep is the most important thing right now. And don't forget to drink enough, and get some sunshine if you can."

Dinah's monosyllabic response was muffled against her grandmother's waist.

Joan released her, kissing the top of Dinah's head, and then headed to the corner of the living room. She bent over the bassinette, stroking the sleeping baby's cheek and cooing until Griffin jangled his car keys and said sardonically, "Joan, you know how Eva hates long good-byes."

As he turned to go out of the apartment after Joan, Griffin caught a glimpse of Dinah, standing forlorn and pale in the middle of the vast living room, as Eva began to wail. Griffin really hated it when Eva cried. She looked like she was suffering so much, her face scrunched into soft pink

216

folds, like an overripe peach, and her mouth gaping, all red gums and rigid little tongue. The noise was searing. How did parents stand it? Griffin wondered. And how did they know what a baby needed? It wasn't always hunger or wetness, he'd discovered; sometimes Eva just seemed to cry out of some primal anguish. He closed the door on the noise, feeling sorry for his sister, yet relieved to be leaving.

As they drove to O'Hare, Joan agonized again about leaving Dinah alone.

"She had a baby," Griffin said. "It's not life or death, you know."

"Well, neither is a broken leg," Joan said, though she clearly was also anxious about her friend back home.

"I know, but I'll be here, too, so Dinah won't be alone. Don't worry about us."

Joan smiled. "You have no idea, sweetheart. I never stop worrying about any of you."

Griffin looked at her, with her crown of white hair, and realized that his grandmother had gotten old without him noticing. She'd survived the loss of her husband, her son and daughter-in-law, and had faced her own mortality through cancer. Griffin didn't *want* her to worry anymore. Though Joan had hinted several times that Dinah could move back east to live with her, so she could help with Eva, Griffin knew she didn't need the extra work. Neither did he, but he was sure it was temporary.

"I promise I'll take good care of them," Griffin assured Joan, looking back at the road, veering around a taxi that had slowed without warning in his lane.

After a lull, Joan asked, "Does it seem to you that Dinah's . . . not quite herself?"

"No. I don't know. She's just adjusting, I guess."

"I know, but she seems overwhelmed, and more than a little distracted."

"Well, not sleeping every night doesn't help," Griffin said. "I can attest to that."

Joan was silent. "Maybe you're right." She paused. " 'This, too, shall pass.' "

Once he deposited Joan at her departure gate with a hurried hug, Griffin turned around to head back into the city. As he got closer, he realized he was heading in the wrong direction, away from home and Paradiso—and not entirely by accident.

Ray's windows, a bank of them, were filled with dangling glass crystals, each turning and casting shards of color along the walls and floor. Ray said his sister, Carrie, had hung the crystals with fishing lines on a recent visit.

"She said they have special energy," Ray said. There was no hint of mocking in his voice; in fact, as he watched the glass teardrops turn, he seemed convinced.

"So, are you into New Age and all that?" Griffin asked, half teasing. They were still new enough to each other that they trod carefully into areas of discovery. Thus, whenever Griffin arrived, there were a few initial moments of small talk, which invariably led to revelatory discussions.

Ray laughed a little. "No, I'm actually a devout Catholic."

"Very funny."

"I'm serious. I go to Mass twice a week."

Griffin looked at Ray carefully, still waiting for the punch line.

"What about confession?" Griffin asked. "What about, uh, the church's stance on *homosexuality*?"

"I know," Ray said, and shrugged. "I keep hoping things will change, but nothing's perfect, right? Anyway, I love the liturgy and the music and the stained glass." He paused, pointing to the crystals. "Like that. It just sort of makes you feel there is something holy about being a part of this world, in spite of it all."

Griffin didn't know what to say. It seemed that every time he was with Ray, another door opened and he walked in, to find that the man was comprised of endless, fascinating rooms. It made Griffin want to be a better person when he was with him; he even wanted to keep his clothes on, to just keep talking and opening those doors.

But now, as if they'd sufficiently warmed up, Ray came closer and wrapped his arms around Griffin, sliding his face down along Griffin's chest. Griffin moaned, eliciting a yelped response from Holly, who'd been tucked as usual into a large crate in a corner. Ray had purchased the crate, along with a plaid cushion and some dog food for such visits; it seemed a sign that things were moving along.

His belt was being unbuckled. His jeans, rumpled from sleep, were pulled loose. Ray was trying to guide Griffin to the bed or the sofa, or the floor—it didn't seem to matter which—but all at once, Griffin felt so exhausted, he simply slumped against Ray's shoulder.

"I'm sorry, Ray. I'm just so tired. Could I just lie down?" He pulled his clothes back on clumsily and sprawled on the sofa.

"You all right?" Ray asked, perched beside him and placing a hand on Griffin's forehead. "You don't feel warm." He paused. "Or hot, either," he added, a joke that Griffin, with his eyes half closed, caught a little late.

"Sorry," he repeated. "Really. I was up all night with the baby. Again."

"First it was Theo, now it's Eva."

"What do you mean?" Griffin asked, perking up.

"I mean you still have someone at home who needs you more."

"It's temporary," Griffin said quickly. "Till Dinah can find her own place and Eva is old enough for day care—I guess. I really don't know what they're going to do. I'm sort of afraid to ask."

"Why? She's your sister, right?"

It occurred to Griffin that Ray's relationship with his sister must be very different from his own with either Dinah or Alice. Griffin felt he was just getting to know the grown-up Dinah, but so much had changed so fast. She suddenly wasn't even the same person, and she had a tiny stranger in her arms.

Griffin closed his eyes again, blocking out his thoughts and the light scattered across the wall, and Ray's disappointed face.

When he awoke, it was to Holly's impatient bark, to the light grown brighter in the living room, and to a gnawing hunger, all at once. Griffin sat up, groggy, hushing Holly. He spied a piece of paper on the floor beside his shoes.

It was a note from Ray: "Go ahead and use the shower. I had to head in to work. Call me later if you can break free. You look so damn cute when you sleep."

Griffin smiled, but knew he already had stayed too long, trying his dog's patience, and that he was late for work. Griffin stumbled to the door with Holly pulling him along, and then out to the street, where the dog promptly peed against the nearest tree. As he rushed to Paradiso, Griffin thought about Ray, inevitably comparing him with Theo—and the other way around.

It amazed Griffin how understanding Ray seemed. In the early stages of his love affair with Theo, if Griffin had been more interested in sleep than sex, Theo would have wanted to analyze his feelings, turning them over to inspect for cracks. Or he would have turned pensive, hurt. Looking back, it occurred to Griffin that on some level, he'd always wanted to protect Theo from pain.

But Theo was the lightness that had buoyed Griffin— and recently Dinah. He was the cheerleader, the one who believed the world was a wonderful place, a place into which one should bring children. Theo wanted a baby, and after all the Lamaze and tending to Dinah the past months, he had wanted *this* baby. It probably crushed him more than Griffin knew to be left out when she finally arrived.

Ray never even asked about the baby. He was more interested in Holly, which at first had been in his favor. While Theo had thought of the dog as a nuisance, Ray immediately "adopted" her, always kneeling down to rub Holly's ears and back with a sure, gentle pressure. He was the same with Griffin, intuiting how he wanted to be touched, stocking his kitchen with food he knew Griffin liked.

But some things bothered Griffin. For one, Ray wasn't ever funny. After years of "married" life—from the beginning, actually—Griffin and Theo had shared the same sense of humor, inside jokes, and inane observations. When Griffin told Ray a political joke (something, he realized now, that had also involved the Pope), Ray had feigned a half-hearted snort.

And then there was the matter of family. Griffin had yet to meet the supposedly darling Carrie, but she was it. She and Ray had other relatives, but they were far-flung and had never been close. Griffin thought of the numerous Steins and wondered what Theo had told them. The thought of Theo's parents hearing the news made Griffin's heart constrict. For the first time, it struck him that he'd lost even more than his longtime lover and friend; he'd lost his in-laws, Jon and Lil; he'd lost an entire family.

Pausing mid-stride, he let Holly go nuts over a half-gnawed chicken wing dropped on the curb. Then Griffin bent over, taking a deep breath. To his great surprise, he began belatedly to weep. He wept for Theo, for all of their years, for their end, and with great gulping sobs, he wept for the loss of the Steins, *his* Steins.

Images whirled through his head of holidays at the Lake Michigan compound—the crowded, overheated house, and tables piled with food that Griffin had helped cook. He thought of the attic, where he and Theo would lie in bed and watch the stars twinkle through a small scratched skylight. Like children, they would make preposterous wishes, topping each other's until they were convulsed with laughter.

Griffin wept on, till Holly trotted to his side and dropped the chicken wing on his shoe for consolation.

"You all right, sir?" a voice was asking, and Griffin straightened up, to see a young police officer studying him with genuine concern.

Griffin managed to nod, while surreptitiously wiping

his nose on his sleeve. "I'm fine, thanks. I just—I've just had a death in my family," he said, which was not entirely untrue.

"Oh. I'm so sorry, sir." The officer put a hand awkwardly on Griffin's shoulder. "My condolences," he said carefully, as if it were a new word he was trying out. He looked no older than fifteen.

Maybe Griffin was just getting old—was thirty-two old? (*Sir?*) It seemed he had lived so much life already; maybe that was why he was so bone-tired. It wasn't just a newborn's erratic sleep patterns; it was grief piled upon grief. Some days it felt like living inside a mud hut, another shovelful tossed on top, weighing it down. Losing Theo was the latest mound, heavier than Griffin had realized until now. How could he explain *that* to this child officer?

So he simply thanked him again and gently tugged Holly's leash, hurrying the rest of the way to work, trying to pull himself together. His heart sank heavily in his chest and his head throbbed even more than before. Worst of all, around the edges flitted the thought that he had made a terrible mistake. What if Theo really was the One?

Two weeks later, Griffin was deep in a pattern of compartmentalizing. In one part he was the doting uncle, sharing as much of the burden of infant care as he could; in another, he was a newfound lover; in yet another, he was an ex, trying to suppress his sense of loss and regret; and finally, and most comfortably, he was a chef.

At eleven o'clock in the morning, Griffin focused only on what was right in front of him: mounds of chopped onion like crusty snow; leaves of pungent basil, shredded with his bare hands, which carried the scent for hours; delicate strings of saffron; and the flame on the stove—or rather, six flames on different burners at different heights. It felt like he was standing at the edge of a live volcano, different areas active, all of them threatening to singe his wrists or face if he got too close. And sometimes, after a rushed battle with fresh cuts of beef, he looked like he'd just come out of surgery.

Today, the specials, thankfully, tended toward the tame and sublime: pastas, white fish, quiche, and orange-apricot crêpes smothered in cinnamon-laced whipped cream. Griffin ate three crêpes with two cups of espresso, and then two more when the lunch rush died down, standing at the enormous prep island. He ate as if his life depended on it, stuffing in the dripping, syrupy bites without pause.

"Want some sprinkles with that?" teased Steve, one of the line cooks. Steve habitually wore a black bandanna over his hair, which was white-blond and baby-fine, as were his eyebrows and lashes. Griffin suspected the bandanna and his frequent swearing were part of Steve's effort to appear less ethereal and more macho; sadly, it didn't work.

"Have you actually tried it?" Griffin asked, his mouth full. "It's amazing."

"Fuck no. I'm on the braised-fig diet this week," Steve said.

Griffin laughed. A running joke in the kitchen referred to the latest diet crazes, which often showed up in the kinds of special requests that came from the clientele. Sometimes it was for broth soups ("Could you just, like, leave out the milk?" a woman once asked when cream of leek was the soup du jour), or just cabbage, or eggless egg dishes. One customer wanted a burger, but without the bun—or the beef. "Just the toppings; you know, the 'everything' that comes on a burger."

"Hey, I forgot—you had a phone call," Steve was saying while gulping something Griffin couldn't see; Steve tended to nip into the rum used for glazes. "Your sister."

"Dinah?" Griffin asked. "Did she say what she wanted?"

"I didn't answer; Javier did," Steve said.

Dinah never called Griffin at work; no one did. The only time Theo had ever called Paradiso was when the pilot light went out on the stove at home and he smelled gas. Griffin had advised him to open the windows and call the fire department; then he'd hung up, annoyed that Theo hadn't figured it out for himself. Then he'd begun to worry that it might be serious, that Theo would be asphyxiated, so he'd called home ten minutes later to check on him, and heard a fireman in the background, laughing.

Griffin called his apartment now, wiping his sticky mouth with one hand, telling himself that Dinah just was stressed and it probably was nothing—a stuck faucet or a mouse in the kitchen. The phone rang nine, ten, fourteen times.

He hung up and yelled, "Steve, you'll have to clean up. I have to go." He grabbed his keys and then Holly from the enclosure and dashed for his car.

As he drove, running red lights and dodging dawdling drivers like pinball obstacles, Griffin realized that his flight instincts had taken over. Not only did he not want to know what terrible thing had happened, he wanted to keep driving right past his own street, up Lake Shore Drive, through

Evanston, and onward till he passed Green Bay and Sault Ste. Marie and the Canadian border. Perhaps if he drove there, he might never have to know what latest tragedy had befallen his family. He would be safe.

Of course, his own safety was not the issue. Griffin pulled up in front of his building and left his car beside a fire hydrant. He stepped out running and didn't stop until he was up both flights of stairs and at his door.

Once inside, he glanced around the room for evidence, though he had no idea what he was looking for or would find.

Dinah appeared then from the bedroom doorway, looking stricken. Her clothes appeared hastily chosen and all wrong for the weather; it was a mild spring day, but she wore a sweater and was struggling to fit her arms into the sleeves of a coat.

Griffin automatically went to her and gently tugged off her coat. "Wait. What happened?" he asked in a hush, fearing the worst. "Where's Eva?"

"She's gone." Dinah said flatly, letting her arms hang loose.

"Gone?" Griffin repeated. It had to be a mistake; she couldn't mean it.

"Theo has her," Dinah replied simply. Her eyes were a little blurry and unfocused, and she behaved like an unreliable witness.

"Theo!" Griffin cried. "What do you mean? *Why?*"

"He's been coming over, you know, and . . ." Dinah's voice trailed off.

Griffin stared at his sister. "Coming over when?"

"When you're at work," Dinah said. "Because of how

things are between you guys; because of what's-his-name."
Griffin refrained from comment. "You know I've always
loved Theo," Dinah said. "He's been really helpful, and after Joan left, I didn't have anyone else."

Griffin felt stricken, but she was right. He hadn't
helped very much. He'd watched Dinah struggle with the
baby, as if Eva were something wild he himself wasn't
trained or equipped to handle; as if Dinah, just by giving
birth, were an expert. Clearly, she wasn't.

"This morning, she wouldn't stop crying," Dinah was
saying.

"So Theo just . . . *took* her?" Griffin asked.

"No," Dinah said, meeting his gaze. "I gave her to him."
She sat down then, as if deflated. Griffin sat, too, and waited.
Then, after a long, pained silence, Dinah tried to explain.

Theo first had showed up at the apartment with crisply
cut red tulips and a pure white baby blanket wrapped in tissue and satin ribbons. He took one look at Eva and seemed
to fall in love. Everyone said she was beautiful, and Dinah
supposed it was true, with her exquisite doll features and
dark hair and eyes, but Theo seemed "transformed." He
picked Eva up and held her as if she were a rare creature
he'd been looking for his whole life.

In the days that followed, Theo showed up almost as
soon as Griffin had left; it seemed like an illicit affair whenever Dinah opened the door and peered around it to make
sure the coast was clear. But then immediately, Dinah
would relax as Theo lifted her crying daughter from the bassinette. He walked around with her, whispering and cooing until she calmed in his arms. He offered to feed her
with Dinah's bottled breast milk so Dinah could rest.

This morning, Theo had expertly nudged the baby's limbs into a clean cotton sleeper and then zipped it up. He fed her, rocked her, calmed her.

"It was like he was born knowing how to do everything," Dinah said, her eyes watering. "Unlike me." She paused, wiping her eyes. "I wish you'd stayed together. You'd be perfect parents." She looked at Griffin and then away. "At least I know Theo would be. That's why—"

"*Why?*" Griffin echoed, still not comprehending the turn of events. "Why did you do it?"

"I couldn't handle it another minute." A pause. "I couldn't handle her."

Griffin waited, choosing his words carefully. Their grandmother had been right to be worried that Dinah didn't seem herself. She never slept, and she was overwhelmed.

"Do you mean," Griffin asked gently, "that you just needed a break? Theo took her for the rest of the day, or what?" For a fleeting moment, Griffin wondered if Theo was so desperate for a baby, he would take one offered out of despair.

Dinah didn't respond to the question. She slumped farther down into the chair. Then she said, "I'm so tired all the time, I could just lie down in the middle of the street and not care. I don't think this is normal." She paused. "You know, sometimes, when Theo comes over, I just go out for a while to see the guys, and I feel like myself again. And I really don't want to come back."

Griffin knew about the homeless men and a few women Dinah had tended to in her small way for the past months. They'd come to count on her kindness, her offerings of warm food and coffee from the bakery, and a wadded dollar bill or sometimes a bit more. They knew her by name and she knew all of them; she'd listed names, but Griffin only remembered one, Merlin the Magician, of all things.

"I feel like I have this calling," Dinah said. "Everyone thinks it's some kind of do-gooder thing. But it's more than that. I feel it every single time I've passed a homeless person on the street, anywhere. I feel drawn to them like a magnetic tug, like I have to do something, and I want to do something."

"I understand that," Griffin said. "But Eva needs you, too."

"I know," Dinah said. "I never should have had her. I can't—I just didn't know what to do." She took in a deep gulping breath and pressed her hands to her breasts. "I'm leaking."

"Let's go," Griffin said, standing up. "Let's go get her back, Dinah."

"You must think I'm a terrible person," Dinah said miserably.

"I don't. I just think you're overwhelmed. And I'm going to help you more, I promise."

Dinah wiped her nose on her sleeve, leaving a shiny trail on the wool. "Theo tried to call you, too, when he got here this morning, but you weren't at work yet and no one knew where you were."

Griffin guiltily remembered that this morning he'd been at Ray's again, relieved to be away from his sister, and Eva's squalling. It was starting to become clear that Theo hadn't taken Eva at all, but was trying to rescue Dinah; he must have known how bad it was and that he had to intervene, at least temporarily. And he had tried to call Griffin, though no one relayed that message.

Silently, Griffin led Dinah down the stairs to his car. He nudged Holly into the backseat, and she obeyed, happily sticking her nose between the front seats. Dinah sat with her hands still pressed against her wet shirt, trying to staunch the flow. She looked heartbroken, and lost.

It occurred to Griffin that perhaps he just never paid enough attention. If he had been listening to Dinah, and to Joan, he (like Theo) would have known that while she seemed to be coping, his sister actually had been falling to pieces.

He wondered if things would be different if their parents had survived, if someone had been there to offer more guidance, to show them how to care for each other, and for another. Maybe as it was, they just weren't cut out for family life.

It might seem we judge, watching and eavesdropping thus. But we don't. We once lived on Earth, said the wrong things, broke vows, and hurt the ones we loved. All of it recorded but now erased as a clean blackboard, no sign of the chalky accusations or even their dust. So we cannot shake our heads or wring our hands over the tangled messes others make.

From my beautiful room I watch the waves curling and whales moving across the horizon in a long dotted line. The view shifts as in a child's View-Master, each one as pleasing and wondrous as the last, and better than 3-D.

James appears and sits on the edge of the broad plush

seat with me. It is made of something wondrous, like—there really is nothing like it. We sit for a while and neither of us speaks as Griffin and Dinah drive tensely through Chicago, in one car among thousands crawling along Lake Michigan.

"Is it really our fault?" I finally ask.

"We didn't kill ourselves," James says, lightly touching the spot where his damaged heart once resided.

"You're right," I say. "It just seems they are so cut loose, even now, when they're all grown up. They still haven't figured things out."

James laughs, and at first I think it is because of the dodos flapping past, looking at us with their round bug eyes. "Who ever has things figured out?" he says.

Life on Earth indeed can seem but one hard-earned lesson after another, with moments of grace and beauty in between to keep people sane, and hopeful. While some die peacefully at the natural end of a long, well-lived life, even they still haven't completed everything they meant to, or lived without regret.

And some of us thought we'd have more time to get things right. I tell myself that at least we planted some seeds—ideas of love, and faith, and loyalty—that are starting to show signs of growth. Time will tell.

Our gaze follows one car along the city streets and the curve of the blue, blue lake. We cannot help but notice that Dinah's arms are restless in her lap, with nothing to hold, and that Griffin glances at her sideways, unsure of what to do or say.

"He used to be so good at cajoling, even when they were little," James says. "He's out of practice."

"Fraternal instinct will take over," I say.

And sure enough, Griffin reaches across the front seat to take his sister's hand, which he finds disturbingly slick with her own milk. Dinah squeezes her other arm across her chest, and Griffin just keeps holding her wet hand. He knows that words will not suffice, only speed. Instinctively, his foot presses down harder on the accelerator.

For once, as by divine intervention, police radar does not pick up a signal as a car races blatantly past, right through the middle of a busy intersection in Lincoln Park, running a red light. The officer, whose squad car is half-hidden in the scrub of an overgrown parking lot, looks the other way, scratches his ear, and thinks about french fries.

PART III

Lost and Found

Thirteen

The brigade of parents and nannies lining the fence of the preschool grounds reminded Alice of the fans outside the stage doors of the theater. Their faces (most anyway) were as expectant, and—when the doors opened—as aglow with adulation. Alice smiled to herself, thinking how she used to love that look turned toward her, and how she was now one of the adoring fans. Much had changed in a year.

She searched the crowd for Adam, and when he appeared and saw her, he grinned, which made Alice's heart soar a little; the feelings were mutual.

"Alice," he said breathlessly. "You won't *believe* what happened!"

"What?" she asked, taking his backpack and slinging it over her arm, grasping his hand in hers.

"Bob the chinchilla had babies! Two of them!"

"Twins? Wow!" Alice paused. "So, Bob is a girl, then?"

Adam looked at her. "Yeah. She had *babies*." Then after

a few steps, he added, "I don't think they're twins. They're separate."

Alice laughed a little to herself, and then remembered that Adam had been inquiring about Siamese twins recently. "They can be twins, even if they're separate," she said. "I mean, it's actually a lot more common than Siamese twins."

"I know," Adam said patiently, and then dropped the subject, as he often did, moving without transition on to something else. "We need to buy pesto," he said.

"Right. For your pasta."

"I don't like plain anymore."

"I know."

They walked hand in hand amicably for the twelve blocks home, stopping now and then to look into store windows, and for Adam to try to retie his own shoelace, until he finally gave up and grudgingly let Alice do it. The "commute," as she had come to think of it, took a long time, no matter the weather, and Alice had learned to take it in stride. Some days, though, she just wanted to stop and sit in a coffee shop and stare out of the window without being badgered with questions or the urging to leave, *please?*

"I like the smush," Adam announced.

"Smush?"

"The snow that's all wet and mushy."

"Oh," Alice said, not correcting him. "I like it, too." Though, really, she didn't. She hated slush and March's erratic weather patterns. A morning rising blue and sunny could turn into a frigid, rainy afternoon. Alice considered ruefully that she used to be in rehearsals most days, so she hadn't paid much attention to what was happening outside.

Since her last play, *Cat on a Hot Tin Roof,* had closed early due to a financial dispute between producers, Alice had been at loose ends. She liked spending more time with Adam after school, but she missed work. She regularly sought auditions, but nothing felt right, and she even considered a long-standing offer from a friend to join his theater troupe for guaranteed parts. Alice always had liked the freedom and possibilities inherent in being a free agent, always hoping that a plum Broadway role might finally come through.

The only work she had had in four months, however, was far from Broadway or any theater, though it was still "acting," and at least it was employment. Alice was doing voice-overs for radio and television commercials. She adopted a firm but sprightly tone for an insurance company ("You won't be in better hands anywhere else, and that's a promise"), spoke with gentle professionalism for a women's hospital ("We look after you the way you look after everyone else—you're that important to us"), and employed husky flirtatiousness for a men's club ("Come on over to our place—we know how to keep customers coming back"). When Ian heard the last one on the radio, he roared with laughter and teased Alice, begging her to repeat the line in bed.

"I, for one, keep coming back," Ian had said, pulling her close.

"Thank God no one else knows it's me," Alice said, rolling her eyes.

Ian grinned wickedly. "Oh, I told everyone at work, and now they're all going to the club, hoping you work there."

"Very funny. If things keep going this way, I might have to."

"You'll find something," Ian said tenderly. "I think you're smart to be picky."

"You think I'm being picky?"

"I meant it as a compliment," Ian said.

"Oh."

Alice worried, though, that she was missing opportunities because her expectations were too high, and that she was being passed by. Apparently, good reviews and even a flattering profile in *The New York Times* were no guarantee for an actor. Directors Alice had known for years weren't calling her for their new plays. When she found out that Calvin Heinz was casting Ibsen's *A Doll's House*, she called him about auditioning (suspecting he wouldn't even ask her to). He apologetically told Alice that she was "too thin" for his current production.

"Are you kidding?" Alice said, laughing. "I think I've gained another five pounds being home at night, eating leftover macaroni and cheese."

"I'm sure you look great," Calvin said, missing the point, it seemed; Alice was practically begging to play the part, any part. "I'm doing a twist and casting Nora as really overweight—playing on the childishness her husband sees in her."

Alice said, "Isn't that a bit . . . denigrating? Not to mention stereotypical: 'You're fat because you eat too much cake and candy, so you're childish'?"

Calvin chuckled. "I love the way you always push, Alice. But no, it isn't like that. I want her to be even *more* sympathetic, so the audience thinks Torvald is even crueler to mistreat her."

"What about Kristine?" Alice asked, trying not to sound

desperate, though she ached with longing—to hold a script, to memorize lines, to dress up and fill her lungs and body with another's imaginary life. "I know the part inside and out, but I'd play it however you want."

There was a long pause, during which Alice grew increasingly uncomfortable. Then Calvin said, "I already cast Janine."

"Janine?" Alice repeated. "Isn't she too young for Kristine?"

Calvin cleared his throat. "She does something with her hair swept up that changes her face," he said lamely, and Alice knew at once he was sleeping with her. Too bad for his wife, Alice thought. She liked Collette.

Alice knew there was one female part left—fittingly, given her current lifestyle—the nanny. But she had suddenly lost interest altogether in the play, in working with Calvin. She wanted to quote Ibsen's Nora: "I've the most extraordinary longing to say: 'Bloody hell!'" But she wished Calvin luck and hung up. Maybe she *was* being picky.

Now she led Adam up the slushy street to their building. In the entryway, he stomped his rubber boots, leaving clots of dirty ice to melt on the obviously just-mopped tile instead of the wide mat, but Alice didn't chide him. She stopped to gather the mail from her mailbox, and Ian's; she still kept hers separate, still kept her old apartment like a secret stashed away. It was the first, and only, apartment Alice had rented since moving to New York after college. At the time, it had been a little expensive for a budding actress, but Alice had been able to afford it until she got more established, because of insurance money she and her siblings received after the death of their father. As a result,

Alice still associated the apartment with him, as if her father's spirit might somehow gently hover there, and thus she couldn't quite let it go.

Shuffling through the mail, Alice noticed that among Ian's was a letter bearing a row of foreign stamps. It was from England. She looked closely and saw Neil Lovelace's tiny initials printed in the upper left corner, as if he were intentionally trying to be cryptic.

"Can we go? I'm starving," Adam said, swishing the toes of his boots through the muddy water as if painting.

"Yeah, sure," Alice said absently, following him up the three flights of stairs to their apartment, still studying the envelope as if she could ascertain its contents if she stared hard enough. Of course, she couldn't open it; it was addressed to Ian. But neither of them had heard from Neil in over a year, since he'd left for England. Alice thought of his apartment in New York left empty, and how in a way the path he'd chosen was no different from hers—living elsewhere, leaving behind ghosts, or at least the ghosts of another life. An other life.

Alice had begun to wonder if the reason Neil had stayed in London so long was because he was attracted to her. The night he'd gone backstage with tulips and then taken her to dinner, the unspoken feelings between them had been as clear as subtitles across the bottom of a screen, relaying what the actors were in fact saying. Alice had chosen to ignore the signals, because she was committed to Ian, and she suspected that Neil ultimately had decided to do the same. Irrationally, Alice had been a little hurt by his extended absence and lack of contact; and of course, it was vain to think he'd left because of her. He hardly knew her.

Alice turned her attention to Adam, helping him butter his toast, a favorite snack, and then she drank two glasses of water so she wouldn't eat any toast herself; she had to start watching her weight, getting back into more disciplined shape.

Alice left the pile of mail on the table near the door as usual, with the letter from Neil tucked in the middle so that Ian would find it when he came home that evening and she could feign surprise. Or act blasé. She hadn't decided yet which was the better reaction.

Instead, when Ian picked up the letter and waved it, saying, "Look! Our old chum Neil!" Alice simply said, "I know. I saw it."

She waited patiently to learn the contents, but when Ian announced that Neil was coming back to New York in a month and immediately throwing a party—"Some kind of fund-raiser thing on behalf of an old friend, and he wants us to come"—Alice had to turn away. Why did Neil have such an effect on her? And after all this time? She knew it was girlish, just the residue of flirtation, of being desired.

But Ian desired her, and he was here with her all the time. Perhaps that was part of the problem of late. Familiarity. Family life: regular (but sometimes less) sex, and grocery shopping, and pediatric appointments, and preschool field trips. Sometimes Alice looked at Ian, filled with longing and happiness at her good fortune; other times she felt they were suspended in make-believe and it would either evaporate or a decision finally would be made. *Are we in this for good, or not?* she wondered, and wished Ian would be the one to ask for more. Alice wanted him to want her enough to ask, and she still wasn't sure she hadn't ended up with him—with both him and Adam—by default. Not knowing scared her. Wanting it to be permanent scared her, too. It was so much easier not caring.

After Ian and Adam were asleep, Alice slipped into the kitchen and phoned Griffin.

"How did you know it was time for change?" she asked her brother.

"I don't think I did. It just sort of happened," he said, apparently unsurprised by the question; it was the shorthand of siblings, reading between—and under and over—the lines.

"On the other hand," Griffin added, "it seemed like it had been coming for a while. Theo and I had grown apart because of, you know, the kid thing." Something in his voice seemed to waver, and Alice wondered if it had anything to do with Eva, who had changed their family more than any of them had expected—another generation of the Stenens, with threads of their lost parents woven into a new person.

Alice said nothing for a moment, sitting in the semi-dark kitchen, listening to the hum of the refrigerator, the ticking of the radiator. "Are you happy, though, with Ray, with how things turned out?"

"Hmm," Griffin said. "I don't think you can know that till you're dead and looking back. But for now, yeah, it's fine."

"Fine?"

"Alice, don't read too much into everything, okay?"

"Okay. Sorry. But do you regret not giving in about kids?"

"No," Griffin said without hesitation. "I still don't want kids. Do you?"

Alice laughed a little, twirled a loose piece of Lego on the tabletop. "I have one, Grif."

"Oh, right. I meant of your own."

"The thing is, he's like my own now. I mean—I'm not his mother, but the closest thing he's got."

"Do you love him?" Griffin asked.

"Adam? Of course." Alice's heart felt suddenly pinched as it dawned on her that she had no sway, no say in the matter if she and Ian broke up; she would lose Adam forever.

"I meant the other one," Griffin said. "Ian."

"Oh," Alice said. *Of course,* she thought, but didn't say. When she didn't answer right away, Griffin changed the subject. He never had been one to pry very deeply into his sisters' lives.

"Joan called right before you did and she sounded a little wan."

"How can someone 'sound' wan?" Alice asked.

"I don't know, she was just a little quieter than usual, not so chortlely and tsk-tsking and all that."

Alice laughed at her brother's vocabulary and told him that Joan probably was just tired. "She's no spring chicken, as she used to tell us twenty years ago."

"I was thinking about the cancer," Griffin said seriously.

"I think she gets checked every six months and she's clean," said Alice, aware that she still acted like the big sister, still reassuring.

"Well, good. But I'll be glad to see her when she comes next month."

"Yeah, me, too," Alice said. Then she said something she rarely said to either of her siblings, for reasons she didn't quite understand; maybe because they were all deprived of what should have come from their parents. "I love you, Grif," she said.

"I love you, too," Griffin said, and the words hung in the air of the phone lines for a long moment until they both simultaneously hung up.

We skim over the waves in our clear-bottomed boat and drift and watch the fish. And we watch Alice drifting through her days with Adam, wishing for a little more. She struggles to be content with these child-driven days, when what she wants is to be onstage, to have her old self back, and parts of her old life with it.

James lies flat in the boat and smiles at the tetra, the clown, the angel, and the puffer faces, which seem to smile back. "So blue," he says, and it's so true. The water still amazes us, just as it did on Earth. "But hopefully it will pass," James adds, and I realize he is referring instead to Alice.

"I don't think she's blue, just restless."

"What color is that, do you think?"

I laugh. "Maybe purple? A little livelier than blue, but similar. Being restless isn't necessarily sad—just discontent."

"I don't think I ever felt that," James says. "I always loved my life, my work, my kids. You."

"But then I left you," I say. "You were awfully blue for a long time."

"Yes," he says, turning to look at me. "A very dark blue. But grief and longing for the lost person aren't the same as discontent."

"Ever the professor," I tease. But words have different

meanings Here. We can parse and name these feelings but don't feel them now. What we feel is more a humming kind of happiness. *Content* doesn't quite come close, though there is a constancy to it.

That's not to say the discontent Alice is experiencing is negative; it isn't. Most growth and change come through groaning and pain. Light comes through clouds, and so on. However, change may come at a price, too. Especially when the wrong path is taken, when the line in the sand shifts a little. Humans like to rub it out with a toe and redraw it a little farther out to justify their choices. "It didn't mean anything," they say, or "No one got hurt."

"She does love him," James says. He sits back up and begins to row to shore through the silvery waves, the fish like streaks of rainbow beneath our feet.

"I know," I agree, though I don't know if he is referring to Ian or Adam or Griffin. It doesn't matter. Alice may love them all (and she does) but still do the wrong thing. And not even intentionally. Just because she's restless, and, yes, a little blue.

I love you, I tell Alice from afar, because she hasn't heard it from me in so long. She can't hear me now, but I hope somehow she feels it.

Fourteen

The line snaked around the block, a restless, undulating collection of humanity. Everyone in line was hot, sweating, and waving pamphlets to stir the air, or holding umbrellas or newspapers overhead to block the afternoon sun. Dinah moved among them, passing out paper cups of water and words of reassurance.

"It's like summer in Atlanta," an old man remarked, lifting a baseball cap from his head, his hair compressed with the hat's shape.

"Yeah, it's weird for March," a younger man agreed.

"Hey, it's after five!" someone shouted, followed by murmurs of assent up and down the row. The speaker, a solidly built woman in her thirties, glared at Dinah, who was approaching.

"Soon, Mirabelle," Dinah said, offering her a fig cookie from a package.

"You ain't ever have Oreos," Mirabelle scoffed, while accepting two figs.

"Sorry," Dinah said. "I'll see if we can get some. But there's chocolate pudding tonight."

"If you ever let us in."

Dinah laughed, patting Mirabelle's arm. Her skin was soft and fleshy, and her hair, unwashed, smelled faintly of tacos. Dinah knew she sometimes worked at a Mexican restaurant washing dishes, and in spite of her persistent orneriness, Mirabelle was one of the more promising members of the homeless community. She didn't want to be in the shelter, and she had confided to Dinah that she came only to keep her friends company. Mirabelle had "bigger plans." Dinah believed her; she believed anyone who claimed she wanted to change her life. "I did," Dinah always told them.

Ever since becoming an intake counselor for the Lakeside Shelter, Dinah had made a point of meeting the residents and visitors one by one. She knew all of the regulars, and greeted newcomers warmly. On rare occasions, her approach backfired. Unused to human contact and kindness, some people bolted at the first sign of it.

Dinah's predecessor, Jack, had advised her not to get too involved, that distance could be helpful in their line of work. He sighed. "I just hope you don't burn out, Dinah."

Though he claimed otherwise, Dinah knew that Jack had accepted his new job as director of a neighborhood center in Nashville for its clean rooms and mostly stable population, as well as for the warmer climate. She couldn't blame him. Homeless shelters were noisy, malodorous, and at times chaotic. And Chicago's weather was hard to take, too, with subzero temperatures in winter, and abrupt current changes—like now, in March, nearing eighty degrees just days after snow. Dinah sometimes thought of moving herself.

But she was settled now. After more than a year, she felt she belonged, in a way she never had before.

She walked cheerfully along the line with her open trash bag like a flight attendant down an aisle of passengers, collecting empty paper cups.

"What's taking so long?" a man named Charlie asked politely as he dropped in his cup, which he'd folded into an origami shape.

"We have more people than usual," Dinah explained, "and problems with a freezer, which flooded into the dining room. We had to bring in bags of ice, and everything just took a little longer than we hoped." She smiled. "I promise it will be worth the wait."

Charlie shrugged and rocked a little on his heels. His Converse sneakers had holes in the toes but new laces.

Others weren't so patient. Some scowled at Dinah or harangued her. She was used to it. She felt it was just a normal part of her day—like Merlin the Magician, who lately had returned after a six-month absence, still scolding her, or in darker moods, threatening to banish her from the "kingdom" altogether. He would stand apart, muttering to some imaginary foe.

When Anne-Marie, the kitchen supervisor, finally waved at her, Dinah hurried to the front of the line to open the double doors to the crowd. One or two jockeyed a little to push ahead, but most of the people knew the routine and simply filed in. They marked their days by the hours of the soup kitchen, the hours of the shelter, and by the hours of the rest of the world, as much as it suited them. Some parked themselves on street corners in the busiest commercial areas, begging or handing out pamphlets for small change. Others had sporadic menial jobs. And a few had actual full-time work that didn't pay quite enough to retain an apartment.

But Dinah and the rest of the staff did all they could to help them rise above the depths of despair and financial setbacks. Dinah had secured jobs on a trial basis for several people, including at Cupcake Heaven, her former employer, and in the kitchen at Paradiso under Griffin's tutelage. One remained there, a skinny man named Roger, who wore cowboy boots with shorts year-round, even with his apron. He had had an innate knack for choosing seasonings and improvising recipes, a talent that Griffin said was exceptional. Roger now lived in a small apartment furnished by the collective of people Dinah had gotten to know in Chicago through Griffin, Theo, and her church. They pitched in when she made specific requests for a mattress, bedding, or pots and pans. Inexplicably, one church member had donated an entire wardrobe of spandex, but it was accepted enthusiastically by several women and one man at the shelter.

But Theo had given the most. Looking around the town house he and Griffin had once shared, he announced to Dinah that he'd grown embarrassed by his riches. "Take anything you want—pillows, extra chairs, whatever. I need to downsize."

After dinner was under way, Dinah checked messages in her office and then turned off her computer for the night. She pushed the chipped wooden chair against the desk and rubbed a smudge from the window of her door with the hem of her blouse. Since her hair had grown, she wore it up in a loose bun, and she shook it out now, swept it back up with her hands, and clipped it back into place.

Yolanda, a social worker, stopped by and asked, "Did you see Atticus?"

"No. Is he here?"

"You just missed him. He was in a rush and just stopped in to deliver some papers." Yolanda added coyly, "He asked about *you*."

Dinah smiled. "Atticus Finch" was their code name for the lanky and dark-eyed public defender, Luc Martinelli, who worked six blocks over and occasionally dropped by the shelter to see clients. He was often distracted and wearing wrinkled shirts, but he was unfailingly handsome, "and *Italian*," as Yolanda had said once, sighing. Both Dinah and Yolanda had developed schoolgirl crushes on Luc, but Yolanda reluctantly relinquished first rights to Dinah, since she was "alas, already married."

"You know I don't have a prayer," Dinah said now, sighing.

"Why not? He likes you. It's obvious."

"Um, in case you're forgetting, Yoli, my life is a little complicated."

"Oh ye of little faith," Yolanda said. "You have to take chances in life."

"I think I've already done that in spades," Dinah said, and kissed her friend and headed out.

It was already dark, and she kept to the lighted main streets, though she felt perfectly safe. Dinah never had been afraid in Chicago, or in D.C., or anywhere, really. She'd always felt certain that guardian angels watched over her, or God Himself. Sometimes she entertained the thought that her parents watched, too, but she couldn't even picture them anymore, which bothered her.

In one week, her daughter would be one year old, the same age Dinah was when her mother disappeared from her life forever. Thinking of it, Dinah felt her heart clench a little, though she didn't know why. She didn't miss her mother, not really. How could she? There was no memory to miss.

She sped up her pace when she reached Orchard Street, skirting around a couple holding hands, leaning in to kiss. Reflexively, Dinah smiled at them, though of course they weren't looking at her. She tried not to dwell on how long it had been since she'd kissed or held hands with anyone. And she tried not to entertain thoughts of Luc, though she fantasized about him a lot, imagined tugging loose his rumpled shirt, his long fingers running up and down her bare skin. Other women had sex all the time with whomever was available; it seemed acceptable, and yet Dinah didn't long to lie down with strangers. She'd done that once, and it hadn't exactly worked out the way she'd hoped. Not that Luc was a stranger, but Dinah still considered a romance with him almost too much to hope for.

At the back door, Dinah hunted for her keys and let herself in, engulfed in the slightly cat-foody smell of warm tuna, and the sound of a repetitive metallic clang. Spoon against tray, she guessed.

She was right. When Dinah appeared in the kitchen doorway, her daughter's small round face swiveled around, alert. Eva paused, mid-bang, in her high chair with her spoon over her head, then grinned toothily and squealed with delight. She dropped her spoon and raised both arms to her mother. Dinah's heart soared, as it did every time.

"Hey, baby," Dinah whispered, wrapping her arms around her child's soft, solid body, pulling her floppily from her chair. She kissed the folds of skin at Eva's neck, inhaling her scent. She was more in love with her child every day, a feeling that still surprised her. Eva tugged Dinah's hair loose and yanked on it fiercely, making Dinah's eyes water.

"Ow," she said softly, plucking the tiny fingers free and kissing them, too.

Theo smiled at them from the stove. "You're just in time for an old Stein family favorite—creamed tuna on toast."

Cooking wasn't Theo's forte, but Dinah gave him credit for trying. She wasn't picky anyway. Her usual daily fare included apples and granola bars, and coffee from a café on her way to work. Sometimes she stayed for a few minutes to sit at a long dinner table with shelter residents before going home, but she never ate.

"How was work?" Theo asked.

"Fine. How about you?"

"Great. But the boss and his wife are coming for dinner tomorrow. I want you to wear something smashing."

Dinah laughed. This was their fake-marriage banter. Sometimes Dinah worried that it wasn't normal and that someday one of them would find a "real" partner and the dynamic would be upset, their careful routines upended.

But for now, while Eva was small, they operated like a co-operative pair of working parents.

On weekends, Dinah often walked to the Oak Street Beach, or to the zoo, or to playgrounds with Griffin and Eva. It felt like a divorce, where the child was shuttled between the exes, and the situation remained a delicate one. But since the drama of nearly a year earlier, when Dinah, suffering postpartum depression, had thrust Eva at Theo in desperation, she'd been convinced that he was the one who could be counted on.

A few months afterward, Griffin's landlord—whose no-pet policy Griffin ignored—had dropped by unannounced and found Holly Golightly. Griffin decided to move in with Ray, leaving the apartment to Dinah. It came as a shock, however, to her brother and the rest of her family when Dinah announced that she had accepted Theo's offer to live with him instead. Dinah could barely afford the loft on her own, but mostly, she didn't want to be alone. She was no longer suffering depression, but being a single mother still was overwhelming, just as Joan had predicted. Theo loved Eva, and he had plenty of room; it seemed a logical solution.

"Are you crazy?" Alice had asked over the phone the day Dinah started packing.

"Probably—but not about this," said Dinah, glancing at her sleeping baby. "Theo is the most stable person in my life, and I'm not ready to live alone just yet. He *wants* us to move back in."

"I know, but it's just like a soap opera—switching partners, incest, all that."

"I don't think that sex is going to be an issue with us,"

Dinah said drily. Then she added, "I think they're going to get back together anyway, eventually."

"Grif and Theo?" Alice said. "I think that's over, hon."

"But they're soul mates," Dinah said. "They're meant to be together."

Alice had laughed. "You never give up, do you?"

She didn't, but a year later, with Griffin on the periphery, apparently entrenched in a new life with Ray—whom Dinah scarcely knew but disliked on principle—a reunion seemed less and less likely. And she had to admit that her life with Theo was relatively serene. It was platonic and comfortable. And it was a relief that, as far as Dinah could tell, Theo was as celibate as she these days. He had friends over sometimes, but they were already paired off; Theo didn't date, or even talk about looking for another mate. Thus, Dinah kept holding out hope, not so much for a reunion anymore, but selfishly for things to stay the same.

"How was *your* day?" Dinah asked Eva now, nudging her cheek with her nose. Eva giggled. She repeated, "Daydayday," enjoying the new syllables on her tongue.

"Hey, Joan called," Theo was saying. "She wants to bring a friend along to visit next month."

"Really? Who?"

"Some guy called Peter. Her boyfriend, I guess."

Dinah laughed. "I doubt it. After all these years."

"Why? Age has nothing to do with it."

"I guess you're right," Dinah said. "It's just—*Joan*. Hard to imagine."

Theo shook his head. "You never really know everything about a person, you know, not even someone close."

Dinah wondered if Theo was referring to Griffin, but then he brightened. "Guess what, Di?"

"I don't know if I can take any more surprises," she joked.

Theo leaned down toward where Eva sat on Dinah's lap, and said, "Show your mommy, Eva." Eva looked at him quizzically.

"Show me what?" Dinah asked, peering at Eva for signs. She wore the same little sundress Dinah had put on her that morning. She didn't seem to have a new tooth. Nothing about her looked different. Dinah supposed it was a new trick along the lines of "So Big" or "Peek-a-boo," so she waited to see the latest circus act Theo had taught her daughter to perform.

Theo came over and gently tugged Eva from Dinah's arms, holding her by her chubby wrists, and set her on the floor in a standing position. Then he let go. Eva wavered for a moment and then stepped forward robotically, balancing first on her right foot, almost on her toes, and then on her left. She grinned at Dinah, baring all four of her tiny teeth.

"Oh my gosh!" Dinah exclaimed.

"Ya, ya!" Eva said, and clapped her little hands together as she wobbled two more steps forward.

"It walks, it talks!" Theo said, laughing.

Dinah crouched down on the floor, facing her baby as she tumbled; at the last moment, Dinah caught her and swooped her up into her arms, overcome.

It was the small milestone repeated the world over, in kitchens and backyards and in dusty fields and on dirt floors. It was small and also monumental. Dinah felt the shift in the air, the inkling of more to come. More and more and more. Her daughter was growing every moment, her brain firing synapses, storing information. She would grow and learn, and walk away on her own someday.

Dinah felt her heart seize again, a sudden tightness in her chest that felt like the onset of a panic attack. She took a deep breath and then it dawned on her: The reason she was so anxious lately was not because she worried about something happening to Eva, but because she worried about something happening to *her*. That was why her child's first birthday lurking around the corner made her nervous: What if she, Dinah, didn't make it much past that day? What if she fell off a stool or a curb and died?

She looked up at Theo with tears in her eyes. He smiled at her.

"I know," he said. "It's so emotional, isn't it?" He crouched down and wrapped his arms around them both. "Oh, Dinah!" he said suddenly, rearing back a little. "Is it because you weren't here? Because I saw her first steps first?" He shook his head. "I'm so insensitive! I'm sorry, I should have—"

"No," Dinah said into her daughter's hair. "No, it's not that."

Theo didn't seem to hear. "I should have just let her do it on her own, and let you see for yourself."

Dinah laughed. "Like they do at day care? Pretend it never happened? I hear about how they let the parents think the baby took her first steps at home, conveniently after six P.M." She wiped her eyes with one hand while holding Eva with her other. When Eva squirmed, Dinah let her go, watching her daughter crawl off on all fours, show over.

"Are you sure you're not mad?" Theo asked.

Dinah didn't say what she had been thinking. *What if I die?* sounded maudlin and silly even as she formed the words in her head.

"I'm sure," she said. "If I got upset about little things like that, I'd never make it through the day." She remembered Griffin once confiding when he and Theo were still together that even though Theo often reported bad news as a journalist, in his own life he was "as sheltered as a kid in *Leave It to Beaver,* where nothing terrible ever happens and your parents are always there when you come home." Apparently, until Griffin left him, Theo had known almost nothing but true love all around.

Perhaps her brother was right. Perhaps in Theo's world, missing a child's first steps was a kind of loss.

"Let's go for a stroll," Dinah said, standing up.

"What about dinner?"

"I'm not that hungry. Let's wait until after we walk. It's so nice out."

"Okay," Theo said, turning off the stove. "But I'd better bring along some animal crackers, in case the diva gets hungry."

Once they had Eva buckled in the stroller and down the back steps, they took off, walking at a brisk pace. At the corner, preparing to cross, Theo instinctively reached out and took Dinah's hand. She smiled to herself, thinking about how they must look: an ordinary little family of three, out for an evening stroll. For a moment, as they crossed the street, she indulged the fantasy. She squeezed Theo's fingers and pretended he was her man, pretended that all was right with her world. She was happy and in love, and she wasn't going to die.

Hadley Winterthur has died. Clara is beside herself, watching her once husband plunge through, still shaking off the dust, still blinking, stunned from the light. Eighty-four years old, he teetered into the path of a taxicab in Manchester, turning his head the wrong way like a confused tourist (because he *was* confused; he was on Minshull Street but thought he was on Bloom). He immediately was flattened.

Loose-limbed now and astonished, he is followed on the heels by a group of high school athletes from Lagos, rising out of the wreckage of their tour bus. And here come conjoined twins from Brazil, discovering their separate selves, laughing, comparing, then bobbing back together at their heads like magnets for old times' sake. Then they run off, holding hands. These sudden arrivals are always something to behold.

Sitting on a hillside and enjoying all the excitement, I am momentarily diverted from the rejoicing Here to rejoicing There.

I watch Dinah watching Eva take her first steps. And I remember hers, also in a kitchen, on sunshine yellow linoleum—the same linoleum on which I landed, hard, before coming Here. Though Dinah was my third, I thought it was just as new and amazing—a baby pulling herself upright to join the human race, willing herself to go forward. Like Dinah, it made me weep with joy, and a pang of sorrow; she would grow up and go on without me. Little did I know.

James slips away from greeting Hadley and the giddy

Nigerians and joins me. He sits, plucks up some soft blades, and inhales their sweet scent before setting them back down to watch them grow back.

"It's funny," he says. "I once said Dinah and Theo would be perfect together, but it's not an ideal family situation."

I laugh. I don't need to remind him about the Gypsies and communes, the tribes and stepfamilies and dorm rooms. What is a family anyway but a group of people cohabitating, sharing their abode and belongings? From Here, Dinah's arrangement seems to be working quite well.

"It's pretend," James says softly as Dinah and Theo walk hand in hand through the Chicago dusk. "It can't go on like this forever."

Forever. I smile. "No, it can't."

James sighs. It's always a mixed blessing, watching. We can't tear ourselves away; we watch and then they slip from view. And life goes on. And on.

Clara is skipping toward us, with Had beside her, skipping, too. He has a look of sheer joy on his face; he can't believe he's skipping. He can't believe that grass can be this color. He can't believe that Clara is here and she just fell over Niagara Falls one minute ago; it seemed like forever.

Fifteen

Stepping away from Neil's party for a few minutes, Alice stood near a dark edge of the fourteenth-floor balcony, staring at the moon. Through the soft haze of cloud cover, it looked two-dimensional, a paper face. When the clouds sifted apart, though, it seemed to shimmer, full and robust, dominating the landscape. The stately buildings ringing Central Park seemed cowed and diminutive beneath its gaze. When Alice inhaled, the spring air—imbued with the sent of sage and boxwoods set in clay pots all around the terrace—momentarily transported her back to Athens in October 1973, the month before she lost her father.

On nights of a full moon, the Acropolis was open to the public, and one night Alice and her siblings and their father climbed all over the Parthenon. The marble and limestone temple was bathed in an unearthly glow, creating deep shadows along the columns. Far below the hillside, the sound of tavernas—lively bouzouki music and laughter—rose up and made it seem even more festive. It was as if Alice's family was part of some wonderful event that most of the world—including sleepy Athenians and uninformed tourists—was not privy to.

Alice remembered that her father had made her and Griffin and Dinah stop and look around at the decay, though they'd seen it all before on countless trips to the top of the Parthenon in daylight. Then he told them the story of Thomas Bruce, aka Lord Elgin, who in the early 1800s pried friezes and statues from the Parthenon and loaded them into twenty-two ships to take back to England. The pieces, henceforth known as the Elgin Marbles, created an ongoing debate over who rightfully owned them.

"Of course, I side with the Greeks," said their father, leaning against a column, "since the statues were outright stolen from here. They should be returned."

Griffin wanted to know if Lord Elgin was ever caught and punished. Their father responded with a wry grin. "He got his comeuppance from syphilis, which ate off part of his face, and much of his nose, leaving him hideously disfigured. I imagine he looked like the stolen marble sculptures with their chipped noses."

"That's pretty funny," Griffin said.

"That, Griffin," their father said, "is called poetic justice."

Griffin, who was twelve, had nodded then, not really getting it—later he asked Alice what syphilis was, and she didn't quite know, either, except that people got it from having sex.

"I'm never having sex," Griffin had said gravely.

Alice laughed. "You don't automatically get it from

that—only from other people who already have it, probably like catching mono. I think it's pretty rare."

Now she thought with a pang of her father climbing sprightly, cheerfully over the ruins, seeming to have climbed high enough, finally, to escape his grief. And thinking, finally, that life indeed could go on. Having no idea, of course, that his was about to end.

"Life is short" was a maxim Alice knew to be true. You had to make the most of it, no matter what. You had to find what you wanted, and not look back.

Ian suddenly appeared at her side, startling her. "What are you doing out here?" he asked, handing her a glass of white wine, ice cold, the glass sweating. Alice accepted it and drank eagerly.

"Just looking at the moon," she said.

Ian kissed Alice's nape, her favorite spot, causing her to shiver. "You're looking pensive."

"I'm fine," she said. She glanced back over Ian's shoulder at the crowd through the glass; they were polished and groomed, in pearls and silk ties and most in formal black. Alice knew she stood out in her vintage dress, sequined green, nearly dragging the floor. She liked the way people stared, especially, admittedly, the men.

But Neil had embraced her a little too long when she'd first walked in. And when Ian went to hang up Alice's coat, Neil had taken her arm and said, "You know, we never got to have another dinner. I'm so glad you could come tonight." He leaned in and added, "You look more stunning than I remembered."

Flustered, Alice replied, "You're a bigger flirt than I remembered." As soon as Ian went off to phone the babysitter to check on Adam, Alice had slipped out to the shadows of the terrace, and stayed there, afraid to spend too much time around Neil. He still unnerved her. Or rather, her instantaneous attraction to him unnerved her.

"Come on, I want to show you something," Ian was saying now, leading Alice through another door around a corner, away from the party. Alice had to hold up her dress with one hand, and she stumbled a little over the threshold, spilling her wine. She bent to dab at it with her spangled hem. It took her a moment before she realized that they had entered a closed-off wing, which held Neil's bedroom and bath. She protested and started for the door.

"He won't mind," Ian whispered, grasping her hand, reeling her back. But when he tried to kiss Alice against the closed bedroom door, she pulled away.

"We can't," she said. "Not *here*."

"Lovelace is busy; I told you, he won't care."

"I care," Alice said. "It's too . . . weird." It even smelled of Neil's expensive musky cologne, as if he were in the room. Alice liked the scent a little too much.

"Okay, then," Ian said. "Let's ditch this stuffy crowd and go home."

"Yes, let's. I'll get my coat and you go tell Neil I don't feel well."

Before they slipped out, Ian went to Neil and whispered the lie; Alice saw Neil look at her directly, not believing it, his gaze not accusing but bemused.

"'Goodnight, moon,'" Alice said in a hush. "'Goodnight, cow jumping over the moon.'" Adam curled drowsily into her arm, her glittery green dress swept over his bed like a giant fin. Alice turned pages, read on. She could read the book with her eyes closed; she knew every word. It was the same with most of the small stack beside the bed. Adam claimed he couldn't sleep anymore unless Alice read to him first, which had been a challenge on performance nights, when she didn't come home until late. She had recited stories to him over the phone from her dressing room, and then made him promise he would close his eyes after they hung up.

Tonight the babysitter, Miriam, said she had done her best to get Adam to sleep, but apparently, she said sheepishly, "he was faking." The minute Alice and Ian walked into the apartment, sometime after midnight, Adam bounded out of his little room and darted to hug them both.

"I can't sleep," he'd said breathlessly, and though Ian gently chided him, Alice knew there was only one solution. She guided him back to bed, turned on the small lamp with the rice-paper shade, and began to read.

Now, as she reached the "the bowl full of mush," Adam was sound asleep, head cradled in her lap, his weight like heavy fruit. She nudged him carefully back onto his pillow and slid out, turning off the light.

In the elevator after leaving Neil's apartment, Ian, a little drunk, had whispered what he was going to do to Alice after they got home and he ripped off her dress. But when Alice slipped into his—their—bedroom, Ian was snoring heavily. Alice stood for a moment in the moonlight near the window, wide-awake and restless.

She tiptoed out of the room and down the hall, then out of the apartment. She passed Mr. Sechenov's door, which had a picture drawn by Adam taped beneath the peephole. Her bare feet slapped the steps, ringing out in the silence of the stairwell. At the door of her apartment, she fumbled with the keys, first mistaking Ian's for hers.

Once inside, she turned on all the lamps and walked around touching things, as if reclaiming them. She opened the fridge, which smelled of stale cold air and something rotting. There also was a lone bottle of beer and she opened it, drinking as she walked on through to her bedroom.

Her bed was neat, and the lamplight created soft rings on the white quilt. The pillows were plump and inviting. Alice stood looking at it like Goldilocks, as if she'd wandered into someone else's home and was considering the propriety of staying. What if she did stay? What if she went back to the way things were before? Before she knew Ian, before she loved Adam; when she was just Alice and she could have anyone, or no one. Which life was better? And had she really chosen, or like Dinah, just let things happen? Was she just clinging to what had come to feel *safe*?

She lay down, closing her eyes. Her apartment was silent, closing about her like her mother's familiar old coat. The rabbit-trimmed coat was hanging on a hook behind the door, and Alice rose to get it. Then she lay back down atop the covers as she draped it over herself, and fell asleep. She dreamed that her parents were watching her from behind a dark velvet curtain.

A week later, Alice ran into Neil on the street. She was coming out of a drugstore with her birth-control pills in a little white bag and found Neil on the sidewalk, as if planted there waiting for her.

"Are you following me?" she joked. Suddenly, she felt exposed, without makeup, her hair in a messy ponytail. She stuffed her small bag into her coat pocket as if he might know its contents.

"It's sheer coincidence, I swear," Neil said, placing one hand over his heart as in oath. "I happened to see you through the window and waited, just to say hello."

"So—hello," Alice said a little warily.

"Are you feeling better?" Neil asked, and when Alice looked confused, he added, "Since my party? You and Ian left because you were unwell."

"Oh. It had just been a long day and I wasn't up to it, that's all. I wasn't 'unwell' so much as unsocial. Sorry."

"No need to apologize. So, then, where are you headed?"

"Nowhere actually, just running boring errands."

"Do you have time for coffee?" Neil's eyes twinkled at her. "It won't be boring, I promise."

Alice hesitated. She had all day, as she was (still) between plays. "Sure. Why not."

They walked a few blocks without a destination, talking amiably until they passed a small café. Neil held the door for Alice in such a way that she had to dip underneath his long arm.

When they settled at a table beside a window, Neil said, "The pie here is fabulous."

"You've been here?"

"I think I've been everywhere," Neil said wryly. "I'm that old."

"You're not old," Alice said, suspecting he was fishing for a compliment. She glanced at him over her menu. The fan of smile wrinkles, the graying temples, the slight self-consciousness combined with resignation actually were endearing. Alice could see the younger version just beneath the surface, but for some reason she preferred the older one.

"You look especially lovely today," Neil said suddenly.

"I don't," Alice said, laughing, touching her hair. "I'm a mess."

"No, you're just . . . pure essence. No covering. No mask. It's fetching."

Alice found herself blushing. "Well, thanks." She set down the menu and looked around for a server.

"What are you going to have?" Neil asked.

"I don't know. Just coffee, I guess."

"Oh, you *must* have pie! The peach is extraordinary. So is the strawberry-rhubarb, if they have it. And you can't ever go wrong with their pecan."

Alice was thinking that she actually would love a generous piece of chocolate crème pie, but curves were one thing, a mushy belly quite another. She had begun doing nightly sit-ups for the first time in her life, finding that at thirty-six, skipping meals now and then wasn't enough. Skipping pie, however, was essential.

"You order something and I'll just have a bite," she said.

"So you say," Neil said, smiling. "But life is short."

Alice startled at the words she had recently thought herself, but Neil didn't seem to take note. He was signaling a waitress, who smiled and rushed over. He had that effect, Alice thought. Who wouldn't run to him if he snapped his fingers? He probably had dozens of girlfriends on both continents.

"So, have you ever been married, or what?" Alice asked after they'd ordered.

Neil chuckled. "You Americans are always so blunt. Englishwomen just gaze at a man's hand to spy a ring, or ask roundabout questions."

"So—"

"No, I am not 'married, or what.' Haven't been for a long, long time. And I probably never should have been in the first place." Neil paused and said, "I've found I'm not cut of that particular cloth."

For a moment, Alice wondered if he was referring to marriage or obliquely to his sexuality. Perhaps he was gay; it was plausible. His grooming and attentiveness could go either way. His flirting could be a cover, something long practiced, given his generation's closeted attitudes.

"I just like the company of women," Neil said then softly, as if reading her mind. "And sometimes it is nice just to have it 'without strings,' as they say."

"Do you think that's really possible?" Alice asked. "I mean, I always thought that a person could just be with whomever, and it didn't have to become some long-term *thing*—" She stopped.

"But now?"

"Now, well—you know. I'm with Ian." Alice looked at Neil pointedly, waiting for a reaction.

"I do know," Neil said, sitting back a little, meeting her gaze without guile.

The waitress was back, setting down coffee cups and creamer, and a plate of peach pie with two forks. "Enjoy," she said brightly.

"We shall," Neil said as she walked away. He lifted a forkful of crust and fruit, oozing over the sides, and immediately reached over and fed the bite to Alice.

She had no choice but to accept it. The crust was flaky and sweet, the filling as perfect as a fresh peach but warm and gooey. *"Wow,"* Alice said after she'd swallowed.

Neil's eyes lit up with delight. "I told you so," he said. He pushed the plate toward her. "Have the rest."

"No, no, we have to share."

"I'm all for that," Neil said, and then laughed as Alice dug in.

When they'd finished, they walked back to the street. The sky was overcast, clouds pressing down over the city as if muffling it. The sidewalk was deserted as a movie set, and Alice glanced in the direction of the busier intersection.

"Well, thank you for the pie," she said politely. "I'd better get going."

"Wait—Alice," Neil said, lightly grasping her arm as she turned to go. His hand was large and firm, and she felt something inside her seize—or surrender—as she turned back.

It was no surprise, then, when he pulled her to him and kissed her. First it seemed he was aiming for her cheek, like a gentleman, but then his lips landed full on her mouth and stayed there. Alice tasted pie, and something else, the novelty of new lips and tongue.

"We can't," she said breathlessly as she pulled away.

"I know," Neil said sorrowfully. "I just missed you so."

Alice looked into his eyes and said nothing. Without another word, they parted ways.

"Always the serpent offering the apple, isn't it?" James observes.

"I thought it was peach," I joke.

"He's trouble."

"Charming, though," I say. "Maybe Alice just needs to try different flavors—to be sure."

James looks at me like I might have kept something from him.

I laugh. "You came along, my prince, and I never thought about anyone else." To tease him, I add, "Also, I was too young to find out."

In the summer of 1954, I was seventeen and bristling with my newfound luster, full of that wonderful arrogance of the young. I wondered who before could have known what it felt like to wake to such days full of possibility. Or to such new, perfectly formed breasts.

One day, waiting tables at a café in Georgetown, I was wiping the dust and pollen from the outdoor tables when I first saw James. He rode past on his bicycle. And then he rolled past again, more slowly, in the other direction. I smiled and looked down at my own reflection in the surface of the metal table. And I saw it all there like a crystal ball: He would stop and ask me a pointless question, and then my name, and we would talk, and later kiss. And not much after that, I would be in a gleaming satin dress pressed against the crisp white shirt of his tuxedo.

"I fell in love on the spot," says James, remembering, too.

"We were lucky," I say.

"I hope Alice doesn't do something silly."

I smile. Just like James to understate. "She already has," I say. It is just as I expected. Like Griffin, Alice is distracted by novelty, by kisses, by the flattery of being pursued. "They want to have their cake and eat it, too."

"I thought it was pie," says James.

I laugh. "You're eternally entertaining."

Stars begin falling around us with little musical *plinks*. Sometimes when they land, the sparks fly upward and sprinkle down on our heads like incandescent raindrops.

"Do you think you missed something?" James asks.

"Only more time with you, luv."

"Who knows what might have happened if you'd stuck around? If we'd lived," James adds, now holding me in an old-fashioned slow dance. "You might have tired of me."

"Never," I say, and smile at him sweetly, brushing something shimmering from his shoulder. "I'd never tire of you."

Sixteen

He had a pattern now. Like any practiced stalker, he knew the best time to catch them at home, and the best vantage point for watching, well hidden. And he didn't do it all the time; he wasn't really obsessive. It was just that he missed them. All of them.

Griffin stood across the street from his old house on Orchard Street and saw through the lighted windows that Theo had Eva in his arms. He carried her easily on one hip while he walked around the house. She squirmed, though, and Theo passed her to Dinah, who didn't seem to be having any more luck.

Whenever Griffin was with Eva lately, he'd noticed that she strived for independence, though she was still wobbly on her feet. She protested being put in the stroller, and lit up triumphantly when allowed to toddle alongside. Her pudgy fingers would turn bone white where she tightly gripped the padded side, her other hand engulfed in Griffin's own. He loved how she smelled—her skin, the little wisps of hair on her scalp, her palms when he kissed them. He'd had no idea children could be so literally sweet; the air around them lighter, and also denser with goodness, it seemed.

He counted down the days until the weekend, when he could meet his sister in a park or on the waterfront to play with Eva. Sometimes they met during the week, though rarely, as Dinah spent days at the shelter and Griffin now worked evening hours. Once in a great while, he convinced Dinah to come to his apartment for lunch or dinner on his nights off, but she was still reticent around Ray. They recently had fought about it.

"You don't give him enough credit, Di," Griffin had said. "Ray's a really great guy."

"I'm sure he is. I know he's . . . nice."

"*Nice?* That's all you can say? I've been with him for almost a year."

"That was your choice."

"What's that supposed to mean?" Griffin demanded.

"You chose to run off with someone else. Am I supposed to be happy about it?"

Griffin gaped at his sister. "You should talk! You moved in with my ex. It's like a soap opera!"

Dinah didn't say anything at first. "That's exactly what Alice said," she said. "But that's not really fair—Theo is just like family to me."

"What about me?" Griffin asked.

Dinah's eyes watered then. "I'm sorry. I love you, Grif, but I can't live with you and Ray."

They let it go at that, though Griffin had never suggested she move in with them, and he was left wondering why Dinah couldn't just live on her own, or with a real partner. But of course he knew how it was: Theo was the perfect surrogate father. And sometimes things just happened. Like with Ray.

Lately, though, something had swept over Griffin like a fever and he found himself taking detours past his old house. He rationalized it as a longer walk for Holly, but of course that wasn't the truth. He simply was desperate for a glimpse, like the Little Match Girl huddled in the cold, peering into warm, lighted windows to spy on happy families. Griffin wanted to see them in action—the "family" of Theo and Dinah, with Eva at the center.

Holly Golightly barked at a homeless man passing by and Griffin shushed her. The man had a dirty white beard, like a character from a fairy tale, and he was talking to himself. He didn't seem to notice Griffin at all and narrowly missed walking into him. Griffin stepped back, yanking Holly out of the way. After the man was gone, Griffin glanced back across the street. Ignoring common sense, he crossed over and ventured closer, around the back of the house, until his head was level with the kitchen window.

Then he was peering through the half-tilted slats of the blinds—blinds that he and Theo had picked out and hung together one Saturday years earlier. Griffin knew he should leave, but he lingered. Inside, his sister was at the kitchen sink, holding Eva awkwardly, trying to get the tiny girl to wave her hands under the flow of water. For some reason, Eva, who loved playing in water, was protesting. She arched her back and seemed to be yelling. Theo rushed in from another room and swept Eva out of Dinah's arms. He smiled and cooed into the baby's face, and expertly distracted her while Dinah wiped Eva's hands with a wet cloth. To anyone else, the scene would convey a perfect nuclear family, the parents equally attentive and involved, relying on each other's skills to tend to their child.

While Griffin watched, he saw that they were suddenly, all three, moving toward the back door. He bounded out of the way, jerking Holly's leash and silently begging her not to bark. He stumbled backward toward the fence and hid, crouching, behind the trash bin and a folded patio table. Tiny crocuses, the first heralds of spring, sprouted at his feet, barely visible amid rotted leaves. Griffin held his dog against his shin, with one hand gently muzzling her. She seemed not to mind, merely wagged her tail and obediently sat.

Theo came out of the house first, with a folded stroller that he bounced noisily down the steps. Then he struggled for a moment to open it, thrusting it against the pavement until the wheels locked into place. All the clatter excited Holly, who wriggled against Griffin, but he held her fast and she settled down. Theo seemed not to hear anything, because he simply reached up to lift Eva from Dinah's arms. He strapped her into the stroller as she jabbered some nonsense, then waited as Dinah locked the door.

"I hope they're still serving," Dinah said, clomping down the steps. "It's nearly nine, you know. And we said we were going to start working on a more regular bedtime, remember?"

"I know. But one more night won't make a difference, will it? Besides, we're starving, and they love Eva—they'll fawn all over her and give her crackers as soon as we're seated. It'll be fine. And she'll probably fall asleep on the way home."

Eva was squealing with frustration, and Griffin, with his ears perked, could deduce that she was trying to wriggle her way out of her straps.

"Come on, sweetie, just stay put. It's not for long," Theo said in a patient, soothing tone. "Eva, baby, you're fine. It's just for a little while." He paused and said to Dinah, "She's just gotten her sea legs, you know."

Dinah sighed. "She'll want to walk the whole way. It'll take an hour." There was a muted debate that Griffin couldn't make out, but the end result was Eva's release. Griffin peered around the trash bin in time to see her toddling merrily beside the stroller as Theo pulled it behind them like a wagon.

Whatever was said next was out of Griffin's earshot as the three turned down the narrow walkway beside the house and were gone. Griffin sat a moment longer, stunned by the ease with which Theo and Dinah discussed "their" child, and how paternal Theo was with Eva. Griffin still couldn't believe things had turned out this way. And that for the past hour—as he'd been walking Holly and then spying on his sister and his ex-lover—he hadn't once thought of Ray.

Ray was probably wondering where Griffin had gone and what was taking so long. Griffin had told him he was going to walk the dog around the block, or a little farther. Ray had said, "Okay, hurry back" as he dialed the local Chinese restaurant. He wanted to time the delivery to coincide with the airing of a Hitchcock film on television. Griffin realized that the movie had started a half hour earlier, and he still crouched behind a trash bin at his old house. He could never tell Ray the truth, because it was too weird, and, in a way, awful, sneaking around the way he had when he'd first met Ray.

And the truth was that he had hoped that by watching Theo, he could convince himself that he had made the right choice, that nothing really was lost. But all he felt was bereft.

"You spoil her, you know," Ray said the next morning. His tone was teasing but seemed vaguely critical, as if Griffin should have known better.

"I think she's doing fine, actually," Griffin said. "She listens to me." Then, out of old habit from humoring Theo, he joked, "Maybe she thinks you're too far down in the pecking order." He knelt down to pet Holly, who wagged her tail furiously.

Ray laughed snidely. "Yeah, I'm at the bottom of the pack. In my own home."

Griffin looked up then, recognizing the slight. "I thought we agreed that if I paid half the rent—"

"I know, I know. I'm sorry. That came out wrong," Ray said. "It's *our* place." He bent down then to rub Holly behind the ears as if to say *No hard feelings*, but it was Griffin who was waiting to be placated. They didn't meet each other's eyes, and Griffin told himself it was just part of the adjustment period, after moving in together. Yet, it had been nearly a year.

At first, Griffin thought the fault lay within himself. Walking home from work one night he had passed the Episcopal church that Dinah belonged to, and which he'd attended for Eva's christening. He hesitated at the massive red doors and then pushed his way in; after all, the sign beside the entry declared ALL ARE WELCOME ALL THE TIME.

Inside, the church was quiet and candy-lit from stained glass. Only three or four other visitors sat in pews, far apart, lost in their reverent thoughts. Griffin took a seat near the back, head tilted so he could take in the high arched ceiling, the leaded Gothic lamps, and, amusingly, a child's Mylar balloon that somehow had gotten lodged at the peak.

Seek and you shall find, Griffin thought. But what he was seeking, he still wasn't sure. Sometimes, he thought the one he was looking for wasn't his heavenly Father but his father in Heaven. Griffin still missed him after twenty years. He wondered what it would be like just to talk things through, feel his father's hand—even awkwardly—on his back. The absence of his parents, but especially his father, still had the power to make him swoon with grief. He choked it back, like he always did.

When he left the church, rather than enlightened, he felt more burdened. But perhaps that's how it is with God, he thought; you talk to Him and He listens, and like an insightful therapist, waits for you to understand yourself better and to act according to your newfound wisdom. The point, Griffin suspected, was that a person had to keep searching, even though it wasn't easy.

He had tried to explain these thoughts to Ray, but he couldn't find the right words.

"Maybe you need to go to an actual service," Ray suggested. "You know, hear a sermon, take Communion. That's what people do."

Griffin laughed. "You make it sound so easy. Add a cup of religion and a dash of status quo and mix well!"

Ray looked at him. "I wasn't joking."

Neither was I, Griffin thought, but once again, their signals had crossed. Though he'd believed at the outset that Ray was a kindred spirit, perhaps even more of a soul mate than Theo, Griffin had found that shared tragedy wasn't enough. In fact, neither of them really liked to talk about it, so it was as if they both had scars hidden underneath their clothes. And even though they ate together, went to movies or galleries or stores together, and slept together, they didn't really seem . . . together. They clashed in small but niggling ways.

In addition to his rigid dog-training principles (Holly needed to have regular hours in her crate; shouldn't have so many treats), Ray was more particular than Griffin had realized. He was territorial about closet and drawer space, and wanted cleared countertops in the kitchen—no room for Griffin's battered cutting boards and mixer with the chipped enamel base. Theo had been similarly neat, liking order, but he also was generous, and considered all of the contents of their house—*his* house—as shared, right down to the washcloths and razors. Ray kept his razor in its plastic case in a drawer beside the sink. When Griffin reached for it one morning, Ray asked, "Uh, don't you have your own?"

Griffin replied, deadpan, "Don't worry, I've got that chin fungus all cleared up."

"I'm probably weird," Ray said, frowning, "but I don't share razors or toothbrushes or towels." Then he wrapped his arms around Griffin and proposed that they keep their things separate but promise to share their thoughts and feelings. "If we can't be honest," he said, "then what's the point?"

The words burned now as Griffin crouched on the

kitchen floor beside Holly and thought about the previous night—nights—when he'd gone to spy on Theo. He could stretch the truth if he wanted and claim that he was just dropping in to see Eva and Dinah, and that Theo wasn't even home. But instead, he simply lied and said that his walk had turned into a jog and he'd lost track of time. Indeed, he had run the entire way back home, bursting through the apartment door in a corroborating sweat.

Ray sighed. "Well, she's officially your dog, so I shouldn't judge." He smiled at Griffin. "I'm sorry. I just forget sometimes that she's not Audrey."

"It's okay," Griffin said. "She's just a dog, you know."

Sometimes he had to remind himself of that fact, but he was continually surprised by how happy he was to see Holly at the end of the day. Happier, often, than he was to see Ray.

"She's a good dog, though," Ray said. "I hope you know that I love her, too."

At this, Griffin stood up and embraced Ray. *Love the one you're with,* he thought. And for a moment, he believed that he did. Or could, if he just tried harder.

The rain should have been an obvious deterrent; he shouldn't have gone out at all. But bad habits were hard to break, and Griffin grabbed an umbrella and the leash and told himself this was the last time. He intended to reform, to stay home from now on.

Yet, *home* was a nebulous term. Griffin had learned very early that what he believed was a safe haven could be anything but. His mother could fall in her own kitchen and die. His father could take his children away from the sorrowful memories and try to create a temporary home in another country, but that could shatter, too. Joan had done her best to make a home for her bereaved grandchildren, and to draw them all together at holidays, as if there really were a "home" to come back to, but to Griffin, it had all been pretense. And the home that Griffin had spun over nearly a dozen years with Theo—overflowing with cozy comforts and extended family, photographs and proof of happy times together—had disintegrated over a matter of days when he confessed his infidelity.

And now, though he lived with Ray, Griffin felt unsettled and displaced, even though it had been his own choice. He had slammed his own door in his own face; there was no going back.

Even so, here he was again, standing on Orchard Street in the pouring rain. The umbrella was useless. Griffin was soaked, and Holly's fur was as slick as an otter's. It was late, after eleven, and only one light appeared to be on in the house—the one with the linen shade in the study Theo used for writing. Griffin knew without seeing that it was littered with reference books and papers; that the shelves were filled with books vertically and horizontally, like the wrong puzzle pieces jammed into place; that the cup of pens on the desk held only one brand, a fine-tip marker from Germany. Every Christmas, Griffin had stuffed a new boxful into Theo's stocking. He guessed that Theo was working under a deadline now.

Griffin wavered. He could return right now to Ray,

who was curled in bed and probably asleep. Or he could cross the street and knock lightly on the study window. What he would do or say next, he had no idea. All he knew was that he had a burning desire to set foot in his old home. His only home.

Heart pounding, Griffin took a deep breath, wiped his wet face with one hand, and tossed the limp umbrella into a trash bin. Then he stepped off the curb.

Distracted by his own blood pumping, his nerves on edge, he failed to hear tires shushing on the wet pavement, a taxi coming fast around the corner. Holly, leading instead of following as usual, yanked the leash so hard that its loop slipped from Griffin's grasp. The impact was quiet but for a thump and a truncated yelp, but it stopped Griffin in his tracks. He was stunned and sickened all at once. Halfway down the block, the taxi slowed, red brake lights beaming through the dark and the rain. Then the driver seemed to rethink stopping (*Oh, thank God, just a mutt*), and drove on, disappearing.

And so there was just Griffin, kneeling in the street and weeping over the still, soft body of Holly Golightly. He lifted a front paw and it was so small in his palm; even though full-grown, she was puppy-size. Griffin lifted her chin and saw that her face was smashed, blood trickling from her mouth in a gelatinous thread. He wailed then, and threw up.

"Theo!" he yelled, shoulders heaving. "*Theo!*"

It seemed like hours—no one came; no other cars passed by—but suddenly the front door opened, and there in silhouette was Theo. He stood for a moment, peering intently into the darkness; half of the streetlights were burned out, and the rain was coming down in torrents.

"Oh my gosh, oh *gosh*," he said aloud, and ran barefoot into the street. He dropped to the oily pavement, instantly drenched, and gathered Griffin into his arms.

"Come on," he said finally. "Let's get you inside." Somehow, he managed to force Griffin to stand.

And then Theo—who never had warmed to Holly, had griped about her dander and paw prints, and had scarcely even stooped to pet her—bent and lifted the soggy, bloody body into his arms and carried her across the street to his house as Griffin staggered behind.

A half hour later, Holly lay wrapped mummylike in a beach towel in a corner of the mudroom. Griffin and Theo sat hunched at the kitchen table, a ceramic pot of tea between them, untouched. The wall clock ticked like a metronome and the refrigerator hummed familiarly; everything was the same except for a high chair pushed against a wall and baby bottles drying on a rack beside the sink. Theo reached across the table and squeezed Griffin's hand, then handed him more tissue.

They spoke softly, so as not to wake Eva and Dinah, but Griffin couldn't have raised his voice if he'd tried; he was half in shock, hoarse with grief.

"I can't believe she's dead," he said for the third or fourth time.

"I know."

"I shouldn't have—"

"It was an accident, Grif. Don't beat yourself up."

"But if it were a kid—if it were Eva—you would never

say that," he said, wiping his eyes. "I was responsible for her, and she got killed because I let go."

"But Griffin," Theo said patiently. "She ran, right? I'm sure there was nothing you could have done to stop it."

"If I hadn't come," Griffin said, more to himself than to Theo. He looked up and met Theo's eyes then. "I shouldn't have come."

"It's okay," Theo said, not seeking an explanation. His gaze was so kind, his face so smooth and familiar, Griffin felt a rush of love and anguish all at once.

Theo was the same, but different, too; he seemed calmly in charge. Caring for Eva clearly had shifted his focus. He was not unfazed, but he seemed less emotional, less inclined to overreact; he could handle someone else's troubles now.

"You're wearing Old Spice again," Theo noted, smiling a little.

Griffin nodded sadly. "It was my dad's."

"Really?" Theo said. His voice softened. "I never knew that."

Ray knew, but he'd asked Griffin to stop; he said his father had used the same cologne, and he didn't like to be reminded.

Griffin's gaze drifted over toward the mudroom, to the inert mound in the corner where Holly's bed had once sat. "What am I going to do?" he said, his voice cracking.

"You can bury her here, if you want, in the back."

Griffin looked at him. "That's not what I meant."

Theo looked back, his expression unreadable. He seemed to be sifting his emotions just beneath the surface. He seemed to be assessing Griffin, separating the various versions—the one he knew before, the one who'd left, the one who sat here now—and trying to make them fit, or trying to decide if he cared beyond pity for what had happened tonight in the street.

Finally, he said, "You should sleep here tonight. You're too tired to think. Just call . . . Ray and tell him what happened. Tell him where you are and why. It's always best to be honest, you know." He paused. "Then the chips fall where they will."

Griffin nodded and stood, then picked up the phone.

She comes bounding over to us as if she knows us, as if we smell like him. It is uncanny. James kneels down first, covered in dog-kissing, tail-wagging glee.

"Oh, we should send her back!" I say. "It's not too late." I'm delighted to see her, but I am thinking of Griffin. Of his loss.

We see it happen all the time in emergency rooms and ambulances, in houses and tents and the backseats of cars, or veterinary offices. A person or creature on the brink of death—teetering at the portal, glimpsing the light—suddenly is yanked back to the temporal body of flesh or fur.

Griffin's dog was only just smacked by the car, only just crumpled in the street; a few moments left of warmth and breath and beating heart. Griffin isn't equipped, though. He doesn't know CPR or any other means of canine rescue. Before anything can be done (if anything could be done), he has collapsed in grief. She's gone.

"She's Here to stay," James says. "Aren't you, girl?" he asks the dog, grinning.

I hug her, too, and then I realize that she smells like *him*. How, I do not know, but she does. I bury my nose in her fur, in her clean, soft new scruff, and inhale traces of my son. My wonderful, flawed, and floundering son.

"I'm so glad he's home," I whisper.

"You mean 'she,'" James says.

"No," I say. And James smiles.

Seventeen

"What a mess," said Dinah. She crawled around on her hands and knees, scooping up clotted tortellini, wiping buttery sauce and bits of cheese from the lower cupboard doors. Above her, Eva's feet dangled from the high chair, clanged against the metal foot bar. Now and then she leaned heavily over the side, chortling at her mother on the floor.

"*Meth,*" Eva lisped.

"Yes, it is a mess. So are you, girly." As she stood, Dinah muttered to herself, "So is everything around here."

While it was what she'd once hoped for—a reunion—everything had changed since Griffin's return. Dinah realized that she had come to depend on the simplicity of her life with Theo. He fed Eva breakfast while Dinah took a shower. They trundled off to day care, then to work. At lunch, Dinah visited Eva until her naptime, and then went back to work. In the evenings, Theo picked up Eva from day care, since his schedule was more flexible, and the three of them ate dinner, played, and read books, and then went to their respective beds. Or at least that's how it had been.

Now, Griffin and Theo shared a bed again. And though it had been only a week—since the tragic death of Holly Golightly—theirs seemed indeed a full-fledged reunion. Griffin and Theo talked late into the night; Dinah heard their murmurs, the sounds of secret pleasures, their deep, quiet laughter. Then she heard one or the other or both getting up in the middle of the night for a drink of water, or scotch. Though neither smoked, Dinah half-expected to find cigars stubbed out in the den. The house seemed undeniably masculine now—whereas with just Theo, it had seemed predominately feminine, and chaste. Even Theo had seemed so, adapting to Dinah's and Eva's needs. They had been a contented threesome, nearly a family, an illusion Dinah had grown used to, like pants that didn't fit quite right (an off-center zipper, or a twisted inseam) but still functioned fine. With Griffin's arrival, Dinah felt that she was the one who suddenly didn't fit.

It occurred to her that she might just be jealous.

Eva loved the change, of course. She was in her egocentric glory with one more person to dote on her, play with her, or chase her around the house while she screamed with delight.

Dinah rinsed the dishrag again. Then she turned to clean her daughter's face and lift her free. When Eva was in her arms, Dinah relaxed. *This* is what matters, she reminded herself. Nothing is easy, or simple.

And then there was Joan, who had called to inform her grandchildren in a too-high voice, "Everything is fine, but they want to run a few more tests." It wasn't until later that Dinah remembered the "more" part, indicating that Joan had already been seeing a doctor. When Dinah called back to ask for details, Joan remained vague and upbeat. Her cancer might have come back, she explained, as if it were a mere cold.

"It's probably nothing," she had said.

"Well, how are you feeling?" Dinah persisted.

"Oh, fine, just fine, really. Maybe a little achy in places, but it's just old age."

Dinah feared it wasn't. But Joan would be coming for a visit soon, and Dinah decided she could see for herself how her grandmother was faring. And finally meet her boyfriend, Peter. Joan had been coy on that subject, too, though Alice said she thought Joan had been seeing him for the better part of a year.

"Why didn't she tell us?" Dinah had asked her sister over the phone.

"Oh, you know," Alice said. "It's her generation. She thinks we're 'too young' to know that our elders might have, *ahem*, sex lives."

"*Alice!*" Dinah said, aghast.

Alice laughed. "Well, I guess in your case, she's right."

Now Dinah walked around the house with Eva on her hip and found her brother and Theo engrossed in a game of chess, each with a bottle of imported beer at his side. They were deep in thought but smiling secretively at each other. They practically glowed.

"No!" Griffin cried out in mock horror as Theo moved his knight. "I can't believe I didn't see it coming."

"You didn't see it coming because you weren't paying attention. Plus, you don't really know how to play chess, do you? You're a faker." He glanced up. "Eva! Lovey!"

Eva grinned and reached out her arms to Theo, who took her easily onto his lap. Dinah noticed a faint yet perceptible shadow crossing Griffin's face; Eva adored him, but she was more attached to Theo. Thankfully, she had never begun calling him "Daddy" or even "Dada," as most babies did. Even when strangers mistook him for her father, Eva called him "Tee-oh," which sounded like the Spanish word for uncle.

"You guys remember that I have to work tonight, right?" Dinah said.

"Yes, lucky us, right, Eva?" said Theo, nuzzling her.

"Do you need a ride?" Griffin asked Dinah.

"No, thanks. I'll walk. It's not far and I think the rain's let up. But you aren't going to get drunk on the job, are you?"

Both men laughed. "No. Of course not," Theo said. "We're quitting right now, don't worry. I'll get the babe to bed."

"I can do it," Griffin said eagerly. "I mean, I'd like to help."

Theo smiled at him. "Yeah. That would be great. Why don't you read *The Quiet Noisy Book*, or that one about the farm? She loves them both."

Griffin reached across the chessboard to take Eva, but she coyly turned away, burying her face in Theo's chest, clutching the fabric of his shirt in both her tiny fists.

"Hey, Eva," Theo said to the top of her head. "Why don't you go to Uncle Grif. I'll go fix your bath." Eva just stayed pressed against him.

"She's too young to be given choices," Dinah said authoritatively. "Just hand her over."

Theo gave her a questioning look, and Griffin said a shade testily, "It's okay, Di. You don't have to monitor everything."

Dinah gritted her teeth. "Fine. Whatever."

Theo glanced at Dinah and caught her eye, as if he wanted to say something but shouldn't. They hadn't spoken about the change in the household dynamics, except after the third night Griffin had slept over, and seemed to be staying for good.

"I feel like things might finally be righting themselves, you know?" Theo told Dinah then. "Like we had a really bad winter and now it's clearing up."

"So, you *forgive* him?" Dinah had asked. She knew she was being petty, and punishing. Didn't she believe in grace? And besides, she was talking about her own brother. She'd always known he and Theo belonged together; they were the perfect couple.

"It's not perfect," Theo had said. "It never was. But after you've been married for ten or fifteen years, you'll understand." He sighed. "The thing is, it's kind of exhausting holding a grudge. So when he came back . . ." He paused, smiling. "What happened before didn't matter that much anymore. The past is past, and I wanted him back. Griffin has just always been *it* for me."

Dinah wondered what it meant for her and Eva now. Theo seemed to think that nothing should change, the more the merrier. For Dinah, though, things were shifting. She didn't know in what way, but she felt that something was bound to happen.

Eva finally turned to acknowledge her mother, and beamed up at her toothily, as if they were in on a private joke. *"Mom-mom-mom,"* she chanted.

"See you later, monkey," Dinah whispered, kissing her. Then she turned to go to work, ignoring both her brother and Theo.

Once outside, Dinah felt glad to escape. Glad to be on her way to a place where the problems, though deeply complex, could be boiled down to one immediate, solvable one—the need for food and shelter.

The windows were slick with rain and the floor covered in a dizzying maze of wet footprints. A heavy aroma of beef Stroganoff and pungent body odor hung in the damp, warm air, and Dinah retreated to her office. She had returned for a rare late shift, to fill in for Jon, a coworker who was recovering from surgery. He'd wrenched his knee playing basketball, and Dinah thought it was not exactly a surprise, given his size, which was 250 pounds (and much of it, frankly, beer gut) on a five-and-a-half-foot frame. Everyone was taking turns covering his night shifts. At least, Dinah thought, things were relatively quiet late at night.

Dinah worked in her office for an hour, until she was alerted to a new arrival. The woman's name was Angel, and though she was the same age, if not a little older, she kept referring to Dinah as "ma'am." Angel's brows were like tiny wings and her bangs were cut in a peculiar zigzag, which, if clean, might have made for a modish hairstyle. She was small and wiry, with a hint of prettiness that, Dinah surmised, had not served her well. She had been living on the street for two months, since an eviction. She had no children, no partner; she had trouble maintaining relationships.

"Where have you been staying lately, Angel?" Dinah asked.

"In a beach house," Angel said, and laughed. "Made of cardboard." Then she scowled. "Some damn kids kicked it in when I wasn't home."

When Dinah suggested she deserved better than a cardboard box, Angel said, "Yes, ma'am, but at least I owned it. It was all mine."

Dinah led her to the women's wing, to a clean bed in a corner, near a window. It was barred, but at least it had a view; a sliver of Lake Michigan was visible between the buildings.

"This is all right, I guess," Angel said, shrugging. Dinah left her to get settled, and when she turned at the door, she saw that Angel was fingering the quilt, then pressing her face to the pillow and inhaling, eyes closed in bliss.

Dinah's church members recently had donated four dozen quilts to the shelter. Spending hours stitching small squares together and then stuffing them with cotton sounded exceedingly boring to Dinah, but the end results were wonderful. The beds were draped in welcoming swaths of rosebuds, gingham, and paisley.

Sometimes the shelter felt to Dinah like an orphanage, and she a surrogate mother like Miss Clavel in *Madeline*. Sometimes she wanted to walk though the rooms and kiss the foreheads of the sleepers as if they were children. She often thought that they really were just lost children, wedged inside tired, beleaguered adult bodies.

Many—or most—had been victims of abuse along the way; many had turned tricks on the street, or had seen people murdered, and narrowly escaped death themselves. Some of their stories verged on the fantastic: mothers who allegedly had dropped them out of ten-story windows; fathers who had single-handedly robbed banks, or driven motorcycles over rooftops like Evel Knievel to outrun the law; lovers who were famous but wouldn't admit to fathering their now-homeless children. The truth didn't really matter. For one reason or another, sensational or predictable, they had ended up in a shelter, their lives on hold, or held together by string.

Near midnight, the end of her shift, Dinah made one last sweep of the shelter, and checked on Angel, who was asleep and snoring. Then she locked her office door and walked down the long hallway to the reception desk, where Gregory, the night guard, rocked heavily in his chair, a paperback in one hand. He looked up from his reading and smiled.

"Hey, precious," he said. To him, everyone was "precious"—staff members, residents, and Llydia (née Lloyd), the transvestite mail carrier.

"Would you mind calling me a cab?" Dinah asked. "I forgot to do it before I locked my office."

"You betcha."

As Gregory dialed, there was a loud rapping at the main door, and Dinah turned, startled to see Luc Martinelli there, peering in through the barred window. When she rushed to unlatch the heavy bolt, Luc explained that he had heard she was working late, and wondered if he might walk her home.

"I was in the neighborhood anyway, after a late dinner," he said, his tone casual.

"Dinner? Wow, that *is* late," Dinah said, then saw Gregory smirk. Luc blushed, and Dinah realized that he'd stretched the truth: He had come just for her. Her heart beat a little faster and she turned to ask Gregory to cancel her cab.

"Sure thing, precious. But watch yourself," he joked. "He's trouble."

The rain had slowed to a faint mist that clung to their coats and hair like fine netting. Luc's hair was dark, his eyes darker. Every now and then Dinah's eyes met his and he smiled impishly. He really was nothing like Atticus Finch; he was far more boyish up close, awkward as a teenager. Their talk was easy but filled with lulls as they searched for common ground that didn't involve work. Work, however, kept coming back, a comfort zone.

"Did you hear about Sam?" Luc asked. Sam, a frequent resident at the shelter, suffered from lifelong diabetes. In recent months he'd had several toes amputated due to gangrene. Dinah hadn't seen him in a while, but that was typical for their clientele. People came and went, and some returned, but many never were heard from again. Sam, however, was a favorite of the staff, and Luc had helped him sort out his medical insurance and, Dinah knew, privately paid some of his extra expenses.

"No—what about him?" she asked.

"He's back in the hospital," Luc said. "They had to take his whole left leg this time."

"That's *awful*."

"I know. I don't know how much longer he's going to last. I saw him yesterday, but I don't think he knew who I was. It's probably for the best if he goes at this point."

Dinah sighed, sorrowful. "I've always loved that guy," she said.

"You love them all," Luc said.

"No, not *all*." Dinah truly tried, though, to see Jesus in every face. But some people were not easily lovable.

She and Luc had reached a corner where there was an all-night pharmacy, and Dinah stopped walking.

"I hope you don't mind," she said, "but I need to stop in here for some diapers before I go home." As soon as she said it, she regretted it.

"How old is your daughter?"

"One year. How did you know about her?"

"I asked around." Luc shrugged, looking sheepish.

"What else do you know?" Dinah blurted. She was out of practice when it came to flirting.

"I know you're single, that you live with a friend—Yolanda assured me he's 'just a friend'—and I've been trying for ages to figure out how to ask you out."

"Really?" Dinah felt herself blush.

"So, do you want to have dinner sometime? Friday?"

Dinah nodded, smiling. "Wait here. I'll be quick," she said, slipping through the door of the drugstore, floating down the overlit aisles.

She couldn't stop smiling. She felt as if the blood was rushing through all of her veins like the clean, rain-washed air. She unclipped her hair and let it fall around her shoulders, and paused before a tiny mirror in the makeup aisle to pinch a little color into her cheeks. Then she bought the diapers and rushed back outside, where Luc was waiting against the wall. He grinned when he saw her and stepped forward, his brown eyes shining.

Dinah couldn't wait; hadn't she waited long enough by now? She stuffed the diapers under one arm, grabbed Luc with the other, and kissed him full on the mouth. He seemed momentarily taken aback, but then his hands were in her hair and he kissed her back, slowly and sensuously, as if he had all the time in the world, as if they weren't standing on the sidewalk outside a drugstore with its ghastly fluorescent lighting flooding through the windows.

As if aware all at once where they were, they pulled away and looked at each other, and laughed.

"Well," Luc said, smiling. "I'm glad we got that out of the way before our first date."

"Sorry," Dinah said. "I couldn't help myself."

"Me, neither," Luc said, and started to list toward her again.

Suddenly, just beyond him, a shadow moved in the alley. Dinah tensed, but then she recognized the figure coming toward them. The filthy white beard, the long coat.

"Merlin!" Dinah exclaimed. "How are you?" She hadn't seen him in months; it was as if he'd vanished. He didn't look quite right—not that he ever did.

Merlin said nothing, his eyes wild in the streetlight, and before Dinah could react, he pulled a sword from underneath his soiled coat. It flashed past Luc, who cried out, but too late.

The blade sliced her side, and Dinah flung out her arms

as she fell, the diapers flying into the street. Her head hit the pavement and she was stunned, trying to work out what was happening as the world spun about her.

Wait! she thought. *Merlin, why*— And then, *Eva!* The rest of her family skated across her mind like little paper boats, out of reach. *Griffin and Theo, don't forget to*— *I need to*— *Joan*— *Alice, I*—

Dinah grew vaguely aware of the wetness of her shirt and the hardness of the pavement beneath her cheek, and of the smell of rain, and of blood, which she also faintly tasted. Voices surrounded her from all sides, like in one of Alice's plays when an ensemble cast was calling across the stage. Dinah knew one voice but couldn't at the moment remember the name it belonged to. Atticus? Precious?

"Someone get help!"

"*Omigod* . . . what happened?"

"Joey, go call nine one one. . . ."

"Where is . . . Did he get away?"

". . . a *sword*?"

"Damn it, someone, hold this. . . . Hold it on her firmly, but not too hard. . . ."

"Can she talk? Miss, can you talk?"

"Her name's Dinah."

"*Gosh*, there's a lot of . . ."

"Shit, they better hurry. . . . Press down!"

"Miss? Miss? Miss?"

Dinah tried to respond; she even tried to smile. It was funny, like on a TV skit, someone saying "Miss" over and over. Someone had called her "ma'am" earlier. How old *was* she anyway? She couldn't say. Whoever was speaking thought she was young. She *was* young, after all—fifteen?

Nine? Where was her father? She thought she saw him coming down the street. Maybe it was a dream. She struggled to wake. Yet she was awake; she heard sirens; she still felt the hard pavement and the sogginess of her shirt and someone pressing on her lung. It didn't hurt, but she couldn't breathe. She tried to lift an arm to push them away—*That's too hard. I can't breathe. Where'd my dad go? Wait, I'm not ready*—but then she fell over into darkness

"Dinah! Stay with me!"

and then farther into light.

Here comes Sam from the shelter, marveling at his new legs, scissoring them with delight. He passes Dinah and turns to glance at her in surprise: *Oh, you, too!* But she isn't quite catching up.

"*Oh,*" we say.

"We can't let her."

"It's out of our hands."

"But I want her. Let her come!"

"We can't, she must go back."

I don't even know which of us is speaking when. Our words and feelings zing and boomerang. We feel the same. Yes. No. She is. She isn't. Is she? Others gather to watch, curious.

We reach for her. We push her away. We . . .

Our daughter tumbles through the light, not knowing which way is up.

Eighteen

"You haven't been yourself lately," Ian said. He was slouched on the sofa, with Adam asleep across his lap. Adam's lips were parted and moist, a droplet of drool inching out of the side. Alice wanted to scoop him up in her arms and hold him. She knew well his weight and warmth now; she couldn't imagine life without him. But Ian was prodding her. She turned to look at him.

"I'm an actress," Alice said wearily, a shade defensively. "I'm never myself."

Ian scoffed. "That's lame and you know it."

Alice said nothing. She had just come home from another unsuccessful audition and was in no mood to argue.

Ian glanced down at Adam, then back up at Alice and asked in a low voice, "Alice—is there someone else?" His eyes clouded; he seemed already resigned, as if he'd been waiting to ask the question for weeks.

"*No,*" Alice said too vehemently. "Of course not!" *Not like that anyway*, she thought. But it was impossible to explain to Ian what she didn't understand herself.

"I just feel like we're in a rut or something," Ian said. "I don't want us to be."

"I don't, either," Alice said, and sat down beside him, with Adam between them. She waited, expecting Ian to say something else, but he just took her hand in his and leaned back against the sofa and closed his eyes, as if shutting out further discussion.

The day after he kissed her, Neil called Alice to apologize.

"There's no need," Alice said, her voice calm, cool. "It was just a mistake. No big deal."

"Right. *No big deal,*" Neil repeated in a flat American accent, mirth in his voice. "I really am sorry, though. I had no right. I hope you'll forgive me."

Alice said nothing for a moment. She knew Neil wasn't solely at fault. She had agreed to go with him to the café; she'd suspected that something once again was buzzing between them and she'd allowed herself to walk closer to the wire, to feel the voltage. She'd *wanted* to. Part of her craved it, missed it—the attention of other men. It was a struggle to maintain fidelity. It wasn't about sex, she realized, just the flirting and the company—the same thing Neil had said about himself.

"I think we should just let it go," Alice said. "It's just between us, right?"

"Don't worry, luv. I'd never say anything to Ian."

Luv, Alice thought after they hung up. Neil wouldn't relent. Or perhaps it was just habit with him, with women. An offhand endearment tossed around without thinking, the way some waitresses called customers "hon," or cabdrivers sometimes called Alice "baby." It meant nothing, just an innocent form of flattery or camaraderie.

The problem, though, was that since Neil was a friend of Ian's, and living once again in New York, Alice would have to continue to see him. And now when she did see him (or even thought of him), she knew she would be tasting peach pie—and him.

At the coffee shop, Imogene handed Alice her new three-person play, called *Boxing Day.* Taking place entirely in a stalled elevator, it was "an exploration of human limitations, incest, grace, and forgiveness." It had taken Imogene longer to write than she'd first hoped, she said, having suffered a bout of pneumonia and then writer's block. She claimed the latter was far worse.

Alice smiled at Imogene across the table, happier to see her than she'd have expected. Imogene was like the teacher who demanded too much but, in the end, was the one who transformed education for her students. Alice flipped through the manuscript, afraid to show her excitement, to let on how much she wanted the work.

"I'll read it as soon as possible," she said calmly.

"Good. I want to start rehearsals in a week," said Imogene. She stared at Alice from behind her dark-rimmed glasses, eyes glittering.

"I haven't even looked at it yet, Imogene," Alice said, laughing, but she was elated and deeply flattered; there was only one female role in the play and she was it.

"Oh, I know that," Imogene said. "But I have thought about this for nearly a year. And without you, there is no play."

"No pressure, huh," Alice joked. But then she finally let her guard down and allowed her joy to shine through unabashedly. Imogene laughed, which was a first, as far as Alice knew.

"I know you, Alice, better than you think. I got you as soon as I met you. You just need the right board to leap from and you'll go far. This play could be the start."

"Gosh, I hope so," Alice said. And though Imogene said nothing more, Alice could see in her sharp eyes that she wanted the new play to be a leap for herself, too. They both had endured long "dry spells" and were eager to be past them.

Alice read the first half of the play on the subway home and was astounded; it was the best thing she'd read in years. And the confinement of the stage space made the words all the more potent.

When she got home, she excitedly told Ian she was going to do a new play, finally.

"Oh, that's great!" he said, hugging her. When they sat down in the kitchen with glasses of celebratory wine, he asked what it was about.

"An incestuous love triangle, in an elevator," Alice said.

"That sounds salacious," Ian said, then paused. "So, it's just you and two men?"

"Yes," Alice said, and teased, "Isn't it great?" She saw

by the expression on Ian's face that he wasn't amused. "Don't worry," Alice added blithely, "there's no sex onstage; from what I've read, it's mostly just the aftermath of the trysts." She wondered how Ian could be jealous of a figment of imagination—Imogene's, or his own. He obviously still felt suspicious, though Alice never had been unfaithful, not technically, and they weren't even married, technically.

"Anyway," she sighed, realizing the celebration was over as soon as it had begun, "it's just a story."

"What story?" Adam demanded, suddenly bounding between them. "I want a story!"

Ian said nothing, quietly brooding, and Alice steered Adam out of the kitchen. "How about if I tell you one in your room?" she asked, leading him there.

Adam plopped onto the mattress beside Alice. The lights were off, except for the strand of fairy lights still strung around the walls. A few of the tiny bulbs were burned out, which made the others look more like scattered stars if Alice squinted. She caressed Adam's soft hair, felt the pulse at his temple.

"Tell me," he prodded her breathlessly, though he didn't pull away. He liked Alice to stroke his head, and curled more deeply into her arms like a cat. He'd once told Alice that he liked her because she was "nice and soft." *He's so sweet and uncomplicated,* she thought.

"Okay, but it's not exactly a story," Alice said. "What do you know about elves?"

"They're really little, like this," Adam said without hesitation, holding his thumb and forefinger apart an inch. "And they live inside trees. I look for them in the park with Dad."

Alice smiled. "Have you seen them?"

"No! They hide *completely* from big people. They're sneaky."

"That's true," Alice said. "But sometimes they come to visit."

Adam swiveled his head to look up at her. "Really?"

Alice nodded. Then, repeating what her own mother had once told her, she described in detail how elves slip into houses over window ledges, sliding in on the ends of branches or sometimes dropping gently off the backs of birds. "If you listen really carefully, you can hear them whispering just outside your window."

Adam sat up a little. "I don't have a window in here."

"That's okay. They'll come to any window. Maybe the kitchen or bathroom; you never know."

"What else?" Adam asked, his eyes shining.

Alice thought. She heard her mother's faraway voice, just above a whisper. "If you leave little bits of kiwi or watermelon on the ledge, they'll come and eat it. They love watermelon."

"Did you do that?"

"Yes," Alice said.

"Did they come?"

She nodded. "But not when I was looking, of course. They're very discreet. Sneaky, like you said."

Adam seemed to be thinking this over. "How did you know they ate it, and not the pigeons?"

"I just knew," she said. "I saw their tiny footprints."

Adam looked at Alice again, studying her face as if for evidence of teasing or deception. At four and in preschool, he was growing slightly more skeptical about fantasy. However, he seemed desperately to want to keep believing.

"I'll buy some fruit and we can try it out," Alice promised. She heard the phone ringing, Ian's muffled voice answering.

"Kiss me," Adam suddenly demanded, flinging himself dramatically onto his back. Alice laughed and obliged, kissing both of his round cheeks and his nose. He strung his arms around her neck and held on, breathing softly into her hair as if he never wanted to let go. Alice dreaded telling him that she was going to be working in the theater again, and home a lot less for a while.

Suddenly, Adam hopped up and announced that he was going to brush his teeth. "I got a new toothbrush. Want to see?"

"Sure, in a minute," Alice said.

"In a minute is never," Adam moaned, before darting off to the bathroom.

"He's too smart for his own good," Alice said, half laughing as she walked back into the kitchen. Ian was still sitting at the table, but now he was reading a magazine (or pretending to) and eating yogurt from a small carton.

"Hmm?" he said, not looking up.

"Never mind. Who was on the phone?"

"Neil. He wants us to have dinner next week."

"Didn't we just go to a party at his place?" Alice asked. She turned her back and opened the refrigerator. Her cheeks burned; the cool air helped, but not much. She was ashamed for the secrecy, even if all she'd done was have pie. And a too-long kiss. It was more than that, she knew; it was a door nudged open, waiting for her to decide if she was going to walk in.

"He's just social, I guess," Ian was saying. "Or he likes you." He laughed.

Alice was eager to change the subject. "Do we have any more Pinot Grigio? Or anything?"

"Sorry," Ian said, licking his spoon. "There's just an opened bottle of that awful Merlot or whatever you bought. I think it's gone off, though. Not that it would make a difference."

"I didn't think it was that bad."

"So, you don't want to have dinner?"

"I'm not that hungry," Alice said absently.

"No, I meant with Neil."

"Oh. I don't care. It's up to you."

"Don't you like him?" Ian asked.

Alice turned to look at him, but his expression appeared neutral. "I like him fine," she said levelly. "But I'd rather go out with just you. We never go out anymore."

"Oh. I guess between your plays every night and a kid . . ." Ian said, and shrugged. "I mean—you know it's not that simple."

"You know I haven't been in a play in months, until now, and I haven't even started rehearsals yet."

"That's not the issue, though, is it?" Ian asked.

"What is, then?"

Ian shrugged and said nothing. In the silence, Alice turned away from the open refrigerator to stir the pasta Ian had forgotten. It irritated her that he seemed to defer cooking to her most of the time.

Without looking up from his magazine, Ian asked, "Where's the madman?"

"Brushing his teeth."

"He hasn't even eaten yet," Ian said. "His pasta's on the stove."

"I know—I'm stirring it; it's almost like glue now."

"You're letting all the cold air out, by the way."

Alice shut the refrigerator door so that bottles rattled. "That was an annoyed-roommate comment if I ever heard one," she said coldly. "*By the way.*"

"*I'm* not annoyed," Ian said as the tension filled the air. "Is that what you think we are—roommates?"

Alice looked away. "I have to go out for a while." She had no idea where, but she just needed to breathe.

"Great. Fine. Just leave when things get testy, right?" Ian tossed down his spoon and it clattered to the floor. "Is that why you won't give up your apartment? You just won't commit?"

"*Commit?*" Alice asked, taken aback. "Me? What do you call what I've been doing for over a year?"

Ian regarded her now with an intensity that she had not seen before. But then his expression changed, collapsed a little, and he looked desperate, as if he wanted to say something else but didn't know how to say it.

Alice didn't know what to say, either. But the look on Ian's face convinced her that she knew what she had to do. She picked up her coat. She turned to leave just as Adam raced back into the room, sliding in his socks, skidding gracefully to a halt.

"Where are you going, Alice? To the palace?" he asked, blinking up at her.

"I have a meeting, sweetie. I'll see you later, okay?"

"You're always going away," he said, pouting.

But I always come back, Alice wanted to say, although stubbornly she didn't, as she knew Ian was listening. Instead, she simply kissed Adam on the head and left.

The well-oiled doorman seemed to recognize her from the party, and probably assumed she was the latest paramour. He smiled and opened the door for Alice, then reached for the phone, asking her name so he could announce her arrival.

"He said to come right up."

When Neil opened the door to his apartment, Alice was surprised to see him slightly disheveled, as if he'd just woken from a nap, though it was evening. He wore a brown sweater with a small moth hole near the neck, revealing a white undershirt beneath. He looked almost vulnerable.

"Come in!" he said cheerfully, holding the door wide open.

Alice walked in. The apartment, which she had seen only in candlelight and full of guests, seemed spacious and warm. The aura of glamour was lessened, though it remained a lovely apartment, and far larger than any Alice had ever been in, with its tall windows and broad balcony. Ian told her at the party that Neil had owned it for over thirty years. When Alice allowed herself to do the math— Neil had lived here, as a grown man, off and on, since Alice was in kindergarten—she realized how far apart they were in age, in worlds.

"I admit I'm surprised," Neil said, motioning Alice to a chair near an unlit fireplace. With one switch, Neil turned it on. The gas logs ignited, and though it didn't crackle, the fire gave off heat, and Alice kept her gaze on the flickering flames. She ignored the romantic implication of two people before a blazing fire. Maybe Neil was just feeling cold, or thought she might be. The nights were still chilly, spring not quite fully sprung.

"Well, I was just in the neighborhood," Alice explained as she sat, realizing that it sounded like a line. And of course it was disingenuous; even after walking around aimlessly for an hour, deliberating, she had come here intentionally.

"Would you like something to drink?" Neil asked. "Tea? Wine?"

"No, thank you."

He sat on a sofa across from her. "So, Alice—"

"Look," she said quickly. "I don't want to give you the wrong idea. I mean, that's why I came, to dispel any—" She stammered, cleared her throat, and began again more carefully. "I felt like we left it awkwardly on the phone, and I wanted to tell you that I value your friendship—with me, and especially with Ian. I don't want to blow it."

Neil said nothing for a long moment, as if allowing the words to sink in. It occurred to Alice that what she'd said left room for the interpretation that she had been weighing her options. She looked at Neil, silently begging, *Don't get the wrong idea.* But they both already had had the idea, and it stood in the space between them, large and stubborn as a donkey. In fact, the longer Neil sat across from her and said nothing, the more Alice felt the unspoken longing.

Neil smiled at her and then looked down at his long fingers clasped between his knees. He had beautiful hands.

"I understand," he said finally, sounding sincere. Then he looked back up at Alice, as if waiting for more.

Alice had said what she had come to say, what she had come to do, which was to complete unfinished business. Instead of feeling relieved, however, she still felt vaguely unsettled. She stood, not wanting to prolong the discussion. But Neil, ever the gentleman, rushed to his feet at the same moment, and when he did, they were suddenly dangerously close. And then Alice tipped forward, as if the force finally was too strong to resist. At this moment, for a moment longer, she couldn't help herself. Maybe because she and Ian had fought, maybe because she wanted to know what she was missing, what she would always be missing.

She wrapped her arms around Neil's neck and kissed him hard, greedily. *It's just a kiss*, she thought. *Just one more kiss*. She moved her hands to his nape and felt his thick, coarse hair in her fingers. Her body was engulfed in his arms, and he deftly untied the belt of her coat and tugged at the buttons. She slid her hands underneath his brown sweater, the T-shirt. His skin felt warm and surprisingly taut, with just the faintest softness around his torso.

"Alice, I think about you all the time," Neil murmured huskily. "Since I saw you again at my party, since I kissed you, since I first met you—"

He pulled her toward the sofa and she complied, though her heart pounded a warning. They fell together again, and his strong hands moved down her body; his lips slid down her neck, lightly kissing along the way as one hand clutched her hair, the other moved up her thigh. He was pressed against her, nearly on top of her.

He whispered, "Alice," his face close, his eyes staring intently into hers. "Come with me." A smile worked at his lips. "I'm flying to Ibiza next week. Come with me."

"I—" *Ibiza?* Alice wasn't even sure where that was. She wasn't even sure where *she* was anymore.

"I know it's sudden—but is it?" Neil said. "We've been dancing around each other since we met. I know you felt it, too. That's one of the reasons I left. I thought I shouldn't—" His fingers inched higher, along the lacy edge of Alice's underwear. "You *have* to come with me."

The inflection was simply for emphasis, of course, the urging of an almost lover—*Kiss me. Don't go. Stay. Take off your dress. Come here. Please*—but it had the effect of jolting Alice back to herself. She pulled away from his touch, slid out from underneath him with some effort, and wiped her mouth with the back of her hand.

"Oh God. I *can't*. I have to go home."

"Not yet," Neil pleaded.

He looked in her eyes again, willing her, it seemed, to change her mind, but in her mind, she was already gone; it was finished, just like that. Alice stood up, backing a safe distance from the sofa. Neil rose, too, his joints cracking a little.

For a long, silent moment, Alice stood apart, buttoning her coat, while Neil shifted awkwardly, stuffing his hands in his pockets. He looked forlorn, and faintly angry, as if he'd been duped. They stood there as if waiting for the other's reaction, as if they'd had a collision and were standing on the side of the road, inspecting the damage, to see how serious, or minor, it might prove to be.

"Well—" Neil began.

Alice interrupted. "We shouldn't have— I don't know what I was thinking."

"No. It was my fault. I should never have come between you and Ian." Neil shrugged, as if unsure that he meant it—or was desperate to mean it. "It won't ever happen again."

"No, it won't," Alice said firmly. She shook her head woefully. "But I shouldn't have come here. I'm the one who should be sorry. And I am."

"But Alice," Neil said, softly imploring. "Why did you, then? Why did you come here, allowing me to think you felt something for me? You clearly felt *something*."

She forced herself to meet his gaze. "I guess I just needed to be sure."

"That you *don't* feel something?" He looked wounded, petulant.

"Sure that I love Ian," Alice said. And as soon as she said it, she couldn't believe she had waited so long to say it. She realized that until she put to rest any feelings she had for Neil—or any other man—things couldn't truly go forward with Ian. He had to know that he could trust her, and that she wasn't like his ex-wife, who had left and never come back. Suddenly, Alice understood that it was up to her to make things permanent.

And she knew that it wasn't just complacency, or fear of losing Adam, but that she didn't want to leave Ian. Ever.

Alice held out her hand, businesslike, to Neil. He graciously shook it, looking chagrined and perhaps even a bit heartbroken, but saying nothing more.

Then Alice turned and walked to the elevator without looking back. And as she descended fourteen floors, she felt lighter than she'd felt in years, nearly buoyant.

313

"Alice, lookit me!" Adam exclaimed when she rounded the corner of the hallway. He was outside Mr. Sechenov's apartment, lurching along with the old man's artificial leg tucked under one arm like a crutch. "I got three legs!"

Alice saw Mr. Sechenov leaning into his doorjamb, laughing. He said, "I told him to take it for a run—it never gets enough exercise."

Alice felt the impulse to scoop Adam into her arms and hold him tightly, but he was hobbling away, lost in his own weird, childish endeavor, and she was content to let him be. And she needed to see Ian.

She rushed into the apartment, threw off her coat. When she heard Ian in the kitchen, she walked toward him. She was ready to explain (almost) everything; ready to kiss and make up; ready for her whole life.

She was going to propose.

Ian was murmuring into the phone and he turned, startled when he saw Alice. She laughed at his expression; he looked like an actor caught onstage unprepared. She thought how much she loved him, had loved him, really, since the first moment in the Midtown Coffee Shop. Funny to think that his first words to her were *I know you*. She felt vaguely giddy; poetry filled her head, random lines from Shakespeare: *This is the air; that is glorious sun. Will you be mine, now you are doubly won?*

But then the air left the room.

"Alice—" Ian said, his voice cracking.

In that instant, she knew. She knew from the way the blood seemed to drain from her head down. The way her breath stopped, her ears filled with a throbbing, dreadful noise. *Not again.* When you least expect it, when everything seems fine. *Not again.*

"What?" she asked when she could speak. "What happened?" *Please no.*

"Your sister, Dinah. She's— Oh, Alice, honey." Ian's face filled with anguish; he still held the receiver.

Epilogue

They debated about where to scatter her ashes. None of them thought that Takoma Park would suffice, and in the end, on the advice of a friend, they decided to take her to Greece, since Joan had never been. She'd often said she regretted that she had stayed behind in 1973. At the beginning of the sabbatical, during that blissful summer on Santorini, they had spoken to her on the phone and Joan had asked if Greece was as blue as she'd always heard. They assured her that it was, and she sighed through thousands of miles of phone line.

So they carried their grandmother across the ocean. They took turns keeping the vase, a simple fired-clay urn with a Greek-key design in lush black ink, which Griffin had found in a secondhand shop in Chicago. Griffin remarked, when he first held Joan's remains, that he was shocked to find the vase so heavy, and that it rattled a little.

"Bits of bone, I guess," he said in a hushed voice, which broke at the thought.

In the hotel in Athens, where they stayed just one night, Dinah kept the vase beside the bed she shared with Eva; and on the ship to Santorini, Alice wrapped it in extra clothes and nestled it in her suitcase. They planned to take Joan to their last stop and scatter her on the highest, bluest peak.

Nothing in her will had specified her wishes about a resting place, but at the funeral, dear old Peter, Joan's boyfriend, said he had an idea. He was so sweet that the three grandchildren each privately regretted not having spent more time with him and Joan in the past year. But they'd all gathered at their old home in Takoma Park for her last weeks, and were touched by how kind and adoring "Petey" was to Joan.

"So what is your idea?" Alice asked him over coffee after the service.

"She mentioned the Greek islands," Peter said. "She said it was the last time she spoke to her son—your dad—and that he sounded so happy there."

Alice and Griffin and Dinah had looked at one another. None had ever entertained the notion of going back. But the idea struck a chord with each of them. *Full circle,* one thought. *Closure,* thought another. *Why not* was the logic of the third; the past was long since over.

"I'm sure she's already happy," Peter said. "She's already romping in greener pastures, dancing no doubt." He smiled, his blue eyes twinkling through his tears.

On a breezy June afternoon, they made their way on foot along a steep hillside on Santorini, walking behind an impromptu Greek guide with a faded cap and leathered skin. The man, who worked for a nearby vineyard, learned where they were headed and offered to lead. The sun was high and bright, the sky and sea a deep azure. Adam skipped ahead, with Eva scrambling behind, calling his name in a clipped, funny accent she'd adopted, so that it sounded like "Atom." The others strolled in a line along the zigzagging paths, Griffin bringing up the rear, with Joan's vase in the crook of his arm.

For now, they had left behind the bleached white houses and hotels of Fíra, the shimmering swimming pools and checkered-table tavernas spilling over with guests. At this end of the island, the road was less traveled, gravel covered and sprouting weeds. Here and there a tiny shrine emerged, festooned with dried flowers and trinkets, and worry beads draped over a hand-hewn cross. Dinah paused at each one to look.

When the guide left them where they requested, Ian pressed several extra drachmas into the man's palm. After he was gone, the group stopped to peer into the ancient city of Akrotiri, the ruins that James Stenen had happily dug through that long-ago summer.

Alice looked at her siblings. "I think we should leave Joan here, don't you?"

"What if someone digs *her* up?" Adam asked, blinking up at Alice with his serious gray eyes. At six, he expected grown-up answers to his questions; rarely could he be placated with fairy-tale versions. (Though when he asked Griffin what people ate in Heaven and Griffin said, "Angel

318

food cake," Adam had nodded and replied, "I thought so.")

"Well, she's ashes now," Alice told Adam. "I think she'll blend in with the earth."

"Let's go just a little farther," Dinah suggested. "Lots of tourists walk around here, you know." *I don't want Joan to get trampled.*

Alice nodded. Griffin took the lead and they walked toward the lighthouse. The sky seemed to turn a deeper blue, surrounding them on all sides, as if swallowing them, and below, the Aegean glinted turquoise.

Stopping in a quiet, rocky alcove that overlooked the beach, Griffin opened the lid of the clay urn and looked inside and then away, hesitating. No one spoke.

Then Theo cleared his throat and said, "I think this is the perfect place. It seems as close to Heaven as you could get."

Griffin smiled gratefully at him. "You're right," he said. His siblings nodded.

Then Griffin shook out a handful of ashes, and passed the vase to his sisters, who tearfully each took handfuls and then passed it on. Soon everyone, including the children, held tiny bits of Joan, and then all at once let her loose into the wind. Her ashes scattered among the rocks, the brush, against the trunk of a gnarled tree. She dissolved into the blue, blue air and floated imperceptibly down to the sea. Eva looked at her dusty palms and wiped them on her dress. Everyone else wiped wet eyes.

Dinah dropped the empty vase ceremoniously onto the ground, and they all looked at its broken shards, soon to be crushed into the earth, like everything else.

Then Theo slung an arm around Griffin's neck and they walked to the edge of the cliff to look at the sea. Griffin felt sadness ebbing away from him like the waves far below.

Alice went to sit on a small boulder beside her husband, watching the children run tirelessly around. They had been the same way at their wedding the year before, as if weddings and funerals were blissfully the same to them.

Ian asked, "Are you okay?" Alice nodded, and he kissed her nape.

Dinah stood apart, staring at the sea and the sky. She wrapped her arms around her own waist. The slight pressure grazed her scar, which now and then still faintly throbbed. She thought about how she'd arrived here, on this peak—through Luc Martinelli's heroic rescue, and then the mingling of strangers' blood in her veins. And though things hadn't worked out with Luc in the end, he had helped her live, and that was more than enough. Maybe she would meet someone else someday, but nonetheless, she knew she already was lucky. *Blessed,* as Joan would say, correcting her.

"What a view," Ian was saying as he and Alice joined Dinah. "It's even better than I expected."

Alice hugged her sister and smiled. "It *is* beautiful, isn't it?"

Dinah nodded. Instead of the view, though, she gazed at her sprawling family all around. She imagined them later gathering around a table to toast and eat, and talk into the starry night with sleepy children on their laps. She could see their days (good and bad) spreading out to include Theo's family, Ian's, their friends, and even the people at the Lakeside Shelter. She saw how all of them were connected, on and on, further than any of them could imagine. And she saw her parents (now with Joan) watching them from a miraculous distance.

For one astounding, flickering moment, Dinah *had* seen them, and they were smiling. She was sure of it.

Right before they pushed her back here, where she belonged.

We had no choice, of course. It wasn't her time; and it is never up to us. So we continue to watch from the vast sidelines, content Here, but still curious about There.

As always, human beings are endlessly heartbreaking and inspiring, their lives threaded with strands of despair, and brighter ones of hope. They are as predictable and changeable as the weather.

In summer, someone collapses at a parade; an infant is left in an oven-hot car—but also, throngs break open fire hydrants and dance. In winter, people chip ice from inside kitchen windows; or trudge through snowy footprints, lips chapped and split open—and then fly down ski slopes, thinking that nothing could exceed such joy. In between, there are spring jonquils and cotillions; car accidents and first loves. Leaves fall from trees like confetti, and children go trick-or-treating; someone chokes on a bone; someone else makes a wish.

Year after year, the wars unfold: this tribe against that, this religion defying that one, this nation trying to strong-arm another like a boy grabbing a smaller one by the wrist. An eye for an eye and a tooth for a tooth. And yet—people also march into the streets with signs: PEACE. MAKE LOVE,

NOT WAR. They love one another, total strangers. They rush into fires and wreckage to help, to save anyone they can. They stop outside a drugstore to help a woman bleeding in the street.

And in the midst of it all, babies are born, squalling from Bangladesh to Boise to Bordeaux, slipping out of wombs and into arms again and again and again.

And lovers fall in love beneath trees, inside tents, yurts, hammocks. They rock together, on top, from behind, entwined and giddy, as if they'd invented their own limbs. It is wondrous still to behold.

Gifts are bestowed in gold paper and satin ribbon, or tucked into a shred of hemp cloth and tied with a hank of twine. People laugh and embrace, cry and embrace.

They talk, they write, they sing. They fill the air and days with gestures and words, meaningless and paramount: *I love you. Bonjour! See you next summer. I miss you. Cute shoes. I hate you. Be there at eight. Why did you lie? L'Chaim! Marry me. It's only a movie. I'm sorry. Did you feed the cat? Watch where you're going. Don't leave me. Praise God. Pass the sugar. He's dying. She's gone. It's a girl! Looks like rain again. Are you listening? You're so funny. I mean it. Amen.*

It is all new and all the same. A hundred years. A day. Ten thousand moons. For them, each day indeed is brand-new, full of possibility, the unknown: a wonderland.

And because of three who were once ours—and now all of theirs—we cannot help but think so, too. We cannot help but watch their every move when they slide into view.

*

*

*

322

1. The scenes and observations of the parents from up Here are a unique way for the writer and reader to share reflections on the unfolding lives of the Stenen siblings. What stood out most for you from the scenes from Here? How does this possibility of an afterlife fit with your beliefs about what lies beyond?

2. How likely is it that the siblings feel some of the love and concern that their parents are showing for them from the great beyond?

3. The siblings are drawn very sympathetically; their shared experience of loss shapes them each in different ways. How does that loss affect each of them?

4. Which of the three main characters—Alice, Dinah, and Griffin—do you relate to most?

5. The parents say that although the children have changed, they are still the same, "earnestly making their way in a fractured life." Discuss how resilience and love bind them.

6. Each of the Stenens deals with the fact that bad things can happen at any time in a unique way. Alice braces herself for what might come next and escapes into acting to let herself be free. Dinah discovers a strong religious faith in Greece, and her belief in fate and purpose makes her put family first, yet she longs for love and romance. Griffin knows that families are fragile and he loves his partner, Theo, deeply but feels parenthood is for other people—it's tempting fate. What drives each of them to take the risks that they do to create families of their own as adults?

7. How do each of the siblings define family? How do the living arrangements that evolve over the course of the

story reflect their desires and fears about family? How do you define family?

8. Dinah acts out of character by having an impetuous affair on the cruise. Why do you think she threw caution to the wind?

9. As Dinah screams at the falls, filled with disappointment and doubt after finding that Eduardo is to be married, she waits for a sign from God. Her mother comments, "Now she'll have to shake up her life and change things." How do you think Dinah handles the consequences of her actions? What do you think of how heavily she leans on her family to help her through?

10. Why did Griffin adopt Holly, the dog, when Theo was so clearly against it? Why couldn't Griffin talk to Theo about his fears about parenthood and family? How unreasonable was it to expect Theo to understand without really being told?

11. Why was Griffin drawn to Ray? What need did Ray fulfill for him? Why do you think Griffin was willing to give up his relationship with Theo for someone he barely knew?

12. Alice becomes entranced by Adam, the three-year-old son of her neighbor and lover Ian. She thinks perhaps her fantasy of belonging in their lives could be real, perhaps it's where she's meant to be. What is Alice looking for in Ian and Adam? How do her doubts sabotage her desires, especially after she loses Adam for a few minutes in the park one day?

13. Alice notes, "When she was around Neil, she kept reaching for her old self." What do you make of Alice being drawn to being wanted by Neil at the same time

she wishes that Ian would ask to make their relationship permanent? What do you think about her parents' reflection that "Alice may love them all (and she does) but still do the wrong thing. And not even intentionally. Just because she's restless, and, yes, a little blue"?

4. What do you think about Dinah and Theo and Eva pretending to be the happy family? And Griffin sneaking around watching them, stalking the old homestead?

5. After Holly is gone and Griffin moves back in, Dinah feels like she doesn't fit in anymore, and she is surprised that Theo can so easily forgive Griffin. What do you think of the shift back for Theo and Griffin?

6. What do you think the title of the book means? Where do you imagine the three main characters' lives going from here?

For more reading group suggestions, visit
www.readinggroupgold.com.

*A
Reading
Group
Guide*

St. Martin's
Griffin